ROMANTIC TIMES BOOKreviews RAVES ABOUT AWARD-WINNING AUTHOR ELAINE BARBIERI!

CRY OF THE WOLF

"The final release in the Wolf series is as masterful and satisfying as readers could desire. Barbieri pulls out all the stops, drawing together every loose thread in this strong Western, beautiful romance and powerful story about family."

NIGHT OF THE WOLF

"Western sagas are Barbieri's forte and the Wolf series is an excellent example of the memorable characters, broad scope, intrigue, tragedy and triumph that make her sagas memorable."

SIGN OF THE WOLF

"Barbieri captures the essence of a time and place, the spirit of the characters, the jargon, the superstitions and the culture of the Old West. She sets her plot against this colorful backdrop and delivers what her fans most desire: a strong story and the aura of the era."

HAWK'S PRIZE

"A wonderful and satisfying conclusion to the four-book series…Barbieri's engaging characters touch your emotions and you get a totally unexpected surprise at the end."

HAWK'S PASSION

"This is an enjoyable read."

TEXAS TRIUMPH

"Barbieri brings the Texas Star trilogy to a powerful close, leading readers through a maze of deception, dishonesty, magic, hatred and justice's ultimate triumph."

A LOVER'S CARESS

Dagan clutched Rosamund closer. "Nay, you are meant for more than de Silva's crude intentions. You are too intelligent...too beautiful...too worthwhile in both body and spirit for a man who has the reputation of having used so many, only to discard them when his interest waned."

Intoxicated by her scent, by the feminine warmth of her, Dagan stroked Rosamund's hair. He marveled that the pale tresses were as silken as he had imagined and whispered, "Your hair glows despite its cut, you know. Although my vision was impaired when you first tended my wounds, I recall that your hair looked like a halo surrounding delicate features that I struggled to see. As I recovered, I spent hours imagining how it would feel to stroke those gleaming tresses...to feel them slip through my fingers. I longed to smooth the curve of your cheek...to follow the contours of your ears with my tongue...to follow a course that could only lead to your lips..."

ELAINE BARBIERI

THE ROSE & THE SHIELD

LEISURE BOOKS   NEW YORK CITY

To my readers, with love.

A LEISURE BOOK®

March 2009

Published by

Dorchester Publishing Co., Inc.
200 Madison Avenue
New York, NY 10016

ISBN 10: 0-8439-6014-0
ISBN 13: 978-0-8439-6014-3
E-ISBN: 1-4285-0610-1

The name "Leisure Books" and the stylized "L" with design are trademarks of Dorchester Publishing Co., Inc.

Printed in the United States of America.

10 9 8 7 6 5 4 3 2 1

Visit us on the web at www.dorchesterpub.com.

The Rose & the Shield

Prologue

Harold was crowned King of England on the day of King Edward's funeral in January 1066, but he enjoyed his royal title for less than a year. Duke William, the illegitimate son of the Duke of Normandy, was enraged at Harold's ascension to the throne. Claiming that Harold had broken his promise to support him as Edward's heir, Duke William launched an invasion of England.

Harold was killed defending his royal title at Senlac.

Duke William was crowned King of England on Christmas Day, 1066, as vanquished Anglo-Saxons mourned.

Standing proudly with Duke William as he donned his crown were knights who had proven their loyalty to him in fierce battles for the throne. These men were rewarded for their fealty with the land and titles of those they had conquered. They imposed their will on the Saxons under their reign. Some were generous and fair despite the rancor that naturally followed bloody battles.

Others were not.

Chapter One

1075

By what right do you dare to refuse me your services?" Baron Guilbert de Silva demanded. "You are my vassal! You live on this land because of my generosity. You may be evicted from your meager dwelling at any time and left to wander homeless if that is your wish."

"That is not my wish, my lord!"

From inside the meager hut she shared with her father, Rosamund listened to the heated exchange outside. "I wish only to serve you as you wish," her father continued, his tone placating. "I desired only to explain that age has left its mark on me. I am not the same person who raised the castle walls for you years ago."

"You look fit and well to me."

"Yes, but—"

The baron's voice was soft yet threatening. "Tell me now if you refuse to gather the laborers needed to finish the cathedral I envision. The former master mason failed to make the progress he promised. He was not worthy of the title *master mason*. Indeed, he no longer bears it . . . or any name at all." His point coldly made, the baron continued, "The necessary artisans are gathered at the site of the cathedral, but they argue incessantly, awaiting the leadership of a knowledgeable master to guide them. The walls you built for me still stand strong. You proved that you have the ability that is needed to accomplish this task. The cathedral that I envision may not be large in size, but it will be so awe-inspiring as to have no match on William's soil. It will be my plea to God to forgive me for the lives I've taken in battle." The baron paused to add, "And I *will* have my vision realized."

Peering through a crack in the door of the hut, Rosamund assessed the baron with a gaze steeped in animosity. His innate arrogance was obvious in his manner, and his flawless, magnificently tailored attire of red and black was silent testimony to the wealth he had wrung from the simple people of Hendsmille. Yet she had to admit the baron was handsome in a sinister way. He was tall and fit despite the gray hair sprinkled among the dark at his temples. His cleanly shaven, aristocratic features had besotted many a maiden. Rumor had it, however, that he lost interest in even the most comely of maids after he had had his way with them.

Nine years ago, the baron's army had overwhelmed the simple Saxons defending their fief with rakes and pitchforks. He had not hesitated to shed the blood of those brave, poorly armed villagers. Now, after nearly a decade ruling the people of Hendsmille—after the Saxons had lost their heritage to the Norman invader and had become chattel on land they had once considered their own—he still felt no hesitation shedding their blood.

Rosamund was brought back sharply to the present

when her father protested, "Your purpose in raising a cathedral is noble, but I—"

Unprepared for the baron's fury, Rosamund stumbled backward when he bellowed viciously at her father, "It is not for you to judge my intentions! I come to charge you with the privilege of building my cathedral—my edifice to the Lord before whom we all bow. I demand that you tell me now yea or nay, if you will undertake this righteous project." He lowered his voice as he warned, "I caution you, consider your answer well."

Rosamund saw the color slowly drain from her father's face. Perspiration appeared on his forehead and upper lip as he scrutinized the baron's expression. She saw him stare for long moments into the dark eyes that glared into his. Only she heard the reluctance in his tone when he replied, "I will see to the construction of your cathedral and gladly, my lord." He paused to lick his lips before he added, "I ask only that you allow my assistant to aid me when I see fit to lean on his youth, and that your soldiers not protest his presence or his help when it is needed."

The baron scoffed, "Is that all?"

"That is all."

"The favor is granted."

"Thank you."

"Do not thank me." The baron continued, with true menace in his tone, "You will find that I am a meticulous taskmaster who will demand the best of your skill—for only the best will do."

With that last warning, Baron Guilbert mounted his great black steed and turned away.

Her expression dark with intensity, Rosamund straightened up as the baron rode off. At eighteen years of age, she was a true Saxon beauty, with finely sculpted features that appeared too fair for a common woman. Her long blonde tresses swept over shoulders that seemed too delicate for her unusual height, and her silver-blue eyes flashed with emotion. Narrow-waisted and high-breasted, she had finally grown into the long legs that had marked an awkward youth.

She frowned uneasily when her father stood unmoving where the baron had left him. She knew the fear that the short, stocky, rapidly balding Hadley Wedge concealed was not for himself. He had always put her well-being ahead of his own. Nine years ago he'd insisted on keeping her by his side when he took advantage of the "wander years" allowed a master mason to travel throughout the country. Even engulfed by sorrow, she had sensed his true reason for doing so: not to learn the latest ways of working at his craft as he claimed, but so that the passage of time would bring about changes that no one would question.

During those years of travel, she learned as much about the silent hatred the Saxons bore for the Norman invaders as she had learned about the intricacies of his trade. Yet what she remembered most was her father's emotion when they stepped once more on the soil of Hendsmille. Tears came to his eyes when his wood-and-wattle hut came into view. It was then that she realized fully for the first time that Hadley's real motive in leaving was to ensure her safety, and that, true to the promise he had made, he would guard her with his life.

She also knew that if not for the sudden reversal of

their positions—if not for his present *need* for her—
she might follow another path.

In truth, she was still unsure which to take.

Rosamund emerged from the hut as her father
turned to walk unsteadily back toward her.

"Take care, Father," she warned. "There is a stone on
the ground in front of you." Grasping his arm, Rosamund guided him into the hut and helped him to a
chair.

"The baron wants you to oversee the building of his
cathedral, but you know as well as I that God has nothing to do with his intentions. He has ambitions that far
exceed his position here. By building this cathedral, he
seeks to gain the approval of influential figures within
the church. You will function as nothing more than a
slave who will allow him to gain a stronger connection
with William."

"I tried to explain my deficiency to him, but he
would not listen."

"I know."

"Do you, Rosamund?" Hadley concentrated on
Rosamund's sympathetic expression as he said, "I have
made a decision. I am the only person who knows your
secret, and for that reason I am necessary to your future."

"Father, I—"

"No, do not speak. Allow me to finish. I asked permission to lean on a youth because of my age. Do you
know who that young man would be?"

"One of the many apprentices you have trained in
your craft."

"You are my right hand, Rosamund. I have come to depend on your expertise where mine has faltered."

Rosamund took a breath. "Father . . ."

"I am unable to meet the baron's demands without you."

"But I am a woman!"

"A *beautiful* woman. The baron would use you and throw you away as he has done so many women before you."

"Father, the baron's words were clear. Your life relies on your ability to provide what he desires."

"I would strike a compromise, although it would entail some sacrifice on your part."

Rosamund looked lovingly at the small, portly man who had protected her through the years. "My life is yours."

Rosamund stroked the long length of fair hair she held in her hand. Morning light seeped through the windows, illuminating the hut's oak and chestnut frame and its wattle walls plastered with clay. The meager furnishings sat close to a central hearth that glowed day and night.

Rosamund stood before the small mirror that her father had bought during their travels. She should have seen a Saxon maiden with pale hair, fair skin, and blue eyes that flashed silver when she was angry. Instead, she saw a fair, spindly youth with cropped hair that concealed her brow and all but hid the frustration in her eyes as she viewed the short, shapeless garment she wore belted at the waist with a leather thong, the baggy

Gallic breeches, and the worn hose gartered below the knee. She glanced at the calf-length mantle draped over her arm, knowing that the simple article of clothing was to be fastened at her shoulder so it might cover her head when needed. Her father had purchased her new attire from a young serf traveling through the fief with his master. Rosamund's only consolation in donning the costume was that her ample breasts, presently bound, were hidden by the loose garments, and that the bulky fabric concealed the narrow waist that had come to her with womanhood.

"Are you ready?"

Rosamund jerked her head toward the sound of her father's voice coming from outside the hut. He had allowed her privacy in order to complete her costume—and to shear her precious hair.

A tear slipped from her eye, and Rosamund brushed it angrily away. The sacrifice was little in light of all Hadley had done for her.

"He is approaching, Rosamund!"

Rosamund's lips tightened. The baron wanted to see for himself that her father had complied fully with his wishes and gathered laborers from the nearby village. She knew what the outcome would be if he had not, and she ground her teeth tighter.

"Rosamund, hurry!"

Rosamund tucked the shorn length of fair hair beneath her mattress beside the treasured ring that she also hid there, and then walked to the door with a long, exaggerated step far different than her normal tread. As the baron drew near the group of men her father had gathered, she murmured, "I hope you warned the others to hold their tongues, Father, and that they will remember to refer to me as Ross."

Hadley sighed. "I did. They will keep our secret because they know the baron's reputation and despise him for it. You must remember to call me Hadley, just as the others do."

Rosamund nodded. She grasped her father's arm and walked beside him toward the assemblage. Everyone knew that Hadley's vision had declined, but no one realized that the deterioration had recently escalated and that at times Hadley saw only foggy outlines rather than clear images. Rosamund had resolved to be his eyes. His secret was safe—just as hers was with him.

The baron halted his mount and waited for them to approach. Her head held high, Rosamund was unable to conceal the contempt in her gaze when she saw that he had arrived with three men-at-arms following close behind him.

Protection . . . against lowly peasants.

The baron's dark brows rose in an arch as he asked bluntly, "Is this the youth you spoke of Hadley?"

"Yes, my lord. It is he."

"He has little muscle to recommend him."

"He is thin, but he has proven his worth."

"Then you had best advise him not to expect his youth to protect him when he taunts me so openly."

"Yes, my lord." Turning toward her, Hadley ordered, "You must look at your betters with respect, Ross!"

Blood colored Rosamund's face at Hadley's words, but she lowered her eyes dutifully. She raised them again to find the baron staring at her.

"Were this youth not important to you, Hadley, and

were the task before you not so critical at this time, I would find work for him in my personal service . . . for I find him surprisingly intriguing, considering his gender."

Hadley blinked when the baron laughed. He then turned toward his men to say, "The privileges of position are many, are they not?"

Rosamund saw the baron's men turn to regard her more intently. Their eyes crawled over her baggily clad figure, and she experienced a sudden urge to retch; yet she refused to allow them that acknowledgment. Instead, she jerked her gaze hotly toward the baron. Then, remembering, lowered it to the ground.

"That's better." The baron's expression darkened as he added, "But I fear that more than a mere reprimand will be necessary to tame the fire in this youth's eyes. Perhaps further *personal instruction* . . . "

Rosamund's heart pounded. Barely controlling the retort that rose to her lips, she glanced at Hadley, then lowered her gaze.

"That is better." Abruptly glancing away from Rosamund's lowered head, the baron said, "But the sun rises and a full day's work lies ahead."

The baron followed his comment by digging his spurs cruelly into his mount's sides as he urged it forward. Similarly mounted, his armed men fell in behind the force of workers, who remained silent as they trudged toward the work awaiting them.

Allowing himself to fall behind them, Hadley whispered to Rosamund, "Take care. The baron watches you."

"He may watch me all he wants, but I will not fall

10

into his trap." Looking directly into her father's concerned gaze, Rosamund whispered more softly, "I will stay by your side and become lost in this throng."

She frowned when Hadley stumbled on the uneven terrain and took his arm more firmly.

Rosamund did not see the baron glance back from his position ahead of her. Nor did she see dark interest spark again in his obsidian gaze.

It was unseasonably hot.

His dark hair slick with perspiration, Dagan pulled uncomfortably at the neck of his heavy traveling attire as he moved relentlessly forward on the king's errand. He swayed weakly in the saddle and glanced around him at the empty wilderness of primeval forest and heath, aware that although men ventured out by day through the thickets, streams, and marshy places of Hendsmille in order to herd the remains of their livestock, few of them would attempt to spend the night there for fear of the wolves and *spirits* that were said to roam the woods.

His sharply chiseled features drew into a frown. He did not believe in spirits. He struggled to clear his mind and recall the evening when William had summoned him secretly to his chambers. He remembered that William's infrequent smile had been spontaneous when he entered. Dagan had been little more than a youth when Duke William had accepted him as one of his soldiers. Like William, he had been ridiculed throughout his youth because his Norman father had chosen an English bride—the same English bride who had insisted he become fluent in her language as well as in his father's native French. His language skills had served William well, but it was Dagan's intelligence and loyalty that had earned him his knighthood and William's favor. He had truly earned William's full trust and confidence, however, when he risked his own life to save William's.

His fluctuating lucidity returned to the moment when William confided that he had heard rumors of unrest in the fief awarded to Baron Guilbert de Silva. William had received reports that the baron employed every opportunity to indulge his mastery over the people of Hendsmille and the surrounding environs awarded to him after victory; that the villages, fields, and woods had become places of doubt, fear, and secrecy; and that even the children were made to know that de Silva was their master.

Dagan remembered William's distress at that last statement. He insisted that as regents, his barons should enforce the adoption of a Norman lifestyle in England, but his goal was for loyalty to the throne and for harmony in victory. If he were to believe rumor, he could only conclude that neither had been accomplished in Hendsmille.

Dagan jolted forward unexpectedly when his warhorse stumbled underneath him; yet when he glanced down at the animal, Dagan saw that Conqueror's gait was steady and true. The copse had begun wavering strangely, and the terrain had become uncertain to his eye. He winced at the pain in his leg when it throbbed more boldly, and silently cursed as he realized that his unhealed war wound was causing his fever and delirium.

The rapidly darkening glade was silent when Dagan studied his options with growing uncertainty. Another pain stabbed his leg, and Dagan made the decision to allow Conqueror his head. He knew the animal would find the nearest source of water—which Dagan would use to treat his wound. After a good night's sleep, he would arrive in better condition.

Dagan was hardly conscious when Conqueror halted at last. He slipped awkwardly from the saddle, hearing the trickling sound of a stream. As he stumbled toward it darkness overwhelmed him.

When he regained consciousness at the sound of Conqueror's soft whinny, Dagan heard rustling in the surrounding bushes. He forced himself to sit up and strove to clear his mind.

Conqueror whinnied again, and Dagan stilled.

Danger threatened.

Dagan struggled to his feet and sought to withdraw his sword from the scabbard on his saddle. A painful blow from behind staggered him, and he cried out in rage. He turned to strike back but was unable to focus on the wavering shadows in front of him. Another shattering blow struck his chin, and Dagan sank to his knees, only to be bludgeoned again and again. He fell to the ground as the savage battering continued.

When a sharp command brought it to an abrupt halt, he peered out through a bloodied gaze as the three men standing over him began stripping him of his clothing. Turning him roughly this way and that, they did not stop until he was left in naught but a breechcloth.

A harsh voice barked another command the moment before a blade slammed into his chest.

A hot flow of blood surged.

Unconsciousness threatened.

And then . . . Dagan felt nothing at all.

It was dark when Rosamund and Hadley returned from their first day at the site of the new cathedral. She ushered Hadley through the entrance of their hut and pulled the door closed behind her. Rosamund moved quickly toward the fireplace as Hadley sat weakly on a nearby chair. The fire was low, but she raised it again with the expertise of long practice. She stirred the pottage in the cauldron before turning back to scrutinize her father.

Exhaustion marked his face, and she said softly, "This will never do, Father. The long walk has wearied you. You must accept the offer to occupy the former master mason's hut for the duration of your work on the baron's cathedral."

"The hut is too isolated from those of the foreign artisans."

"It is close to the site where the cathedral will stand and will forestall the walk you would need to make each day."

"The baron watched you throughout the day. I saw him. He followed your every move, even though he believes you to be a boy. I fear the proximity will tempt him further, Rosamund."

"I am but a lad who works beside you, Father. I will be forgotten by the baron when a young wench diverts his fancy."

"Would that were true."

"Do not fear for me, Father," Rosamund said defi-

14

antly. "There is more to this Saxon maid than meets the eye."

Hadley did not reply, and Rosamund's shoulders stiffened. She knew her place, and it was not in the simple wood-and-wattle hut where she presently resided. Nor was it in the bed of a rapacious Norman.

Hadley was correct. She was destined for more.

Chapter Two

Wet lips nuzzled his cheek. Low snorts of encouragement accompanied the nuzzling as Dagan groaned and realized he was lying on the hard forest ground with Conqueror standing over him and dawn brightening the sky.

He attempted to rise, but halted at the sharp pain in his chest. The acrid taste of blood was strong in his mouth and his eyes were almost swollen shut. Dagan shivered with fever and cold as he realized that in addition to being wounded, he was totally naked except for his breechcloth.

Conqueror snorted again. Blood marked the horse's hide—blood that he was somehow certain bespoke the animal's resistance—and he gradually remembered.

His war wound had incapacitated him. An assault had surprised him. He had been unable to thwart it.

He had been robbed . . . beaten . . . stabbed . . . left for dead.

Dagan looked around him. He saw discarded clothing lying nearby and realized his own garments had been exchanged for the dirty rags that his assailants had left behind.

Dagan reached for them with a bloodied hand and pulled them toward him. Conqueror snorted at his movement and stepped back. Judging from the animal's wounds, the thieves had attempted to take Conqueror along with his other possessions. Yet it seemed that the loyal animal had somehow managed to escape, and had returned to his side.

Dagan managed to don the discarded rags, and with a momentous effort, raised himself to his feet and boosted himself up onto Conqueror's bare back.

Leaning heavily over the brave animal's neck, Dagan gripped his silky mane tightly. He whispered into his ear, "The rest is up to you."

Rosamund glanced around the dirty master mason's hut that Hadley had decided to accept. She had spent the morning making their new abode habitable by setting out fresh straw for their mattresses, cleaning the refuse out of the hut, and brushing the fireplace free of the spiders and other creatures that had established their homes there.

The previous master mason had obviously had as little concern for cleanliness as he'd had for his work. Actually, if the empty containers smelling of ale were any indication, the former master mason had had only one pursuit in mind. In light of the depressed situation in the country under William's reign, she wondered if she could blame him.

It galled Rosamund to admit that a foreign master was now in charge of the destiny of free-minded Saxons. She still remembered the day nine years earlier when a party of knights and soldiers led by the Baron de Silva came charging into the fief. At his orders, the baron's soldiers slaughtered the livestock, confiscated their stores of food, and set fire to anything they could not carry away. The baron had watched as his pillagers ravished the women and killed anyone who had attempted to stop them. If Hadley had not spirited her away and hidden her, she probably would not have survived the day.

The entire countryside that the baron had so secured for William had been awarded to him, including faraway wilds of forested land. The Saxons who had been living there for generations had become the baron's virtual slaves.

Rosamund frowned. She would not have Hadley suffer the same fate as the poor man who had once occupied this hut. For that reason she had pressed him to accept lodging closer to the construction site so he might exert his best effort. However dangerous the situation might be for her there, it would be far more dangerous for both of them if he did not satisfy the baron.

Rosamund glanced at the dispersing crowd outside the hut. She was thankful that Hadley was presently capable of supervising the artisans gathered to await his direction. He was having a good day, perhaps because the morning light was bright and clear; perhaps because this temporary home had momentarily relieved some of his concerns; but most probably because the baron's absence from the scene had alleviated his agitation.

A familiar desperation assaulted Rosamund. She approved of Hadley's decision to endure his infirmity in silence and believed that Saxon herbs and cures proved more worthwhile than a Norman physician's care for the most part. On days like this, when Hadley's vision appeared so improved, she could not help but think that much of his problem was caused by the stress that the rapidly aging fellow had suffered over the years because of her.

Rosamund had believed since early childhood that she had survived the Norman invasion for a reason. That reason had become clearer as she had grown, until she became convinced that she had been spared to become a pivotal figure who would help the Saxons regain their pride. She had attained womanhood with that silent conviction in mind. Toward that end, she had taken note of the insurrections to the north, where expatriate Saxons united with Irish and Scottish forces to continue revolt against William's rule. She had learned all she could about invasions from other foreign sources, hoping their aspirations for England's throne might be turned to the advantage of her people. She had scrutinized news of the seemingly ceaseless battles marking William's reign. In doing so, she had decided that time and circumstance had finally come together to provide the perfect climate for her to make her move.

Yet she still hesitated . . . because Hadley's life now depended on her.

"Ross . . ."

Responding belatedly to the unfamiliar name her father used, Rosamund called out, "I'm coming . . . *Hadley.*"

He turned toward her and whispered, "I have sent the workmen back to their jobs, and I need to make certain before work progresses that the former master mason's efforts were sound and the foundation will support a structure as heavy as the one the baron proposes. I cannot trust my vision in calculating so important an issue. You must confirm what I see."

"Of course, Father."

Rosamund attempted to take Hadley's arm, but he shrugged off her hand as he said more softly, "It will not do to make me appear less than able in the event the baron is watching. I will act as if I'm instructing you." He sighed. "It is a necessary deception, I'm afraid."

Hadley squinted into the rising sun as he walked across the busy construction site with Rosamund at his side. With her fair hair chopped boyishly short and her feminine curves concealed by the shapeless garb of a youth, not an eye turned to scrutinize her. He nodded, grateful that her disguise appeared to suffice.

That concern thrust aside, he stared at the confusion around him. Horse-drawn wagons delivered huge stones to various sites as stonecutters and apprentices worked to shape the heavy rock. Others dumped supplies into great mounds that awaited his distribution. He saw that other apprentices carried sand in buckets to be mixed into mortar, and yet others transported the mixed mortar to the places where the masons worked with hammer and chisel. Hadley glanced at the guidelines that had been strung to mark the positions of walls and walkways yet to be constructed, knowing that he dared not allow progress on the massive project until he had had time to examine all the work that had been done. The knowledge that the former master mason had been haphazard in so many respects nagged at him—as did the necessity of the additional labor needed to excavate a foundation that might be found unsound.

His vision clouded, Hadley squinted more intensely into the distance as a horseman approached the site. The rider's stance was awkward and his mount's step was uncertain. Hadley noted that laborers halted their efforts to stare in the man's direction, and that beside him, Rosamund gradually stiffened.

"What is it, Ross? Who is that rider and why is everyone stopping to stare at his approach?"

Rosamund responded breathlessly. "I do not know, Father, except that the man is bleeding. Wait here. I'll see to it."

Hadley watched with limited vision as Rosamund rushed to the rider's side.

Rosamund gulped at the sight that met her eyes when she reached the motionless horseman. Lying limply astride a great warhorse, the fellow wore ragged clothing soaked with blood that had begun to dry. His face was battered and swollen into a grotesque mask.

Judging from his clothing, he was a common man, yet he was riding a Norman destrier. She could only surmise that he had stolen the horse from one of the baron's knights and had had the misfortune to meet up with soldiers before managing to escape on it. The thought pleased Rosamund. She admired the man's pluck for winning out over those who had taken so much from them, and for his success in escaping with his treasure despite an obviously vicious attack.

Aware that the thief might be followed, Rosamund made a quick decision and ordered, "Lift this man from his mount and carry him to the master mason's hut—quickly. Then hide the horse in the stable so I may tend to him later."

The apprentices did not move.

Anger flashing, Rosamund was about to repeat her orders when Hadley spoke from behind her. "Do as Ross says. You will obey his orders as if I have spoken them." He instructed the gathered workmen more softly, "And you will maintain any secrecy that Ross demands—do you understand?"

Rosamund saw immediate acquiescence register in the gruff workmen's eyes as they hastened to pull the rider from his horse. In that moment of stark revelation, she saw that with his words, Hadley had satisfied a lingering resentment against their enforced labor, and that both artisans and common laborers alike shared a loathing for the baron who had driven them into servitude with his demands. The silent courage visible in their expressions also indicated that they would keep any secret Hadley asked of them, and that if any among them desired to challenge those sentiments, they would do so under threat of their lives.

Rosamund glanced around her as the bloodied fellow and the great warhorse were swiftly taken in different directions. She turned boldly toward the approaching soldiers the baron had left on watch at the site. She stepped back as one of them addressed Hadley, asking, "Who was that man and why are those workers carrying him toward your hut?"

Hadley shrugged as he responded. "I don't know who he is, except that the poor fellow was obviously set upon by thieves. I directed those men to take him to my hut, where my assistant will determine the extent of his wounds." Hadley smiled. "The fellow looks to be well built. I have no doubt he will be grateful for our help and will become a valuable asset when he is well."

The soldiers nodded. Their approval of Hadley's seemingly high-handed expectations turned Rosamund's stomach. When they were far enough away, she turned back to Hadley and whispered, "Thank you, Father."

"Go to the fellow, Rosamund," Hadley whispered in return. "I will make my way to the foundation and follow the procedures there until you are available. Do not worry about me."

Nodding, Rosamund turned toward their hut as workmen carried the wounded man inside. The poor man had chanced upon the right place for help. She would not abandon any loyal Saxon who needed her help. She would protect him with her life.

Dagan awakened upon a mattress of simple straw in a primitive hut. He attempted to move, but groaned softly when pain throbbed to life at the effort. A slender youth kneeling at the fireplace turned toward him at the sound, and then approached him carrying a wooden bowl. He blinked, attempting to see more clearly, but it was to no avail as the young man drew closer and offered him a drink from a cup at his side.

"Where am I?"

The boy responded in a voice that had yet to mature. "Your horse carried you into the construction site of Baron de Silva's cathedral, but we are all friends in this place. I have asked others to hide the great warhorse that brought you here. It will be confined among the draft animals in the barn while I tend to you. We are not concerned with where you obtained so valuable an animal."

"The horse . . . is mine."

"Its ownership does not matter to me. I am the head apprentice to the master mason at this site. He asked me to care for you."

"No doctor!" Dagan's gaze wavered, but his sentiment remained strong. "Bloodletting . . . weakens."

"You need not fear. We have no Norman doctors or leeches here." A semblance of a smile touched the young man's lips. "I will use only Saxon herbs and remedies that have proved their worth in curing, but I must first wash away the debris covering you."

Dagan struggled to clear his uncertain vision. The young man's features were delicate and perfect. He had seen similar young men like him before, and was aware that those of their like often worked harder than others to prove their usefulness on the field of battle.

Another painful spasm convulsed him, and Dagan bit back a groan as he closed his eyes. He could only hope the young man was as skilled as he appeared to be.

"You will have to help me."

The voice drifted into Dagan's semiconscious state and he opened his eyes.

The youth clarified, "I need to remove your clothing so I may tend to your injuries fully. You are too big . . . too heavy for me to lift without your cooperation, and I dare not ask for help."

Dagan raised himself with an extreme effort and allowed the fellow to remove his shirt. Darkness edged his vision as he heard the young man say, "I need to remove your breeches, too."

The loosened breeches slipped down his legs, leaving only his breechcloth in place as he mumbled, "My chest burns."

"I see the wound. Do not worry. I will take care of it. Just close your eyes and rest."

The young man's voice was strangely melodic and reassuring. Closing his eyes as he was bidden, Dagan felt himself slipping off into unconsciousness with the thought that the boy's clear blue eyes had been honest and sympathetic as they had looked down into his. He had seen something else there, too—something he could not quite define, except to say . . . he trusted him.

Rosamund stared down at the wounded man as he slipped into unconsciousness. She had no doubt his bruises were severe, but she did not believe they were life-threatening. The deep wound in his chest was another matter. He had obviously been viciously stabbed—a wound that might have killed a lesser man.

Rosamund took a shaky breath. The man lying in front of her in naught but a breechcloth was more powerfully built than any she had ever seen. Even covered with bruises and dried blood, it was plain to see he had the body of a warrior. His well-developed arms and legs, as well as his broad chest, indicated he was no stranger to battle. Her heart pounded at the thought that the power he exuded even in his weakened state had probably earned him the trust of many Saxons bent on revolt, and that he would again be a formidable foe against the Normans when he recovered.

If he recovered.

With the realization that the warrior's life was in her hands, Rosamund dipped a cloth into the water she had warmed at the fire. She rubbed it against the special soap she had fused with medicinal herbs and carefully cleansed the wound on the injured man's chest. It began bleeding again under her ministrations and Rosamund frowned. With the dried blood cleared away, she could see that the wound was deep and raw. He appeared to have no trouble breathing, which indicated no complications there, but there was still the possibility that his wounds were beyond her healing ability.

Yet she could not afford to hesitate.

Rosamund picked up the pot of warm salve she commonly used for minor ailments and turned toward the medicine pouch that was never far from her side. Her mother had passed the knowledge of medicinal herbs to her when she was a child. She took a breath as she mixed herbs and salve into a poultice, spread some of the mixture against the wound, and then wrapped the rest in a clean cloth and pressed it against the chest wound.

The stranger began twisting and turning, obviously in the throes of fever. Uncertain how to handle his unexpected behavior, Rosamund sat back helplessly until the fellow began shouting loud, indecipherable orders and, in his delirium, suddenly attempted to rise. Fearing for him and the possibility that he would bring the soldiers down upon them, Rosamund threw herself across his body and whispered against his ear, "Be calm. I am trying to help you. You need not fear anything when I am with you. I will protect you."

The man's protests halted abruptly. He looked at her, his swollen eyes small slits of amber as his arms folded around her with unanticipated strength. Holding her tight against him, he demanded roughly, "Who are you?"

"My name is Ros . . . Ross. I am your friend."

"My friend . . ."

The fellow searched her face for long moments. She felt the flat of his hand caress her back just before his eyelids closed and he released her.

Rosamund drew back, shuddering. She had felt the strength of the fellow's grip even in his weakened state. He could easily have crushed her—could have broken every bone in her body—but he had instead chosen an incredibly gentle caress. She remembered the scrutiny of that narrowed, amber-eyed stare. He had trusted her, and she was determined to be worthy of his trust.

The injured man slipped into an unnatural sleep. He began shivering despite the warmth of the hut, and Rosamund pulled the worn coverlet up to shield him. She took a deep breath before dipping a cloth into the warm, soapy water and washing the blood from his face. The swelling there appeared to be increasing. His eyes would soon be completely closed, and he would soon no longer be able to breathe through his nose. She rinsed out the cloth when his face was clean, changed the water, and then ran the cloth across his lips again. Rosamund saw his tongue slip out to seek the moisture, and she raised a sip of ale to his lips. She did not see the moment when his eyes opened briefly, when he glimpsed her face, and then closed his eyes again to a more restful sleep.

Lowering the coverlet as her work progressed, Rosamund washed the full length of his muscular body—the powerful arms that had gripped her so tightly and the broad chest against which he had briefly clutched her. She paused at the breechcloth covering his vitals, her heart pounding. Determined to ignore her trembling hands, she bypassed the stained cloth and washed the dirt from his muscular legs. It was then that another inflamed injury came into view. The wound was clearly an old one that had festered from neglect or inadequate treatment.

No doctor . . . bloodletting weakens.

She agreed with the stranger's statement, but not with whatever alternate treatment he had employed. Taking another strained breath, she squeezed out the cloth and began washing the wound. The fellow reacted violently, thrashing and mumbling until she whispered against his ear, "Trust me. I am your friend."

When he stilled, she washed away the discharge and considered the wound quietly. She had no choice but to cauterize it in order to burn away the festered, weeping flesh.

With slow deliberation, Rosamund placed a broad knife on the coals. She removed it with a cloth when it was heated through and approached the injured man. She knelt beside him and whispered into his ear, "This treatment is necessary. Please forgive me for the pain I will cause you."

Rosamund pressed the flat of the hot blade to his wound. She swallowed sharply when his eyes snapped open with an instinctive protest that halted the moment he saw her face. The scent of burning flesh rose between them as she whispered sincerely, "I am sorry."

She saw the perspiration that rose to the man's battered face in reaction to the pain of the hot blade. She was not aware of the tear that slipped down her cheek, and was startled when the stranger raised a shaky hand to brush it away. He whispered thickly, "I do not feel pain when I look into your eyes."

His hand dropped to the mattress and his eyes closed. Rosamund's heart leaped in her chest. No! It couldn't be! He couldn't be dead!

She caught her breath when she saw the pulse in his throat throbbing strongly. She raised her hand to the spot where he had brushed a tear from her cheek. Somehow the stranger had not doubted that the pain she had caused him was necessary, and his touch had been an acknowledgment of that fact. Why did she wish that the brief caress had meant something more?

Hadley looked up from the part of the foundation that had been laid according to the former master mason's instructions. He had spent the past hour staring blankly at the plan and walking beside his friend, Horace, as they scrutinized the construction. The fellow had been one of many who had accompanied him to the site to add their talents to the project two days earlier. Horace had many comments about the work already executed there—most of them negative. Hadley had not liked what he saw either, however little that had been. He was as aware as Horace, however, that his friend's true talents lay in carving the great blocks of stone that would be used on the exterior of the cathedral. He was a true artisan despite his age, but he was not educated in the intricacies of construction. Horace had merely done him the favor of assisting him while Rosamund was absent. He appreciated his friend's effort, but it only demonstrated more clearly than before how dependent he was on Rosamund's presence.

An approaching horseman neared and Horace went still. Hadley could not see the fellow's face clearly, but further identification was unnecessary. No other man rode so arrogantly, nor wore colors so vibrant as to proclaim without speech that his station was far superior to that of the common workmen who labored there.

The baron halted his horse and Hadley stiffened. Horace slipped away, granting them privacy as the baron inquired, "I see that a different fellow accompanied you on your rounds today. Where is the young apprentice so necessary to you that you were willing to challenge my authority for him?"

"Ross is presently at the hut that we will share."

The baron's handsome, clean-shaven face twitched as he repeated, "The hut you will share . . ."

"Ross is my apprentice, and he is almost a son to me. He has lived with me since . . . since William became king. He is presently in our new home tending to a fellow apprentice who had an accident."

"So . . . Ross is a physician as well as being practically *a son* to you?"

"Ross is not a physician. He is merely versed in

Saxon remedies . . . knowledge taught to him by his former mistress when he was a lad."

"Ah, yes . . ." The baron's unexpected smile did not conceal the rapacious glint in his eye when he said, "I can understand the need to teach some simple rudiments to a young man such as he. I am sure that Ross has a supremely . . . *gentle touch*. The injured fellow you speak of is fortunate, indeed, to be treated by him." He added as if in afterthought, "I, myself, am inclined to instruct Ross in matters that would benefit both of us. I am sure he would prove an avid student. I may yet avail myself of time with him in order to accomplish that purpose."

His expression hardening when Hadley did not reply, the baron said haughtily, "That aside, it is plain to see that after two days you have altered very little at this site. I cannot be certain if your dependence on your *apprentice* is to be blamed, since he is otherwise occupied at present, but I feel the need to warn you that I am not a patient man."

"I assure you that I am capable of handling the situation, my lord, but certain inspections are necessary before any changes are instituted. I will, however, be sure to inform you if I find . . ."

Hadley's voice trailed away when he realized that the baron's gaze had moved toward a spot behind him, and that the arrogant man was no longer listening. He turned to see a figure approaching. With her boyish garb and rough, elongated step, Rosamund should have stirred little attention, yet the interest sparked in the baron's gaze could not be denied.

"Monsignor . . ."

The baron's head snapped back toward him and Hadley continued softly, "My apprentice now approaches, as you can see. He is an able lad, and I am very fond of him. As I previously mentioned, he is necessary to the performance of my duties here. I find there are ways that I cannot do without him."

"Really?" The baron dismounted as Rosamund drew near. His great stallion snorted as he secured it nearby and swept Rosamund's slender proportions as she approached. He said, "I am drawn to the young fellow. I can understand how someone like him can become indispensable in many ways. I should like to test his abilities for myself."

"I cannot spare him."

"What?" The baron's gaze grew heated as Rosamund stopped at Hadley's side. He demanded incredulously, "Do you lay claim to the time with your apprentice that I would use?"

Hadley persisted, "Ross's time is already heavily divided. The apprentice he is caring for was badly injured. His recuperation will be lengthy and Ross must be available to him."

"I will not abide that loss of time! The fellow can recuperate elsewhere, tended by another."

"The extent of the man's injuries makes that impossible. Ross will be sorely pressed to maintain the fellow's care and to perform his duty to me until the man is well again."

"The injured fellow's condition is of no great importance here or anywhere else. Apprentices such as he are easily replaced."

"His condition is important to Ross, and thus important to me. I demand much of my apprentice."

"You do . . ."

"I demand strict attention to detail so that nothing escapes me—detail that is essential to this project and of greatest importance to its successful completion." Hadley paused before adding with a touch of subservience, "I only wish to do my best for you, my lord."

The baron nodded stiffly. Turning to Rosamund, he put his hand on her shoulder and then slid it upward to force her face up to his when she avoided looking directly at him. He stared into her emotionless features as he stated without embarrassment, "Yes . . . I am strangely attracted to you, Ross. I have heard of the appeal of young men like you but have never deigned to taste the joys they are said to provide. With you, I am tempted." Ignoring the shocked silence that his statement evoked, he continued, "In truth, I am more than tempted. I intend to sate the interest you stir in me, and I will not accept excuses." Moving closer until the stiff proof of his passion pressed hard against Rosamund's hip, he whispered, "What say you? I would hear your response now."

The baron's question hung in the air. Stunned by the hard pressure of his passion against her body and sickened by his belief that she was a young man who would fear reprisal if he refused to consent, she felt bile rise in her throat and did not respond as the baron's hand slipped down from her shoulder. Aware that her secret would be revealed once he encountered the rounded mounds concealed by her voluminous, stained shirt, she stepped back and said, "I have other, more pressing duties that demand my attention, my lord. I have no time for self-indulgence."

The baron's face flamed unexpectedly as he responded, "You intimate that my interest in you is self-indulgent?"

"Is it not?"

Ignoring Hadley's gasp, the baron replied, "Perhaps it *is* self-indulgent, but it is a self-indulgence that I have earned in the king's service."

Rosamund replied to his outrageous statement with spontaneous indignation. "You have *earned* nothing on this land that you stole from simple, poorly trained Saxons who sought to live their lives peacefully—land that William gave you as a reward for your butchery!"

His gaze narrowed, the baron ordered, "Mind your tongue, Ross. My patience grows thin."

"Do you issue another command to me? I thought you had requested a response to your question. I gave it honestly. To my mind, you could not ask for more."

"To my mind, your impertinence is dangerous. If I did not desire you—"

"You desire me, but I do not desire you! I am, instead, appalled to hear that you would have me abandon a man who shares my birthright. You say he may be easily replaced. If that is true, I am Saxon and may be easily replaced by you as well—I would hope by one of the young maids who look at you with covetous eyes, not by a young man like me."

"How easily you speak those words." The baron eyed Rosamund with escalating heat. "Were I not unexpectedly enthralled by your appeal, they would damn you."

"Would they? Methinks you are too *enthralled* with dreams of a great future to forsake the impression you hope to make with the glorious cathedral you plan. Methinks you will realize that I am presently indispensable here and because time has already been wasted on your grand plan, you will sate your desires on a more favorable and willing personage."

"The tongue of a serpent!"

The baron's handsome face reddened, but Rosamund stood fast. She did not see the panic on Hadley's face when he interjected, "My lord, Ross does not mean what he says. He—"

"Silence!" the baron's wrath exploded with a single word in Hadley's direction. Then he turned back to Rosamund. "I find that I admire your audacity in speaking to me without restraint when I requested an honest answer." Closing the short distance between them, he loomed over her with his superior height and said, "For that reason you will escape reprisal this time, but be forewarned . . . I will not overlook your impudence a second time. And I tell you now, sooner or later I will have my way."

The baron stepped backward. In a voice calculated to be overheard by those who were near, he addressed Hadley firmly. "In the meantime, you had best hope that your work pleases me, for in truth, much more than you realize depends on it." With a final suggestive glance in Rosamund's direction, the baron mounted and spurred his steed away.

Turning back to Hadley, Rosamund apologized

softly. "I am sorry, Father. I did not mean to put you in jeopardy, but I could not allow him to speak to me in so insulting a manner."

"I understand. Were I free to act as honestly as I wished, I would have struck him dead." He shook his head. "I originally believed that your disguise would save you from his advances, but the attempt was useless."

"My disguise may still prove effective, Father. The baron is intrigued with me now because he is confused, but his ambitions outweigh whatever sexual fantasies he harbors. I will be safe for the duration of your reign as master mason."

"I will make arrangements for you to vacate this place . . . to disappear so that he will never find you."

"You need me, Father."

"I do not intend to save myself at the expense of your innocence."

"Neither will come to pass. You will see. Neither can I leave now and abandon the man who lies desperately ill in our hut. I will not allow another Saxon to die as the result of William's conquest."

"You have done your best for him. It is time for others to assume his care."

Rosamund shook her head as though she found the thought abhorrent. "The stranger trusts me. He looks to me to aid him, and I will not fail him."

"But you do not know him. We will locate his mother . . . his sister . . . his wife to care for him."

"His wife . . . ?" Rosamund shook her head vigor-

ously. "The stranger has no wife! Nor does he have any other woman whom he depends on. Only me."

"He knows you are a woman?"

"No."

"But you know who he is."

"No."

Confused, Hadley said, "At least you know where he comes from . . . his name."

"No."

"Then how can you be sure?"

"I know. I have seen it in his eyes . . . eyes that speak only truth."

"And the truth is?"

Rosamund took a breath. "The truth is that I have made him a promise that I will not break."

Silent for long moments, Hadley pressed, "What is that promise?"

"I will not desert him."

Silent a few moments longer, Hadley responded, "I will call Horace to my side. Return to the hut. You must not break your promise."

Her eyes suddenly filling, Rosamund whispered, "Thank you, Father."

Dagan awakened abruptly and strained to see through eyes that did not function properly. He managed a glance around the primitive hut where he lay, while fragments of memory began to return. Most vivid was the image of clear blue eyes filled with concern. He remembered a gentle, knowledgeable touch . . . a soft voice that somehow dulled his pain . . . empathy that had evoked a single tear. He recalled stroking that tear away, and the powerful emotions that the touch had raised in him despite his debilities.

But where was that concerned gaze now . . . that gentle touch? His whereabouts were unfamiliar, and as memory of the vicious attack returned abruptly to his mind, the need to escape clamored inside him. Dagan threw back the coverlet and attempted to rise. He placed his feet on the floor of the hut, suddenly aware that he wore nothing but a breechcloth.

Confusion assaulted him, and the heat inside him soared higher. He made an attempt to stand as a slender figure rushed to his side and whispered, "No, lie back. Do not fear. I am here."

That voice . . .

Halting his frantic movement, Dagan squinted into the familiar, blue-eyed gaze. A small, heart-shaped face grew clearer . . . a soft voice reassured him . . . a gentle touch somehow alleviated his pain. He lay back down.

The person leaned over him. He reached up, imprisoning the shadowed figure in his grip so he might scrutinize it more clearly. Myriad emotions overwhelming him, he rasped, "Who are you?"

"I told you, my name is Ross."

"Ross . . . Why do you care for me?"

"You are injured and need my help."

He shook his head and demanded, "Nay . . . *why?*"

The brief silence that followed was finally broken

when the shadowed figure replied, "I do not know why. I do not know who you are or how you came to be here. I only know that you must trust my care."

His strength fading, Dagan heard himself reply, "I do."

Chapter Three

The animal will allow no one near it. It rears. It snaps and bites with its great teeth. Its size is so great that the men fear to approach."

Rosamund frowned at Hadley's pronouncement. The day had been long and difficult and night neared. The stranger lay on the mattress behind her. His fever had escalated despite her greatest efforts, and he had made few coherent comments in recent hours. His face was still grotesquely swollen, and the pain of his body's bruising appeared to be increasing, if she were to judge from the discomfited grunts he uttered with every movement. Although the festering on his leg wound appeared to have been curtailed by her treatment, the deep knife wound in his chest showed no change at all.

As if reading her mind, Hadley looked at the thrashing figure on the straw mattress and whispered, "His wounds are many. It is too soon to expect your herbs to have a healing effect on them; you know that as well as I. But the truth is that he may not survive. In the meantime, the prize this man sought—the great steed that brought him here—stubbornly seeks its own demise. I fear that even should this man survive, the great warhorse will not."

"You are telling me that the great destrier that delivered the stranger to this place has not drunk or eaten since it arrived this morning?"

"Yea, that is what I say. Edmund, the young man who cares for the animals here, cannot fathom a fear that would cause such a problem with the animal."

"Conqueror . . . has no fear," a voice from behind them muttered.

Stunned by the unexpected interruption, Rosamund turned with Hadley toward the mattress where the stranger lay. Deep in delirium, the fellow twisted and turned as if he had not spoken at all. Rosamund crouched at his side. Grateful for the stranger's brief moment of lucidity and hoping for more, she pressed, "If that is so, why does the animal thwart even the best efforts to help him?"

Rosamund waited as the man's head turned toward her. He peered at her for long moments through eyes swollen almost shut, as if attempting to identify her. When he spoke again, he rasped, "Conqueror resents confinement . . . will not abide it . . . at any expense."

"We cannot turn him loose or he will be discovered by the soldiers. Or worse, they will come looking for you because of him."

The stranger mumbled, "What is the choice?"

Slipping back into fevered ramblings, the fellow resumed his semiconscious state, and Rosamund drew herself upright.

"Rosamund . . ."

Rosamund turned toward Hadley and said, "You heard him, Father. The horse must have suffered somehow and will not abide restraint."

"You do not mean we should turn the animal loose?

It is vicious . . . deadly. If the soldiers see it, they will eventually reason that this fellow stole it before bringing it here."

"Not necessarily."

"We cannot take that chance, Rosamund. Your life . . . mine . . . the life of the stranger and of those who helped him depend on it. To choose the life of an animal over the lives of many is wrong."

Rosamund looked down at the fevered stranger. She said hoarsely, "This fellow risked his life to capture that animal."

"And we risk his life again." Hadley took a step back. "I will not argue with you."

"I would see the animal for myself, Father. Perhaps I may help him. If not—" She hesitated "—his fate is sealed."

Satisfied with her reply, Hadley nodded and turned away. He did not look back when Rosamund exited the hut.

Night had fallen when Rosamund walked across the construction site. Small fires grew dim outside huts along the way, indicating that the artisans and workers inside had retired for the night. The small temporary village that had sprung up as a result of the construction was all but silent.

The makeshift barn smelled of sweat and manure as she approached it in the darkening shadows. She heard nervous whinnies as she neared and realized that the great destrier's angry snorting disturbed the keeper, and the other animals as well.

Frowning, Rosamund entered the barn and turned toward a young fellow who said nervously, "My name is

Edmund. I am caretaker here. I know who you are. You are Ross, Hadley's apprentice, who is tending to the man who brought that destrier here. I can do nothing to quiet him. Its agitation makes him a threat to all."

At a loss for a reply, Rosamund responded simply, "It is late. You may retire now and consider that your work is done for the day."

"But—"

"Hadley understands that you have done all you can. He sent me here to tell you that, and to make sure you leave for the night."

Nodding reluctantly as the great horse's whinnies grew ever louder, the young fellow complied. Rosamund waited only until he had cleared the doorway before cautiously approaching the rear of the structure. She stepped back as the animal reared at the sight of her, its eyes bulging and its hooves striking wildly at the air. At the sound of her voice, the animal reared again and snapped at the leather strap confining it.

"The stranger says you do not like to be confined," Rosamund said softly. "He intimated that I should allow you to roam freely in here. I do not know if that is wise, Conqueror."

The great horse eyed her speculatively at the use of his name.

"If I do as the stranger says, you may escape and bring the soldiers down on us. Then all may be lost."

The animal listened to the sound of her voice, moving restlessly as she continued. "If I do not, you will not survive, for no one dares approach you. What is the answer to this problem? What would you have me do?"

The horse's wild-eyed gaze fixed on her. He turned

his head so he might see her more clearly when Rosamund said, "Would you even allow me to loosen your restraint . . . to free you, Conqueror?"

The horse stilled.

"I wonder."

Rosamund approached the animal carefully. Fear a tight knot inside her, she raised her hands slowly toward the leather straps confining him. She noted the nervous steps the horse took . . . the way he watched her every movement. Her heart pounded as she spoke to him softly. Her hands trembled as she unbuckled the straps, saying, "I will free you, but you must not bolt. Instead, you must prove to me that you may be trusted. You must—"

Jerking back when the last buckle was loosened, the destrier reared before Rosamund could finish her statement. She fell back against the stable wall as the creature broke into a gallop, burst through the closed doorway, and thundered out into the night.

Rosamund started after the frantic animal at a run, softly calling his name. She knew he saw her when he looked back, though he did not attempt to elude her. Instead, he slowed his pace, searching the darkness. Conqueror snorted and huffed, breath emerging from his nostrils in white puffs on the cool night air. Rosamund's eyes widened when the horse started directly toward her hut. She gasped when he reached the doorway, then pushed the door open with the power of his strong body and entered.

Stunned, Rosamund followed to see that Hadley had flattened himself against the side of the hut as the great animal walked to the mattress where the stranger lay.

Rosamund entered and came to an abrupt halt when she heard the animal snicker softly as he leaned down over her thrashing patient and nuzzled his cheek. The stranger snapped suddenly awake at the touch. He peered at the great animal, straining to see. She heard him whisper and saw the animal respond with a snort when the man raised his shaky hand to stroke the dark muzzle. The stranger spoke more firmly, and the animal retreated. He turned and came to stand obediently at her side.

Rosamund looked at the bed and saw the stranger glance her way. He muttered, "Take him . . . back to the barn."

Swallowing, Rosamund reached for the reins still dangling from the destrier's harness. When the animal did not protest, she led it out of the hut and back to the barn. She did not attempt to restrain it when it walked to a bucket and drank greedily. She left and closed the ban door behind her when the animal walked toward the corner where feed was strewn and lowered his head to eat.

Breathless, Rosamund returned to the hut and approached the bed. The stranger was moving restlessly. He went still when she asked, "What did you say to that horse?"

"I said nothing."

"You said something."

Pinpoints of amber lingered on her face for long moments before the stranger mumbled, "I told him only to trust you . . . as do I."

Dagan awakened slowly and glanced around to see a small wood-and-wattle hut with a great fireplace. He saw that a young man slept a few feet away on what appeared to be a hastily readied mattress stuffed with straw. Closer to the fire, an old man slept on a similar mattress—all in a space that barely sufficed.

Pain surged unexpectedly in his chest and he grunted and closed his eyes against the searing sensation. The shards of memory that had formerly deserted him returned slowly. He glanced again at the youth sleeping beside his mattress. The young fellow turned toward him unexpectedly, his long eyelashes dark against his pale cheeks, although his hair was as light as the sun. Dagan recalled gradually that eyes bluer than a summer sky lay underneath those eyelids, eyes that reflected concern for his pain . . . and a spark of something else. He viewed again the delicate contours of the lad's cheek, the slender, almost feminine lips . . . and he remembered more. He recalled that the touch of the lad's skin had been soft and smooth. He remembered drawing the lad tight against him to see him more clearly, and that the sensation of holding that slender body close had somehow been like no other. He recalled that the narrow expanse of the young fellow's back under his palm had seemed so delicate that he had been tempted to clutch it closer. He remembered that the soft mounds pressed against his chest had raised a sensation that he—

No, that could not be correct!

Dagan struggled to clear his mind. Yea, he recalled that he had known many such as the young lad before. Yet he had never felt drawn to any of them as he was to this slender youth.

Something was wrong.

Dagan closed his eyes, recalling that a fever had overwhelmed him. He had been attacked and beaten by thieves before managing to mount Conqueror and give him his head. Conqueror had brought him here— wherever *here* was.

"You're awake, and your eyes are clear." In a puzzling lapse of time, the young man was suddenly standing beside him. His blue eyes reflected his relief when he said, "I feared for you when your fever escalated, but I can see now that it has lessened. I am glad."

Somehow annoyed that the boy's relief should impact him so greatly, Dagan said hoarsely, "Who are you?"

"My name is Ros . . . Ross, remember? Your horse brought you to the site of Baron de Silva's cathedral, and we tended to you."

"*You* tended to me."

The young man nodded. "I tended your wounds, and took your clothes and washed them as well." Nodding to the fireplace, where ragged clothing hung drying, she said, "They will be clean and dry when you are well again and ready to don them."

Common clothes of a common man . . . but he was no common man.

Dagan squinted against the pain that surged in his chest when he attempted to speak, only to be halted by the lad, who ordered, "That's enough for now. You are weak. I have only one other question to ask. What may I call you?"

"My name . . ."

"Yea, your name."

Noting that the old man rose from his mattress a

distance away as he was about to reply, Dagan responded cautiously, "My name is . . . Dagan."

Approaching, the old man asked suspiciously, "I am curious how you command such great control over the Norman warhorse that you stole, Dagan."

"Conqueror?"

The old fellow frowned. "An unfortunate name, considering the circumstances under which we Saxons live."

"I did not name him. I rescued him . . . and earned his devotion."

"This man is ill, Father. He should not be questioned in this manner."

Dagan's attention turned toward the young man. "Father?"

The old man replied, "I am like a father to Ross, but he is my apprentice."

Dagan glanced up into the silver-blue eyes looking down into his. Pain surged anew and he gasped and closed his eyes. "To you, he is a son. To me he is . . . somehow more."

Rosamund swallowed as the stranger closed his eyes. She glanced up to see Hadley looking at her. Dagan's mumbling had been all but incoherent. She could not be certain Hadley had understood him, but she had understood every word.

Somehow more . . .

Silently chiding herself at the effect Dagan's confused statement had had on her, Rosamund turned back to the fire. Of course she was *somehow more* to the stranger. She was his only hope for survival. He was totally dependent on her.

But even as she stirred the pot suspended over the flames, Rosamund knew what the stranger had meant. Despite the danger involved in the difficult situation, she felt the same.

Yea . . . he was *somehow more.*

"All rebellion against William is doomed from the start. You know that as well as I."

Baron Guilbert de Silva regarded Sir Franchot Champlain contemptuously as his knight's statement echoed in the silence of his extensive quarters.

It occurred to him that although the fellow was still tall, muscular, and obviously skilled at the butchery of his trade, Champlain had begun showing his age. Not only was his formerly heavy brown hair thinning and his girth widening, Champlain's aging was also marked by a regular and noticeable descent into his cups.

Champlain occupied a position second only to his own in the army of knights to be called up by William at a moment's notice, the terms under which the spoils of the bloody campaign in Hendsmille had been awarded. Although Champlain had fulfilled the demands of his service well over the years, it bothered the baron that Champlain did not recognize William for the fool that he was.

De Silva's sneer deepened. "Nay, I do not see that all rebellion against William is doomed from the start. Unlike you, I recognize that each rebellion William crushed after becoming king was inadequate in some way. I also recognize that it is the thoughts of men like you—men without vision—that have allowed William whatever successes he has achieved."

Champlain responded with unexpected vehemence, "You seem to forget William's vengeance in the north when rebel insurrection occurred there. William allowed no house or human being to remain standing between York and Durham when Earl Edwin and Earl Morcar revolted. He left his subjects with no doubt of his intentions should others attempt to thwart him."

"You doubtless speak of the Saxon populace who still consider us intruders. I tell you they are an inept, cowardly scum."

"That *inept scum* fought bravely, as the amount of blood that was shed can attest."

"You speak of the bloodshed as if you feel a sense of regret in that which was predestined. Shedding blood proves my superiority over those who fall under my sword!"

Champlain responded with continued vehemence. "You know well that I have shed the blood of many in William's service, and that I have no regrets."

"Well, then . . ."

"But I do not shed blood wantonly! I have matured past that part of my life, and I will not participate in mass destruction when it is unnecessary."

Smiling at the spark of determination that had entered his friend's eyes, de Silva responded, "When it is unnecessary . . . yet you know that William's reign will be tested again and again because he is unworthy. He exhibits fealty for his wife but does not acknowledge the efforts of those who have served him as loyally and well."

"He has exhibited loyalty for those—"

"I will not argue with you! Yet I tell you now that the time has come. Cnut, son of King Swein of Denmark, is ready to make his move. I have been in communication with him, and he is readying two hundred ships that he intends to sail against William. I am of royal blood, and I intend to profit from that endeavor."

"Cnut is doomed to failure."

"Not with our help!"

Taking a backward step, Champlain stated firmly, "I am your servant, but I challenge your decision."

"Cnut's attitude is encouraging." De Silva paused, and then asked abruptly, "I would know now if you would join with me and the army I command when that occurs."

His gaze narrowing, Champlain considered his response. Finally speaking, he said, "I have talked freely with you and have voiced my concerns, but I would have you know that my loyalty . . . is primarily yours."

Turning abruptly toward the door when he realized that Martin Venoir had entered and stood listening to their discussion, Champlain added, "I speak for Martin as well—do I not, Martin?"

De Silva studied the younger man who had entered his quarters unexpectedly. Martin had dark hair that bore no streaks of gray, a face that was unmarked by age, and a well-muscled form. Yet the soberness in Martin's dark eyes bespoke a cynicism beyond his years as the younger man replied, "You speak for me, Champlain. Whatever the question, my thoughts are yours."

Satisfied, Champlain turned back to the baron with a frown. "I need ask only one question: If you are unhappy with William's reign, why do you seek his approval by raising a cathedral on this land?"

"I am not a fool."

"Meaning?"

"Meaning . . ." The baron swept the knights with a cunning gaze. "Meaning that should Cnut's invasion fail, I will not go down with him because my devotion to William is obvious by my raising a cathedral to honor his god."

"William's god?"

"Yea, William's god, for I honor no god except when it is expedient!"

Noting approval in Champlain's eyes, de Silva said abruptly, "I will speak to you again of my plans when they are more defined. For the time being, you are dismissed."

Waiting only until the two men left to attend the unceasing warfare training of their trade, de Silva turned toward the mirror. He scrutinized his appearance, smoothing his hair and picking a thread from his impeccable garments before whispering to his reflection, "All goes well, my friend. By whatever artifice necessary, you will soon attain what is rightfully yours."

Smiling at that thought, Guilbert turned toward the door with a definite destination in mind.

"Where is he?"

"My lord . . . to whom do you refer?"

His gaze fixed on the baron's irate figure as he dismounted from his great black steed, Hadley awaited a response to his question. The midmorning sun shone brightly on a site that was only partially visible to Hadley's eyes, but the baron's angry, threatening step was unmistakable as he advanced toward him and said, "You know who I mean! I am inquiring about your apprentice . . . the young fellow who is so necessary to your work that you *cannot spare him,* yet who is now absent from your side."

"Monseignor, I told you yesterday of the worker who was delivered here wounded and bleeding. I also told you that my apprentice is knowledgeable in the art of healing, and that he is the only person capable of treating the man's serious wounds at this time."

De Silva barely retained patience as he growled, "Yea . . . you told me that."

"Ross is tending to him. The man is improved, but his wounds are grave and his condition is still unstable. Ross fears to leave him."

"Ross sacrifices the work you both may achieve here for this unnamed man?"

"His name is Dagan, my lord."

"I did not ask his name! I asked where Ross is. Now that you have replied, I want to know when he will return to his duty here."

"Ross will return immediately upon completing the treatment he deems necessary for the wounded man."

De Silva responded through clenched teeth, "You have not answered me."

"I have given you the only response I am able to give. But I assure you that Ross will be here before the noon hour, when his help will be essential."

"His help is not essential now?"

Hadley stuttered, "Yes, b..but I am presently involved in details that Ross may review later."

"So Ross is presently free?"

"No, he tends to his patient."

"His patient be damned!" Turning, de Silva mounted his horse. He did not turn back when Hadley called out after him, "Where are you going, my lord?"

Digging his spurs into his mount's sides, de Silva goaded him into a leap forward without responding. Hadley choked on the cloud of dust the animal raised in departing and then turned to call out blindly, "Horace, please come to me."

Hadley whispered when Horace responded to his call, "The baron goes to find Rosamund. I fear she will reveal herself in her anger."

"Do not fear, Hadley. The girl is not a fool. She will maintain her disguise."

"I fear that at the least Rosamund will respond to the baron by saying something that will push his anger beyond retrievable bounds. I must go to her and forestall such an encounter."

"I will do anything you ask, so deep is my belief in you, but I warn you, Hadley, that your appearance at the hut has the potential of doing more harm than good. The baron will only turn on you if Rosamund is successful in thwarting him."

"I fear for her."

"Instead, have faith in her. Rosamund will prevail."

Dagan watched through slitted eyes as the lad carried the water he had heated at the fire. His brows knit, he glanced at the midmorning sun outside the hut when the young man placed the water beside him.

Dagan closed his swollen eyes, but he could feel the silver-blue orbs study his bruised features and the darkening marks of abuse on his body. He opened his eyes again as the assessing gaze rested on the deep wound in his chest, covered by a poultice. Blood had coagulated on the cloth. It was time to change the poultice, yet the youth hesitated.

"What is wrong?"

The young man's gaze snapped up to meet Dagan's uncertain stare. "Nothing is wrong. Blood marks the poultice. I was contemplating the best way to cleanse your wound."

"My chest . . ."

"Yea, that wound is the most severe."

Dagan's squinting, amber-colored gaze scrutinized the blurred figure silently before he said absurdly, "I was stabbed."

"I know, by merciless Normans from whom you stole the horse."

"By thieves who hoped to steal my horse from me."

"Normans are all thieves."

Dagan did not reply.

"Do not upset yourself . . . but I would ask you a question." The lad spoke as he ran a warm cloth across Dagan's swollen face, then dipped it into the clean water and ran it across his lips. His touch was gentle as he pulled the poultice from Dagan's chest and stared at the wound more closely.

"The wound appears clean. There is no weeping

that indicates infection—a good sign." The lad pressed a soft hand to Dagan's forehead and said, "You are cooler now."

Struggling against uncertain feelings raised by that touch, Dagan fought to clear his gaze as he mumbled, "Your question . . ."

The lad replied, "The great animal who obeys you is a destrier . . . a warhorse often used by Normans."

Dagan managed a nod.

The lad paused. "You wore the clothes of a common man, yet you rode a warhorse."

Dagan did not immediately respond. His mind was still unclear. Hoping to omit the part of his response that would offend, he chose a half-truth. "I found the animal . . . wounded . . . wandering. I nursed him back to health. He is intelligent and grateful. He has served me well."

"His name . . ."

"His name was engraved on his saddle when I found him—the saddle that was stolen when I was ill with a fever from a previous wound."

"Stolen when Norman soldiers intended to take a valuable animal away from a common man."

Accepting Dagan's lack of response as affirmation, the lad's lips tightened with unspoken anger. He said simply, "Speak no more now. It weakens you. I would not have another good Saxon fall under a Norman blow."

Dagan closed his eyes. He was weak. His words had been misleading because it suited his purpose. He opened his eyes. "Conqueror . . . he is well?"

"The great horse is well. I allowed him to remain loose in the confines of the barn."

Dagan nodded.

The young fellow leaned closer. Dagan breathed in his sweet breath, intensely aware of the clear blue of his eyes when he whispered, "I am sorry. Both Hadley and I briefly doubted you when the horse responded so well to your command. Forgive me."

A resurgence of pain caused Dagan to again close his eyes as the young man whispered, "Have no fear. I will not betray you, and I will care for the destrier for whom you risked your life."

Dagan drifted into a restless sleep to the sound of that ardent promise.

The sound of a horse's hooves pounded to a halt on the turf beyond the hut. The stranger called Dagan had closed his eyes after she had tended to the deep wound in his chest, and now Rosamund leaned protectively closer to him as the baron's shadow darkened the doorway.

Rosamund noted the baron's impatient expression, but she did not attempt to rise from her patient's side as he advanced toward her. Instead, she said coldly, "Did you come to ask after the stranger's health?"

"Do not ask foolish questions!" Halting, the baron glanced around the small hut. "I can offer you quarters much better than these."

"I regret that I cannot accept your generosity. I am needed here."

"Yea, so I am told . . . needed by the master mason and by this nameless fellow as well."

The heat of anger surged as Rosamund replied, "The stranger is not nameless. He is called Dagan."

"He has a name but not much else," the baron scoffed.

"Perhaps that is because all else was stolen from him," Rosamund responded hotly. "Just as many other Saxons lost that which they held most dear."

"How unfortunate for them." Moving closer, the baron leaned down to whisper, "But that is the price of war."

"A war no Saxon sought!"

Jerking upright, the baron replied, "A war that came to them because of the duplicity of Harold, whom they chose as their king! They were justly overrun by a righteous, superior force."

"There was nothing righteous about William's invasion! He stole the country from Harold."

"He took what was rightfully his—which all true men will do in the end."

"Rightfully his? Harold was the rightful heir to the crown."

"A crown that was promised to William at an early age, a promise that was reneged upon after the true king died."

"There was no promise!"

"Deny it if you wish, but that is a truth borne by witnesses."

"William is a foreigner—a Norman! Neither he nor many of those whom he has seated above us even speak our tongue."

"I speak your tongue."

"Only through necessity."

The baron's voice softened unexpectedly as he said, "I have wooed many with the words of your language."

"Yea, I have no doubt that those words slip easily from your tongue."

"But I have never wooed one such as you."

Rosamund tensed. "One such as I?"

The baron extended his hand in an attempt to brush back the fair hair that hung so heavily on her brow. He sneered when Rosamund recoiled from his touch and said, "You do not favor my attentions, but I tell you now that the time will come when you will. You will cry for my touch and you will—"

"I thirst."

Her attention snapping back to the wounded man, Rosamund rose and pushed back the baron's stalwart figure as she strode to the ale bucket. Kneeling at the wounded man's side with cup in hand, she whispered, "Drink. The ale will refresh you, and I will presently make you a fortifying gruel."

"Gruel?" Rosamund did not look up as the baron inquired haughtily. "Where did you obtain the ingredients to make gruel for this man?"

"Would you deprive one of your subjects of that which he needs most, my lord? Is that the action of a benevolent noble?" Contempt in her delicate features, Rosamund responded, "I will answer your question by saying that the ingredients were gathered from many at this site who have seen other Saxons suffer and who wish to see this man survive."

"Are you telling me that I am not considered a benevolent lord?"

"I did not say that."

"What did you say, then?"

Aware that the baron was beginning to lose his

patience, and that the wounded man would suffer if he did, she replied, "I am telling you that resentment against Norman reign runs high among many Saxons . . . and that mercy goes far to diffuse that animosity."

"Mercy . . . for this wounded man . . ."

"Yea, for this *helpless* man."

The baron stood stiffly, his handsome face flushed. Taking a sudden backward step, he said coldly, "If mercy is the tact that will turn those who resent me— including you—in my favor, then this man will receive my mercy." Advancing again in sudden steps, the baron leaned down to whisper, "But keep in mind that my *mercy* will last only two more days, when I will expect you to return to the work that brought you here. Is that understood?"

Refusing to cringe under the baron's heat, Rosamund said, "Yea, it is understood."

Taking her chin roughly in his hand, the baron said more softly, "And then we will see what you have to offer . . . if it was worth the wait, as I envision."

"What I offer? My lord, I offer only my expertise at the work Hadley has taught me."

"Exactly."

Flushing darkly at the inference of his words, Rosamund jerked her chin free and replied, "I promise nothing except my help to build your cathedral, my lord."

"I do not need a promise. I take what is mine."

"Yours? I do not—"

Interrupting, the baron hissed, "Silence! I warn you that another word spoken by you now may be your last."

When Rosamund's chin rose defiantly at his words, the baron added, "Think before you speak. Where would your patient be without you to tend him—and where would Hadley be without your help?"

Rosamund did not reply.

"Consider what I say, for my patience wanes."

Wrapping his hand unexpectedly in Rosamund's light hair, the baron yanked it cruelly. Satisfied that his action had raised tears to her eyes, he said, "Remember that . . . and remember me."

The baron stepped back and turned to stride out the door. Within minutes the sound of his horse's hooves declared his departure.

Swallowing, Rosamund wiped the moisture from her eyes and then turned back to her patient to see that he regarded her intently from a gaze that had been reduced to amber pinpoints of light. His eyes flickered closed, but not before she thought she heard him whisper, "Another offense . . . for which he will pay."

Rosamund was about to speak when the wounded man went still.

Chapter Four

Rosamund walked toward the barn as the rising sun touched the darkness of night. Two days had passed. She had awakened that morning to the realization that she could not afford to spend another day at Dagan's bedside while Hadley worked at the construction site with Horace. If she stayed away any longer, she chanced disproving Hadley's statement that her presence beside him was necessary to his work. She was only too aware that Hadley's claim was true; there was no one other than herself who could provide the kind of support he needed. But the truth was that the wounded man's recovery had somehow become more important to her than she was willing to concede.

Admittedly, she knew no more about Dagan than she had learned that first day. He still suffered from delirium although his fever had lessened. His facial swelling had receded, and strong features were emerging, including an amber-eyed gaze that studied her with heated intensity. The bruises on his masculine body had begun to fade, and she recalled reluctantly the uncertain feelings that assailed her when she bathed his wounds. She had become somehow protective of him despite the power he exuded even in his weakened state. He had too few lucid moments and had spent most of the time since she had assumed his care in avoiding his pain in sleep. She had been reluctant to press him for more information about himself because of his intermittent delirium and because his explanation about Conqueror had cost his strength dearly.

Rosamund's thoughts turned to the great warhorse as she entered the barn and the aroma of heat, straw, and manure grew stronger. She noted that although the animals employed in construction had already begun their work for the day, the destrier remained behind. No longer fettered in any way, he was allowed to roam the barn freely at her insistence. The animal was immediately aware of her entrance but did no more than observe her with a cautious eye as she approached.

It occurred to Rosamund that once the great animal had seen Dagan, he had realized that she was caring for him. The few words Dagan had spoken to him at that time had been received as a rigid command that the warhorse had immediately obeyed. She had come to realize in the time since, while she had cared for the animal, that Dagan had been correct despite his delirium. Conqueror did not suffer fear—only distrust. The great warhorse had demonstrated that truth to her by his immediate acceptance of Dagan's word. She was unsure if the animal's attitude would change when Dagan was on his feet again. She believed somehow that the animal tolerated her simply because of Dagan's brief instructions.

Those thoughts aside, Rosamund approached the great warhorse cautiously. She spoke to him in a low tone as she prepared fresh water and feed, tidied the area, and wondered how the animal had come to exhibit such great loyalty to anyone after having suffered as Dagan claimed. She instinctively felt there was more to the story than Dagan had related and wondered if he would ever tell her.

The echo of approaching footsteps set Conqueror's ears twitching as Rosamund turned toward the doorway. Hadley paused there with Horace at his side.

Leaving Conqueror at the rear of the barn, Rosamund approached the two men as Hadley whispered, "I feared to wait any longer for your return, Rosamund. I leave now with Horace to study the walkways. I left the wounded man sleeping and alone." As her brow knit, Hadley added more softly, "we have reached the deadline that the baron set for your care of the man. He expects you to accompany me today. He will want to know why you do not. I am uncertain what excuse I should give."

Glancing briefly at Horace, Rosamund replied, "I had hoped to accompany you today, Father, but my chores delayed me."

Hadley squinted into the rear of the barn and shook his head. "That great animal complicates the matter. Perhaps it would be best if we left the door open here and allowed it to run off."

"That effort would be wasted, Father." Rosamund glanced back at the warhorse. "Dagan has ordered the animal to wait for him. It will obey until Dagan says otherwise."

Glancing blindly behind him, Hadley said, "I must leave before the baron sends someone for me."

Rosamund declared softly, "Do not fear. I will join

you. I will not allow the baron to direct his anger for me toward you."

"My concern is not for myself, Rosamund. I fear the baron intends to use his position to threaten you."

"I will not be cowed, Father."

Pausing, Hadley replied, "That is my true fear."

Unexpected tears filling her eyes, Rosamund walked a few steps to hug Hadley tightly. She whispered, "Do not worry about me. I will prevail. It is my destiny."

Unable to speak further, Hadley nodded, and then turned on Horace's arm. Rosamund watched his departure for a few moments before turning back to the great warhorse to say, "Behave yourself. Our fate depends on it."

Dagan awakened slowly to the dim light of morning and glanced around the small hut. The slender youth who had tended to him was gone.

Ross's delicate, fair-haired image returned to his mind. The image was *too* delicate . . . *too* fair. . . .

With this realization came a tug of emotion that was equally startling, one that Dagan forced himself to ignore as he attempted to sit up. Finally succeeding, he drew himself to his feet and staggered toward the fireplace. He managed to snatch up the clothing before returning to the mattress and flopping back down with an agonized grunt.

Dagan allowed himself a few moments for recovery before scrutinizing the hut more closely. The two other mattresses lay a distance from his, and a kettle on the fire emitted a pleasing aroma. Ross's image returned again to his confused mind. He recalled the appearance of Baron de Silva and the man's vile proposals.

Dagan's stomach knotted at the thought. Was Ross in the lecherous arms of the baron even now?

No, that could not be so. He remembered the baron's ultimatum—two days, and Ross must return to work or he would suffer the consequences of his absence. Surely two days could not have passed already. In any case, how did the baron dare threaten someone who had tended one of William's own followers?

Dagan sought to clear his mind as he sat on the edge of the mattress. Believing him to be Saxon because of his clothing, Ross had spoken to him freely. The young man had no love for William or for those who had fought with William. The old man . . . Hadley . . . had questioned his arrival on Conqueror, a Norman warhorse, and in doing so had revealed a similar antipathy. Ross had responded for him to Hadley's question with the partially true explanation Dagan had given him—that Dagan had found Conqueror injured and wandering, and had earned the animal's obedience and trust by nursing him back to health. Deliberately eliminated from his explanation had been the reality that Dagan had found Conqueror on the field of battle; that his own Norman warhorse had been killed beneath him; and that Conqueror, similarly injured by a Saxon arrow, would have spent his last hours on the battlefield if not for his care. Nor did he mention that Conqueror had rewarded him for his care with limitless fealty and obedience through the many battles that had eventually won William the crown.

Memory stirred further. Dagan remembered the mission that had brought him to Hendsmille: William had hesitated to condemn de Silva because the baron had comported himself bravely in battle and had earned the land awarded to him.

Dagan recalled that he had originally agreed with William's caution in approaching the matter. Despite de Silva's surprising attempt to involve Ross in one of his sexual aberrations, he did not want to believe that the rumors about one of William's most respected knights were true. Yet he wondered now. Were Ross and his father's antipathy for William and de Silva simply a matter of the vanquished's long-lasting hatred of the victor? Or were the rumors of de Silva's mistreatment of the common man in Hendsmille, as well as of the illegal confiscation of William's hunting grounds and rents from tenants on the land all true?

Dagan's stability wavered. He needed to find out to complete his mission for William. It seemed to him that there was only one way.

Rosamund stepped into the doorway of the hut. She halted abruptly and demanded, "What are you doing?"

The wounded man sat on the edge of the mattress he had occupied for two days. Despite his muscular stature, he clutched his washed and dried clothing as if he had attempted to clothe himself in them but had run out of strength. Determination blazed in his eyes as he said, "I am well. I need to dress."

"You are not well." Advancing to his side, Rosamund lay her palm against his forehead and then scolded, "The unnatural heat in your body has subsided, but you are only beginning to recover. You must allow yourself more time to heal."

"I know myself," Dagan responded. "I am well."

"Are you?"

Her gaze moving down to the circle of blood rapidly widening on the bandage covering his chest wound, Rosamund kneeled immediately at his side. Applying pressure and ignoring his grunt of pain, she looked up to say, "You have lost much blood and it has weakened you. You cannot afford to lose more."

"What?" Dagan replied caustically, "you do not believe that bloodletting will cure me?"

"I have already said that I do not employ that method of healing."

"Yea . . . I recall." Dagan nodded. "Good Saxon herbs . . ."

"Do you dispute the validity of my treatment?" Moving back, Rosamund stood and watched as blood again began seeping through the bandage covering the knife wound in Dagan's chest. She said tightly, "Do you prefer to bleed further so *the impurities will escape,* or will you submit to my simple Saxon remedies?"

Dagan clamped his hand over the wound to staunch the blood draining from it as he replied, "I have seen many battles, but I have never watched emotionlessly as innocent blood flowed."

Kneeling back down beside him, Rosamund replied, "Nor have I." Waiting until the pressure of her hand had slowed the sudden rush of blood, she ripped back the bandage, ignoring Dagan's instinctive protest. "The wound is clean, but blood still flows. I need to employ the methods I used on the infected wound on your leg. You were all but unconscious at the time, but—"

"I was not unconscious."

Rosamund looked up to meet Dagan's gaze. She remembered the way his arm had held her against his muscular body—in protest, or was it more? The memory of his broad palm moving against her back made her flush with heat. In quiet moments since, she had sensed his perusal, only to find, when she approached him, that his eyes were closed. She had wondered if she had imagined his scrutiny and then chided herself at the thought.

"Your leg is all but healed because of my treatment. Will you object if I seal this wound as well?"

"I will not object."

Rosamund hesitated, abruptly uncertain. "There is considerable pain involved."

"Do what you will."

Rosamund nodded. Turning toward the fire, she picked up the broad-bladed knife there, wrapped a cloth around the handle, and heated it to red-hot as she had done before. She turned back toward her battered patient when it was done and walked toward him.

Uncertainty returned. He was weak. Searing the wound would be painful—perhaps more than he was able to bear in his vulnerable state.

"Apply the blade before it cools."

Resenting the attitude of command in Dagan's voice, Rosamund held the flat of the blade to his wound without reply. She winced as the smell of burning flesh rose again between them, but Dagan made no sound. His only reaction was the perspiration that beaded his brow, and Rosamund saw that his gaze did not falter despite his weakened state.

When she withdrew the blade at last, she saw the desired result. With a silent sigh of relief, she said, "Sit back. Allow the wound to settle while I fill a bowl with pottage left from last night's meal. It will strengthen you." She added, "Were the situation different, I would be able to offer more suitable fare hunted on the land and forests surrounding us, but through William's generous victory, landholders were evicted to provide more land for his hunting preserve."

Rosamund grew silent. Left unsaid was her determination that if she were the man she pretended to be, and were she not aware of Hadley's ultimate concern, she would hunt where she liked and when she liked, allowing no one to take that freedom from her.

"I thirst."

Snapped back to the moment by the sound of Dagan's voice, Rosamund turned to fill a crude cup with the broth that she had prepared. She held it to his lips.

"I can drink by myself."

With a short twitch of her nose, Rosamund watched as Dagan raised the cup to his lips and spilled its contents liberally. She allowed the liquid to seep down over his chest before asking, "Do you still thirst?"

A short shake of his head his only response, Rosamund took the cup, returned to the fire, and filled a bowl with pottage.

"I can feed my—"

Rosamund shoved the pottage between Dagan's parted lips before waiting for him to finish. She watched as he slowly swallowed. "Are you ready for more?"

She was almost certain that she saw the flicker of a smile move across Dagan's lips as he replied, "Yea . . . I am ready."

Dagan watched as the young man raised the pottage to his mouth. He saw delicate lips part as his own did, as if accepting the food with him. The comforting concoction made from leftover fare warmed him as he swallowed slowly, watching Ross's elegant features.

Yea, Ross's eyes were blue . . . bluer than any he had ever seen before. The long, surprisingly dark lashes bordering them had not been a figment of his fevered dreams, nor had been the graceful brows all but obscured by the long length of fair hair that had been cut to hang across the forehead. A sweep of that same straight, crudely cut hair fell forward, almost obscuring finely sculpted cheeks, and yet the graceful contours were as unmistakable as the delicate profile and the graceful bow of Ross's lips.

Lovely.

Feminine to a stimulating degree.

Yea, *feminine* . . .

Confusion reigned. Drawing himself up short, Dagan clamped his lips tightly shut.

"Your stomach will hold no more?" Ross frowned.

"Nay." Dagan shook his head, determined to clear it.

"Then I will leave you now."

"Leave?" Dagan's eyes narrowed. He paused and then said, "Then two days have indeed elapsed since we were visited by the baron."

Surprised that he recalled the baron's visit, Rosamund replied, "That is correct."

"You must return to be with Hadley today or suffer the baron's disapproval, is that not also correct?"

"I did not realize you had heard what the baron said."

"I heard him threaten you."

"I do not fear his threats."

"You should. I am acquainted with the influence he possesses."

"Are you? Then you also know how the people of Hendsmille despise his treatment of them, how he imposes his will on them and curtails even the simplest freedoms while still claiming to be a fair and honest holder of the land awarded to him by William in reward for the shedding of innocent blood."

When Dagan did not reply, Ross continued, "You are already acquainted with the wrath of his soldiers, since it was most likely they who sought to steal your warhorse from you."

"Conqueror . . ."

"Yea, Conqueror."

"The animal maintains his strength?"

"Yea, and tolerates me as you commanded."

When Dagan did not respond, Ross said, "I will dress your chest wound, and then go to the building grounds—but not out of fear for myself. Rather, it is my father's fate and the fates of others that I do not trust to the baron's savage idiosyncrasies. My father awaits me there, and you are well enough to tolerate my absence until the midday meal, when I will return briefly."

Dagan raised his chin and said, "I am well. I will dress and I will—"

Ross's eyes widened. He slapped the bowl down on the floor and said, "You will sleep on that mattress until I return or I will not leave!"

Dagan countered, "The baron insists that you go back to work today."

"I do not care what the baron says."

"It is wise to care."

"I have not always been accused of being wise, but I have always been accused of being stubborn. I will not leave unless you promise that you will rest until I return."

"And if the baron comes to force you back to work?"

"I will handle him."

Dagan admired the determination in Ross's eye. He could not help but feel amused that such a slender youth should attempt to threaten him, even in his weakened state, or that Ross would believe he could face down the baron's might.

"I will rest until you return," Dagan responded.

"You give me your word?"

"Yea, I do."

Picking up nearby strips of cloth, Ross bandaged his chest wound, looking up unexpectedly to say, "It occurs to me that although I have tended your wounds, I know little more about you than your given name. The baron may ask for more information. I feel it would be wise to reply, for your sake, and so that I may function without hindrance."

Ross waited for his response. Reluctant to respond with the name Sir Dagan de Lance, since it so clearly declared the Norman side of his heritage, Dagan instinctively replied with his mother's maiden name.

"My name is Dagan *Waterford*." Dagan added, "My home was originally in Horstede, but I live there no longer."

"You need say no more." Ross stood up. "I am aware of the devastation of that shire, and of the hatred that the few survivors bear for the Normans." Ross paused. "Rest. Your time will come."

He left the hut with Dagan frowning behind him.

Hyacinthe Dupree watched Baron Guilbert de Silva pace as she paused silently in the doorway of his quarters. She knew that the day presently dawning was one that he had anticipated. She had seen his temperament fluctuate between anger, anticipation, annoyance, and impatience, but she had sensed there was more. And she had overheard him confide to his friend, Franchot Champlain, that he needed to wait two days in order to keep his word to the one who so intrigued him. He had all but growled as he had said that he wanted his new conquest to be willing . . . very willing.

Hyacinthe had felt the heat of that comment, and jealousy had sprung to life inside her. Guilbert—as the baron had allowed her to call him during passionate moments—appeared more eager than he had ever been before when contemplating a conquest; yet it was unusual for him to wait for his needs to be met.

She could testify to that.

Her full lips twitched at that thought. Dark-haired, with dark eyes, bold features, and a voluptuous figure, she was as well aware of her attributes as she was of her shortcomings. Hyacinthe had worked in the de Silva household since early childhood. She had known Guilbert most of her life, and had loved him as long as she could remember. She had submitted to his sexual overtures with gratitude and delight when she reached puberty at twelve years of age and caught his eye. Then twenty, he had been handsome, well educated and wealthy, and he had seemed so far above her that she had been honored by his touch. In her inexperience, she had truly believed he loved her. As the years passed, he treated her to extended sexual interludes each time he arrived home from one of his sojourns. She had enjoyed his growing intimate expertise, convinced that it simply reflected his maturity. Thrilled and titillated beyond measure, she had told herself that he was not just returning home. He was returning *to her.*

She had since learned the hard way that she could never have made a greater error.

Word of Guilbert's sexual escapades with both willing and unwilling maids became legend as the years passed and he became a knight in William's service. She had realized then that in order to keep his interest, she needed to acquire as much expertise as he and had set about to obtain it any way she could. After countless intimate encounters with men whose faces she could not even recall, she had emerged a versatile bedmate—a woman who had learned limitless ways to enthrall a man. Now she shared her knowledge with only one man.

Hyacinthe had been delirious with joy when Guilbert returned to her more voracious than ever after each military venture. She had prided herself in being a constant challenge to his lust, but she had been totally unprepared when he announced after William was crowned that he was leaving Normandy to claim the new home that William had awarded him for his service.

She had been stunned when he so blatantly intended to leave her behind.

Unable to believe he could do it, Hyacinthe had approached him and pleaded her cause. She had told him of her love, and had been startled when he had laughed in her face before stating coldly that he would not be in need of a resident whore in his new home. She had watched him ride away with the blessings of his parents, who had then turned on her angrily and chastised her for believing that she had provided Guilbert with anything more than temporary satisfaction.

Yet she had not been able to forget him.

Months later, she had packed up her few belongings and traveled to Guilbert's keep in England. She remembered his surprise when he saw her in his kitchen. She recalled the lust that had glowed in his eyes as she had flaunted herself in front of him. Hyacinthe had gone to his isolated quarters in the keep that same evening, and had prided herself in providing him with unforgettable sexual gratification that had lasted long into the next day.

She had suffered through his many peccadilloes in the years since. When Guilbert brought unwilling young women to his quarters to deflower them, or when he spent amorous days and nights with local women who willingly offered their favors, she had told herself that he would return to her in the end. She had borne the ridicule of the kitchen help because she knew that each of his liaisons was temporary—that *she* was the only constant in his life. She had grown more voluptuous with time. Her breasts and hips were fuller, and despite the fear that gray would soon appear in her long tresses, her need to please Guilbert had also grown until she had determined she would do anything to keep his interest.

She had managed to succeed until now.

Hyacinthe recalled the previous evening when she had appeared at the door to Guilbert's quarters as he prepared for bed. He had turned her away with blatant disgust, declaring that he was tired of her, that a new, "unexpected love" would soon take her place; and that until then he needed no woman at all.

With the memory of that statement still ringing in her ears as the new day dawned, Hyacinthe remained silent in the doorway of Guilbert's quarters. She continued to watch his anxious pacing while holding a change of bed linens in hand as a pretext for her appearance there. A chill ran down her spine when Guilbert looked up and asked emotionlessly, "What are you doing here?"

"I came to change your bed linens."

"Get out."

"Guilbert, I—"

"You will address me as 'my lord' like the other kitchen help. I will stand for no less!"

Hyacinthe began again, "My lord, I—"

"Put the linens down and return later, after I have gone."

"My lord . . . will you allow me to relieve your agitation? You know how competent I am at that endeavor."

De Silva sneered. "You are 'competent at that endeavor' with any male who tickles your fancy. I am no longer satisfied to be one of many."

Hyacinthe's heart pounded as she said hoarsely, "You have found a woman on whom you wish to confer your name, then?"

De Silva stopped to glare at her as he said, "I have found another . . . one I am unable to sweep from my mind . . . one who intrigues me as no other has."

Hyacinthe replied boldly, "I can put this other one to shame. I am dedicated to that cause . . . as you well know."

"I know well that you are a whore and, as such, I have no further use for you."

Slowly lowering the neckline of her blouse, Hyacinthe bared her white, rounded breasts. She stroked the taut, brown crests as she whispered, "Can this other one offer you what I offer?"

"Cover yourself!" Stunned at the baron's command, Hyacinthe jerked up her blouse as the baron advanced toward her and rasped, "I await the proper moment before going out to begin my challenge . . . an intimate challenge that I sense will surpass whatever practiced intimacies you offer."

Hyacinthe gasped, "But—"

"Go back to the kitchen and be grateful that I allowed you to consume precious time that I could have passed with someone more worthy. Whatever the outcome of this venture, I do not want you to approach me again, do you hear?"

Hyacinthe nodded.

"Speak to me. I wish to hear you say the words!"

"I hear you."

Looking up at the bright morning sun shining through the window, de Silva added, "The time has come for this new game. I await it with a growing impatience that no one else may sate." Sweeping up his cloak, he reiterated for her benefit, "*No one else.*"

Thrusting her aside as she stood rigidly in the doorway, the baron thundered down the curved staircase and slipped from her sight. Incredulous, Hyacinthe took a breath, and then another. She advanced into the room and placed the clean linens on the bed that they had so often heated with their lovemaking.

But . . . the baron had said their lovemaking was simple lust, and that she was a whore.

Hyacinthe turned to her reflection in the framed mirror that hung opposite her. She stared at her image. That same mirror had often reflected the heat of their lovemaking, yet she saw in it now only an unsmiling woman who had once again been left behind.

Hyacinthe drew herself up straight and forced herself to smile. Her features were handsome and her body was womanly beyond measure. There were few who could offer what she did, and Guilbert would remember those assets when his newest escapade was no longer new. He would come back to her again. If he did not, she would take measures to make sure that he did.

Hyacinthe raised her chin a notch higher. And he would one day make her his lady as she had always known he would. She knew that was true . . . because she would have it no other way.

Rosamund saw her father's expression lighten when she approached him across the scarred terrain where the beginnings of the baron's cathedral loomed. It occurred to her that though his sight was uncertain, he was somehow able to sense her presence. He had been her savior, her protector and provider, through the long years of William's reign and the baron's domination.

Hadley spoke as she drew near. "The baron has not yet arrived although we began work at daybreak. The artisans proceed with their labors as if there is no question of the structure's basic viability. Your keen sight has yet to confirm my findings, but unless my calculations are incorrect, the problems are many. It is my conclusion that most of the foundation and walkways the former master mason laid are woefully inadequate to meet their purpose. I await your closer scrutiny where my eyes fail. I pray that at least some of the present construction may be saved."

Rosamund accepted the plans that Horace placed in her hand without comment. Horace frowned as he said, "This situation is beyond my talents. My experience does not lean in that direction, although I made pretense of affording genuine help to Hadley in your absence. It is my hope that you deem the wounded man in your hut to be well enough that I may turn my responsibilities here over to you."

"Dagan is much improved, but his recovery will be due more to the determination he exhibits than to my care. I thank you for all you have done, Horace. Your friendship and support are well appreciated."

Nodding, Horace replied, "Then I leave Hadley in your capable hands."

Waiting only until Horace had turned away, Rosamund stretched the scrolls out on the ground, kneeled beside them, and then looked up at Hadley to say, "The baron's project is ambitious. The meager force present here will not be able to handle its construction."

Hadley nodded with a darkening frown. "Such was my observance, but I told myself that my failing eyesight imagined a complication where none existed."

"Nay, Father. This plan is grandiose. Without a glance at the present foundation, I feel safe in stating that supplies and artisans presently working here will prove vastly inadequate for so great a project, most especially if a correction is necessary."

"That was the fear I dared not voice to the baron."

"I will voice it for you."

"Nay, that would not be wise."

Rosamund replied with a dark frown, "For the second time today I am accused of not being wise."

"Although I bear no witness to the first, I say now that the wiser course would be to survey the work that has already been done and to formulate a plan to combat the deficiencies before citing them to the baron."

An unexpected voice from behind declared arrogantly, "Before declaring what to me?"

Jumping with a start, Rosamund turned toward the tall, frowning baron as he appeared behind her. She realized that Hadley's failing eyesight had not allowed him to recognize the baron's figure as he approached.

Momentarily at a loss for words, Hadley did not respond. Aware of his temporary lapse, Rosamund drew herself to her feet and said boldly, "Hadley's conclusions are yet uncertain. His experience is renowned, but age has limited the keenness of his sight and he wishes to have me confirm his observations before he declares them to you."

His jaw tightening, the baron repeated, "Before declaring *what* to me?"

"Before citing the viability of the structures the former master mason began constructing."

The baron looked at Rosamund and replied incredulously. "Are you saying that there is some uncertainty as to the safety of the work that has already been done?"

Rosamund raised her chin a notch higher as she replied, "That is what I am saying."

His expression thunderous, the baron exclaimed, "How much longer must I wait for your firm conclusions?"

"That is uncertain. A few days . . . maybe more."

"Because you are otherwise engaged in your hut?"

"Because it will take that much time to dig and measure, and to do all the things that the former master mason did not."

Aware that Hadley remained silent, Rosamund did not look in his direction. Instead she continued, "Hadley has done his calculations. It is now time for me to do mine."

"An unnecessary lapse of time that I will not tolerate," the baron thundered again.

"Would you rather that the walls of this great edifice crumble as you pray, or that the poorly supported roof comes tumbling down upon those whom you wish to impress? If that is so, Hadley and I will proceed more quickly."

"You try my patience, boy!" The baron stared at Rosamund heatedly. He grumbled, "I had intended a far different outcome for this day."

Rosamund responded, "As did I, since my patient has not fully recovered."

"Your patient again!" De Silva flushed. "Who is he, anyway? I know nothing about him except that he was beaten to within an inch of his life."

"His name is Dagan Waterford. His original residence was in Horstede, but he is presently a wanderer who finds work where he may since that place has never truly recovered from its decimation at the time of William's invasion."

"But he survived. Strange, is it not, since so many others fell?"

"Which elevates his importance as a common man in this fief."

"The fellow's condition is of no consequence when greater matters lie in question."

"There is nothing of greater importance than a man's life!"

The baron took a bold step closer as he said, "His *death* would be of equal importance if my patience is tried."

Refusing to cower at his statement, Rosamund

replied arrogantly, "His death would be more detrimental to your project here than you know."

Momentarily silent as his color heightened, the baron asked slowly, "Am I to understand that you threaten me?"

"Nay. I merely state that the laborers here have come to view Dagan as a symbol of all they have borne from the time of William's conquest. His recuperation represents a survival that they had almost surrendered. It also represents the completion of this project you envision. If he were not to survive, they would lose hope, and a man without hope has less to offer because he is far less than he could be."

"You threaten me in a way that leaves me no choice but to conform to your way of thinking if I am not to chance a greater delay in my project than I anticipated." The baron paused. His dark eyes scrutinized Rosamund's face as he said, "If your words were spoken by another, I would doubtless smite him on the spot. Yet when those words are spoken by you, I find myself admiring your pluck."

Rosamund's lips twitched as she replied with an attempt to disguise her disgust, "It would be better if you admired my truthfulness, for that is what I intended."

"Yea . . ." Again the baron paused before adding, "But I intend so much more."

Rosamund moved back and shook off de Silva's hand as he placed it on her shoulder. Stepping to the fore, Hadley stated flatly, "The foundation needs to be carefully scrutinized if we are to guarantee that this cathedral will stand into perpetuity. Work of that magnitude takes time."

"Perpetuity be damned!" The baron's gaze was suddenly hot with anger. "I want this work done and done well! I need no guarantee that it will last forever."

"You need a guarantee that it will stand to support your hope for redemption—is that not what you originally declared?"

"Yea . . ." The baron glanced at Rosamund, although it was Hadley who had asked the question. "That is what I said . . . although another far more personal pressure weighs on me."

"Perhaps it is time, then, for appropriate self-denial."

Turning on Hadley, the baron suddenly raged, "Do you presume to instruct me on what I should do?"

"I make no such presumption, my lord." His failing gaze wavering, Hadley replied, "I say only what may be needed in order for you to realize the dream you intended for this project."

The baron's chest heaved with anger. Pausing for long moments, he directed his next comments to Rosamund.

"I would have you do the work that is necessary for you here—before you tend to your patient. I would have you put him to work on this project as soon as the lout is able—at rough labor if he has no skills. But most importantly, I would have you prepare a report with Hadley of exactly how you expect to proceed . . . so that I may anticipate your progress and the time it will take to achieve your goal. I would have you present it to me personally. Since Hadley values your opinion so greatly and since you presume to speak for him without fear of reprisal, I would have you deliver it to me without Hadley's presence. I would come to know you better. In this way I hope to become more comfortable with the idiosyncrasies of the Saxon nature . . . since I admit that your ways are enigmas that I nonetheless find . . . *stimulating*." The baron prompted tightly, "Are we agreed?"

When Rosamund paused before replying, he added, "I warn you to consider your response well, for your future and the future of many others depend on it."

Hadley responded stiffly in Rosamund's stead. "We will prepare a report for you as you wish, and follow through to the best of our knowledge."

"I did not ask you, old man!" Taking a moment to glare at Hadley, the baron turned back to Rosamund to say with forced sweetness, "I would hear your reply."

Noting Hadley's restless movement when her chin rose in automatic response to the baron's veiled command, Rosamund forced back her temper to reply, "Hadley's word is my law."

"Nay, that is incorrect! *My* word is your law."

Rosamund's lips cracked into a tight smile as she responded, "*Your* word is the law of this shire, my lord. *Hadley's* word is the law to which my heart responds."

"A heart that will continue beating only if I deign it to be so."

"A heart that will continue beating only if the God to whom we all pray so chooses . . . that is, unless you consider yourself above *Him*."

The baron took a spontaneous step back at Rosamund's unexpected response. Unwilling to challenge her statement, he paused and then said flatly, "I will await your report."

Rosamund did not realize that she was trembling until the baron thundered off.

"You challenge him too greatly. You will exhaust his patience soon if you do not take care."

Hadley faced Rosamund in the privacy of the hut, where they had returned after the day's work. Light was waning after the endless toil that the project demanded, but Hadley waited only until the door was closed behind them to address her. He ignored the wounded man who lay silent on the mattress a distance away as he awaited her reply.

Rosamund's face twisted with disgust as she replied, "The baron is a fool controlled by his own lust! I will not tolerate his words without a response of my own."

"His outspoken advances anger me as well. I promise you that I will not allow them to come to fruition."

"You need not defend me, Father. I am grown and can handle one such as he."

"You have no experience with such a one. He is an aberration . . . a ruthless puppet of a conqueror who delights in abusing the conquered . . . a man whose interests lie only in himself, with no thought of the expense to others."

"He is a man who breathes . . . and who will bleed if struck."

"He is also a well-protected man who is skilled at killing. Much brave talk of insurrection has been quelled in the depths of his dungeons. I would not have you chance such a future."

"You need not concern yourself that I would chance it, either, Father. I would take steps to avoid such a circumstance."

"And what would those steps be?" Hadley approached Rosamund falteringly. "I would ask you to be cautious, for my sake as well as for your own. I am not the man I once was."

"I am such a man."

The voice that echoed in the hut behind them was deep and strong. Turning toward her formerly silent patient as he drew himself to a seated position on his mattress, Rosamund assessed Dagan boldly before replying, "You may be such a man, but you are not well and presently are not equal to the task you set for yourself."

"I am well enough."

Rosamund remained silent. She had come back to the hut briefly at the time of the midday meal. Dagan had been sleeping, and she had left a bowl of pottage and a cup of broth beside him for easy access. Believing him asleep, she had barely looked at him upon returning with Hadley moments previously—although she realized as he spoke that he was fully clothed. Further critical scrutiny revealed that the swelling of his features had declined to a surprising degree, and that the visible bruises on his body had begun yellowing. It occurred to her that he grew handsomer as the swelling waned.

Rosamund shook off that thought with the knowledge that being handsome did not make him any stronger.

"You say that I am not yet equal to whatever would

be needed to combat the baron's designs. Yet you refuse to face the reality that you are not equal to that effort, either," Dagan insisted.

Rosamund countered, "I am equal to any effort. Have I not snatched you from the edge of death with my ministrations? Have I not protected you from the baron although he would have thrown you away like common trash? Do I not still protect you with carefully calculated responses to that despicable man—replies that carry the weight of a blow?"

Dagan raised his battered brow. "I do not know . . . do you?"

"Yea, I do!"

"Then my reason for protecting you from him can only be greater than before."

Rosamund's eyes narrowed as Dagan stood up, revealing to her for the first time the full extent of his great size. She replied resolutely, "Perhaps that would be true if you were well, but you have not yet fully recovered."

Dagan sat abruptly as an apparent wave of dizziness struck him. He frowned as he admitted, "Possibly you are correct. I may need a few more days to regain the strength I have lost."

"A few more days . . ." Rosamund's response was mocking.

Adamant, Dagan responded, "A few more days . . . no longer."

Hadley remained silent as Rosamund replied, "You will be ready to handle the heavy work that the baron intends for you in a few more days? I think not."

"I will not labor at the baron's command."

"The baron intends to see your back bent along

with others who work at his site. He allows you to live only for that reason."

Dagan repeated, "I tell you now, I will not labor for him."

"Pride, is that it?" Rosamund shook her head. "Every Saxon in this shire has compromised his pride in one way or another in order to survive. You are no different."

"Yea, I am."

"Are you?" Rosamund took a few steps closer. She scrutinized her patient more closely and saw that despite his battered state, he would not back down. She replied unexpectedly, "Perhaps you are different. Perhaps you will never allow yourself to submit to the baron's demands, no matter the cost to you. But if the cost were to another . . . would you be as adamant?"

"To another?"

"To *me,* for I have guaranteed the baron your presence at his construction site, knowing that he would allow you to survive for only that reason."

"You spoke for me?"

"Yea . . . when you were unable to speak for yourself."

Dagan eyed her coldly. Rosamund saw the anger that tightened his features. She bore his amber-eyed stare until he said abruptly, "The answer to your question is that I would not see you suffer the cost of my refusal to work for the baron. But neither will I suffer seeing him force himself on you."

"I would not allow that to happen."

Dagan replied in a voice that was almost a growl, "Nor would I."

Rosamund released a shuddering breath at his response. She raised her chin and said, "It is agreed, then. You will accompany me to the work grounds when you are well."

"In a few more days."

"When you are . . . *well*."

Dagan looked at her without replying and Rosamund turned away abruptly to see Hadley staring at them. Frowning, she inquired, "Does that not meet with your approval, Father?"

Avoiding a reply, Hadley instructed, "Stoke the fire beneath the cauldron and I will gather herbs that will lend a different flavor to the pottage."

"Herbs . . ."

"The herb garden that a few of the workers planted when construction began is not far from here. I have been told that I am welcome to its produce, and I can find it easily."

"Father . . ."

"My sight may be limited, but my sense of smell is not."

Rosamund frowned and took a step. "Father . . ."

His expression suddenly unyielding, Hadley said, "I will return shortly."

Watching as Hadley left the hut with an uncertain step, Rosamund turned back toward Dagan. Her resolute expression returned and her eyes narrowed as she repeated, "Only when you are well . . ."

Dagan stared at Ross standing so obstinately in front of him. Were he not hindered by weakness . . . were he not so indebted . . . were he not so . . . so *fascinated* by the qualities of determination Ross exhibited in the face of obstacles that would daunt another, he supposed he might be angry at being faced down by the thin, undersized lad.

Dagan unconsciously shook his head at that thought and stared at Ross more closely. Those delicate features . . . those sparkling eyes . . . the smooth, flawless skin . . . those appealing lips . . .

In a moment of sudden clarity, Dagan realized that it made no difference that Ross was half his size. The aura of grace that Ross exhibited, the innate refinement of his demeanor, the gentle touch, the *appeal* that he responded to instinctively despite his greatest effort . . .

Dagan wondered how he could have been even momentarily confused. Ross could not be considered thin or undersized because . . . because Ross was a woman!

An undeniably beautiful, desirable woman . . .

Momentarily angry at Ross's attempt to deceive him, Dagan considered that he had been deceiving her as well. He had had no choice but to falsify his information to make it more palatable to her at this time and place.

But what was the reason for her masquerade as a young man?

The answer to that question was apparent.

Dagan frowned. He had no right to allow Ross to realize that he had seen through her disguise when he was still insufficiently recovered to protect her.

That admission stung. It was important to him to shield Ross from the baron's avaricious demands. He could not allow her to walk arrogantly in the face of destruction—for him or for anyone else.

Ross's comment rang again in his mind.

Only when you are well . . .

He replied aloud, "I will accompany you to the site and I will obey the baron's commands *when I am well,* as you said." He added, "But I will accept that compromise only if you will grant me one in return. I ask that you bide your time with the baron until I can stand at your side and offer you the support you will need."

"I need no one's support!"

"I know the baron's reputation, and I think otherwise. I ask only that you allow me more time."

Dagan saw Ross's expression tighten. Advancing toward him, Ross pressed him firmly back against the mattress with the flat of her palms as she commanded, "Lie back and rest."

Gripping Ross's hands in his, Dagan said, "I ask you to bide your time and your tongue for a few more days. Is that too much to ask?"

"I don't know." Ross frowned more darkly. "The baron plagues me."

Dagan clenched her delicate hands tighter. He struggled against the growing emotion inside him as he said, "I ask you again to bide your time."

Ross's gaze slipped to his lips, and Dagan swallowed thickly. His heart pounded as he awaited her reply.

"All right, I will bide my time and hold my tongue . . ."

Dagan dropped her hands and nodded. He closed his eyes until Ross added, "For a few days."

Dagan's eyes snapped back open; yet he was more relieved than he dared admit despite Ross's addendum.

Ross . . .

She somehow touched him to the soul, yet the outrageous truth was that he did not even know her real name.

Chapter Five

Dagan awoke abruptly and looked around him. The small hut had grown familiar to him, as had the mattress stuffed with straw beneath him. His wounds ached as he perused the still figures on mattresses that lay nearby in the morning shadows.

Rosamund pretended to be male for reasons he had no doubt were related to the Baron de Silva's salacious reputation. He allowed her to believe he was unaware of her gender, knowing that deception provided both Hadley and her with a sense of security even if the precautions they had taken to avoid de Silva's desire had failed. She did not seem to realize that his senses had returned to full capacity before his wounds had fully healed. She was unaware that he had heard the few times when Hadley had slipped and called her Rosamund, confirming what he had already known to be true. Nor did she realize that he had seen her react with a warning finger to her lips and a glance in his direction at her father's lapse. Lastly, she did not seem to be conscious of the fact that the brush of her silver-blue gaze set his heart pounding, or that her gentle touch had become almost too much for him to bear.

She had cared for him meticulously for almost a

week and had virtually saved his life, but her care had not displayed any sign of reverence. Instead, she had chastised him along with her praise, insisting that despite his claims, he was not yet well enough for heavy labor.

Dagan frowned as he stared at her sleeping form. He had promised himself long ago that he would never return to the days when common labor was the only manner of assuaging his hunger available to him. He had fought hard in William's service because he believed in him and in the truth of his causes. He had achieved knighthood, respect, and a position in William's court envied by many. Yet his most cherished achievements were William's friendship and his understanding of the very complex man William was.

It had not been easy to hold his tongue while others described William as a bloodthirsty warrior with no concern for those he had conquered, or when they stated their belief that he had no right to the throne. He knew better. He knew the moral standards by which William conducted his life despite the pressures of the times, and he was aware of the broken promise that had prompted William's invasion.

Yea, to hold his tongue had been difficult. Yet he was only too aware that staying silent was difficult for another as well.

In the dark shadows before dawn, Dagan sat up on his mattress and flexed muscles cramped from inactivity. He frowned at the rags he had been forced to wear instead of his own clothing. Tattered and torn, they barely covered his body, but they were adequate. The same could be said for the worn sandals left behind by his attacker.

Dagan slipped his feet into the sandals and stood up slowly. The week's inactivity had left his balance unsteady. Yet his chest wound was healing, his bruises fading, and he could feel that the facial swelling had all but disappeared. He would allow Rosamund to hold him back no longer.

But . . . first things first.

Dagan moved quietly out of the small hut and closed the door behind him. He walked on the uneven ground in the lightening dawn, feeling stronger with each step. He had no need to ask for directions. He had just to follow the path of a familiar odor.

Dagan approached the barn moments later. He pulled open the door and stood in the entrance, allowing his eyes to become accustomed to the semidarkness within. He had taken no more than two steps into the interior when Conqueror approached him with excited snorts of welcome. His smile full, Dagan caught the bridle of the great gray as he whispered into the animal's ear, "I am pleased to see that you are well cared for, Conqueror."

The warhorse nuzzled him with surprising affection, and Dagan smiled more broadly. The animal pranced around him in a display that made the other animals in the barn restless, and Dagan reprimanded him softly before turning to the bin where the food was stored. It did not miss his notice that Conqueror followed him closely every step of the way and did not touch his food until Dagan gave the signal. When the animal dipped his head to eat, Dagan could not resist a smile at the subtle companionship the horse afforded.

"So, you *can* smile. I was beginning to believe otherwise."

At the sound of the familiar voice, Dagan turned to see Rosamund standing there. Her expression was tense as she said, "I awakened and found your mattress vacant. I assumed that you had taken the first opportunity to escape a difficult situation—that perhaps that was your intention all along—but I knew you would not leave without the animal for whom you had risked your life."

Rosamund paused and Dagan's smile faded. He had not expected her to jump to that conclusion, and he did not like the fact that she had.

Dagan replied, "You are correct, of course. I would not leave this place without my horse, but I gave you my word. I said that I would keep the promise you made to the baron in my stead. I did not expect you to dismiss my promise when it was given in good faith."

Rosamund responded unexpectedly, "I have survived many disappointments since William's invasion. I have lost many loved ones and friends, and have suffered the collapse of many plans and expectations. I did not find it difficult to believe your leaving was yet another—"

"Another disappointment?"

"Another promise broken . . . another solution unresolved . . . another person who—"

When Rosamund did not finish her statement, Dagan prompted, "Another person who . . . ?"

Rosamund raised her chin. "Another person who failed to live up to my expectations."

Dagan faced Rosamund squarely. "You have expectations of me?"

"I balance my father's need for me and the baron's interest cautiously. If you had left, the baron would doubtless have used your disappearance against me. The present situation is difficult enough."

"Why is it difficult?" he pressed. "Because of the baron or William? Surely you did not expect that your life would not see some changes under a different monarch."

"Some changes?" Rosamund's expression was touched with incredulity. "I did not expect to hear those words from the mouth of one who had lived through the devastation of Horstede—or have you forgotten the blood that was shed there . . . the fires that raged . . . the wanton rape and slaughter?"

Dagan raised his chin. "I forget nothing. Those responsible for that debacle have been properly chastised."

"Have they? And if they have, did that effort bring back the dead and restore the village to what it once was?"

"What's past is past. I look forward."

"As would I and those of Hendsmille, did not the baron stand directly in that path by stealing our lands, by charging outrageous rents that the common man cannot hope to pay, by making sure that every one of us realizes that we have been conquered by a foreigner who does not even speak our language."

"Language is unimportant when the intent is sincere. Yet 'stealing your lands . . .'"

Rosamund laughed harshly. "The baron usurps our lands in much the same way William did, only he takes *William's* lands as well. It is for that reason that the baron's hunting preserve has expanded almost twofold over the years while William's preserves have shrunk." Rosamund laughed again. "Though that makes no difference to those of Hendsmille who cannot hunt their own land under penalty of death."

Dagan's lips tightened. He repeated, "You said he charges outrageous rents . . ."

"And keeps a great part of the sum for himself, if I am to believe one in our village who kept his accounts and lost his eyes at the baron's command when he commented on the discrepancies."

Dagan's frown darkened.

"You are displeased at what you hear."

Dagan did not need to reply.

"The people of Hendsmille are similarly displeased."

Aware of Rosamund's prejudices, Dagan made no comment. He needed to discover the truth for himself, and he could not allow his feelings for this woman to affect that resolution.

Reasoning that those feelings resulted from the closeness they had shared while she had cared for his wounds, he said determinedly, "I begin work on the cathedral today."

"Nay, not yet. You are not ready."

"I am as ready as I will ever be."

Rosamund took a step closer. "Are you ready to haul

the great stones that will be needed for construction? Are you ready to mix the great quantities of mortar as the apprentices do? Are you ready to use hammer and chisel where needed, or to raise great timbers, for that is the work the baron would have you do, whatever skills you possess."

"I will do what I must."

"Nay, you will not! The wounds that I so carefully tended will rupture if great pressure is exerted."

"I am stronger than you think."

"Perhaps . . . but not as strong as *you* think."

Dagan's lips twitched at Rosamund's determination. As resolute as she, Dagan said simply, "I go to the construction site to work this morning, either with your approval or without it."

Rosamund's eyes suddenly filled. Strangely affected, Dagan took a step toward her, and then halted as she blinked back her tears and muttered hoarsely, "Stubborn . . ."

Dagan's response was familiar. "I have not always been accused of being wise, but I have always been accused of being stubborn."

She turned abruptly when her own words were thrown back at her. She said over her shoulder, "Hadley prepares breakfast. It would be *wise* if someone who intends to work heartily eats heartily as well."

Rosamund walked away. Dagan found himself staring at the sway of her slender hips underneath the bulky clothing she wore and, aware of the very real danger there, cursed under his breath. He would keep his word and work at the site as promised, and he would gather the information William had requested. Then he would leave as quickly as possible so he might dismiss the emotions assaulting him.

That determination made, Dagan spoke a few words of command for Conqueror to remain behind and followed Rosamund silently.

"Where is he?"

De Silva sat his mount stiffly as the site came to life around him in the early morning hours. Addressing Champlain as his fellow knight sat his horse to his right, the baron glanced at Martin Venoir, who drew up behind them before saying, "I have waited several days for the report on the status of construction to be delivered. I grew tired of waiting and came here only to see that work begins without the master mason and his apprentice."

His gaze knowing, Champlain responded. "Surely there is another reason for your early rising and for summoning our support. Your need to impress a certain person who intrigues you, perhaps."

The baron replied haughtily, "I have made no secret of my fascination with Ross."

"Yet you did not betray your difficulty in convincing him that it would be to his advantage to entertain your intentions," Martin interjected.

De Silva scowled at Martin's unexpected comment. He had thought Martin had the intelligence to know when to hold his tongue. Making sure that he would not have to reprimand him thus again, de Silva replied, "I have difficulty only because I allow it. I admit to being teased by the young fellow's reluctance, but I anticipate a greater reward as a result. Still, I grow weary of delay."

"Then you will be happy to know that both the object of your affections and the master mason approach." De Silva turned to look behind him as Champlain continued, "At their side is the man who was injured."

De Silva turned in the direction Champlain indicated and growled his disapproval. At Ross's side—walking far too close for de Silva's comfort—was a tall, muscular fellow in ragged dress. His wounds were apparent in the yellowing bruising on his face and limbs, and in the slight limp he could not conceal, yet the element of power about him was strong. De Silva recalled Ross's claim that the fellow would be an asset at the site when he was well, but he had not expected he would look directly at him as if in unspoken challenge, or the look of intelligence apparent in the fellow's peculiar light-eyed gaze.

De Silva chose to ignore his presence as he addressed Hadley. "I have waited long enough for the report regarding the situation here. I have come to collect it, or to discover the reason why it is delayed."

"The reason is simple, my lord." Hadley shook off Ross's support as he continued, "I have not finished assessing the work already done. I need a few more days."

"I have heard that before, but I intend to wait no longer."

"My lord," Ross interrupted, "Hadley's report has been delayed by my desire to be certain that all his calculations were reached by correct observations and measurements. I have checked my figures twice, and I—"

"I did not address an apprentice! I addressed the

master mason responsible for this project, and I expect to hear his reply." Gratified when Ross's lips snapped shut, de Silva looked at Hadley and prompted, "Well, what have you to say for yourself?"

"The report is forthcoming. I would not have it lacking in any detail. Hence, the delay."

"Forthcoming . . ." De Silva smirked. "And what does *forthcoming* mean?"

"It represents work that we have yet to accomplish— perhaps another day or so," Hadley replied.

De Silva looked at Ross and asked unexpectedly, "Is that your estimate as well?"

Ross nodded.

Annoyed, the baron ordered, "Speak up! I would not have you play dumb when I ask a question."

"Are you addressing an apprentice now, or do you wish a master mason to reply?"

"Do not try my patience any further, boy."

The big fellow standing silently to Ross's rear took a threatening step, and the knights behind him reacted by drawing their swords. Ross laughed aloud, startling him.

"I do not find the situation amusing, boy."

"My name is . . . Ross."

Signaling his men to sheathe their weapons, the baron repeated, "I would like to know why you find humor in this situation . . . boy."

Ross replied without hesitation. "I find it amusing that you brought two armed knights to protect you from a simple master mason, his apprentice, and a wounded wanderer."

"The *simple master mason and his apprentice* pose no threat to me."

"Then your men must imagine a threat in the presence of a limping man whose wounds are not yet fully healed and whose strength has not yet fully returned."

"They imagine nothing, yet they prepare for anything."

"Then their preparations are in vain, for the fellow standing behind me is a common man who chose to come here to work against my advice."

"Against your advice?"

"He claims he is well and ready to do his part."

"That is wise of him."

Ross smiled and said, "It is his claim that he has not always been accused of being wise, but that he has always been accused of being stubborn."

Unable to see the humor in that response, the baron chose to change the subject. "Work appears to be progressing normally despite your uncertainties as to the stability of the foundation."

Speaking up, Hadley responded, "I did not halt the men's work for good reason . . . for to halt them unnecessarily would mean further delay. I have compromised by having the workmen shape the stones and set them aside. We will have the mortar and supplies ready to be taken up as soon as the decision is reached to go forward."

The baron felt the men behind him move restlessly as he said, "I will wait only two more days for the report you promised."

"It is forthcoming," Hadley agreed.

"It must be delivered personally by your apprentice, as previously indicated."

"But—"

His dark eyes intent, the baron stressed, "I would have it no other way."

Hadley nodded and de Silva smiled at Ross's silence. His amusement faded when the big man standing behind Ross also frowned at his words. He added maliciously, "Put that big fellow to work, too. He appears well enough to me."

"I will see to it that he puts in a full day's work," Hadley responded.

"I am sure he will, since I will notify the guards to watch him carefully, and to react accordingly should his work slacken."

Ross protested, "My lord, he is not at full strength yet. His wounds were severe."

Dagan's reply was cold. "I am well. I will do the work assigned to me."

De Silva frowned at the sound of the fellow's voice. It was deep and steady, and his gaze was direct.

It was *too* direct.

Had he seen the fellow somewhere before?

De Silva asked abruptly, "Do I know you? What is your name?"

"I told you, his name is—"

A stiff glance in Ross's direction halted his interjection, allowing Dagan to reply, "My name is Dagan Waterford. My home was in Horstede."

"Yea, so I was told. Keep in mind the fate that

Horstede suffered and conduct yourself accordingly, for my patience wears thin."

"I will do my part."

De Silva looked at Ross as he said, "I await your report."

Ross's chin rose defiantly, yet he maintained his silence with obvious strength of will.

Smiling, de Silva replied softly, "That is better . . . much better."

De Silva was still smiling when he signaled his men to follow and rode off, leaving only a cloud of dust behind him.

Standing concealed close by, Hyacinthe watched the scene unfold with a whitening countenance. She had suspected that something was amiss in the situation. Yet she had not imagined this—that Guilbert was enamored of a young man!

Stunned beyond belief, Hyacinthe waited only until the baron and his men had disappeared from sight before staggering back toward the keep's kitchen. She entered a few moments later to the knowing glances of the cook and her helper. She ignored the glances of the boys who worked feverishly and silently at the cook's commands, and returned the stare of the gray-haired, elderly cook, Edythe, who resented the influence Hyacinthe had wielded with the baron. She steeled herself as Edythe asked with open amusement, "So your attempts to seduce the baron with your feminine wiles were useless, and now you know why. Will you cut your hair and wear masculine clothing in an effort to further your appeal to him? Will you curb the French accent of which you are so proud and attempt to mimic the voice of the young man the baron now chooses over you? Or will you wait for the baron to take his fill of him and hope he will allow you back in his bed?"

"*Sorciere!*"

"Nay, it is not I who is the witch!"

"*Oui,* it is you, and also that assistant who never strays far from your side. I do not doubt that you and she have an arrangement similar to that which the baron contemplates."

"We do not!" Edythe looked at the younger woman who stood beside her. "I have a husband at home, as does Winifred. Unlike you, we do not function in this place because of the baron, but in spite of him!"

"Spoken with the tongue of one who is accustomed to lies!"

Her face flushing, Edythe picked up the nearby rolling pin and started toward Hyacinthe. "I will teach you that all women are not like you, and *I will teach you* to respect my position in this kitchen. I am in control, and you are merely a common maid—despite your dreams of more!"

Her hand moving toward the nearby table at the older woman's advance, Hyacinthe picked up a knife there and said softly, "Come ahead, then, and I will teach you not to laugh at me."

Ignoring Winifred's gasp, Edythe charged forward. Her advance halted abruptly when a deep voice rang out angrily, "What progresses here?"

Turning toward Martin Venoir as he spoke from

the kitchen doorway, Hyacinthe responded, "Ask the hag! She seems to have much to say today."

"The French whore threatened me with a knife and I but attempted to defend myself from her," Edythe responded. "Is that not true, Winifred?"

"Yea." The younger woman's reply was shaken as she persisted, "It is true."

"I am sure it is true, since your apprentice vouches for you." His reply rang with sarcasm. Martin turned toward Hyacinthe and said, "*Mettez a patience, Hyacinthe. Votre beauté prevloirai.*"

Martin's reply momentarily stunned Hyacinthe. So he knew about the baron's obscene intentions. It appeared everyone had known but her! Yet . . . she had not realized Martin believed she was beautiful, or that her beauty would prevail over the baron's present infatuation.

Hyacinthe regarded Martin more closely. He had the size and muscular girth of the baron, but although he was younger he possessed none of the qualities of her lover. His hair was dark and thick, but it was not distinguished with gray. A scar that ran the length of his cheek from eye to chin marred features that were uneven rather than handsome; and although he had proved his bravery in battle, his stature held none of the instinctive aura of command conferred by noble birth. He was nothing more than a soldier in the command of the man she loved.

Still, Hyacinthe responded gratefully. "The cook lies and her *apprenti* confirms her accusation. I am innocent."

Martin replied, "*Non,* you are not innocent, Hyacinthe. I would never believe that of you, yet I will not allow a countrywoman to be abused by a woman in the service of the baron."

Turning back to the gray-haired cook, Martin said more sternly, "However it began, this discussion is over. It will not be brought up again. Is that understood?"

"Yea," Taking a moment to glance hotly at Hyacinthe, Edythe replied, "If the same pertains to your *countrywoman.*"

"It does."

"Then I will go back to work, and I expect her to do the same."

Martin took an aggressive step forward and, said softly, "I will not abide sarcasm from you, Edythe. Is that also understood?"

The old woman took a breath, then nodded.

His expression stiff, Martin turned and departed, leaving a silent tableau behind him.

In his wake, Hyacinthe felt her first inclination to smile.

"Those guards watch you like dogs guarding a bone."

Dagan looked up from his morning's labor. It annoyed him to realize that Rosamund had been correct, that his wounds had not completely healed. The one on his chest had begun seeping blood again as he sought to move the heavy stones. Rosamund had come immediately to his aid. She had checked the wound and then found another less strenuous task for him. He had seen the guards whisper at that, and he knew what they were thinking. What they did not know was that his own reaction to her worried concern was more intense than he could have anticipated.

Presently engaged in transporting supplies from recently arrived wagons, Dagan paused to wipe away the perspiration that marked his brow. He remained silent in response to Rosamund's comment. Did she feel the the bond between them as well as he? He did not want her to suffer when his mission for William was accomplished and the truth came out. He knew his own frustration with the situation increased at times like the present, when she exhibited tender concern for his well-being. He burned to wrap his arms around her and console her, to whisper that he—

Still staring at Rosamund, Dagan frowned darkly. She felt his change in demeanor and said tightly, "What is wrong? Do you not feel well?"

"I am fine."

"You do not look fine. You look . . . unsettled."

"I am fine."

"All right, if you insist." Rosamund looked at the spot of blood that had previously spotted his shirt. Then she glanced up at the position of the sun in the cloudless sky and said, "It appears that your wound has stopped bleeding, and the day is almost done. You may rest soon."

"I am not tired."

Dagan frowned at the paperwork Rosamund held. He saw the line of carefully marked figures and said, "Your calculations are almost completed, then."

"Hadley and I will compose our report tonight. I will deliver it to the baron tomorrow."

"You will bring it to the baron's keep?"

Rosamund nodded.

"Without Hadley?"

"The baron specifically asked *me* to deliver the report. Hadley is infirm. I would not allow him to incur the baron's anger because of me."

Dagan said coldly, "The baron is more anxious to see you alone than he is to receive the report on the status of construction."

"Nay, I would say he is *as* anxious."

The coldness inside Dagan spread to encompass his voice as he replied, "It will be difficult to say nay to someone as powerful as the baron—that is, if you wish to deny him."

Dagan saw the flush that covered Rosamund's face in reaction to his words, yet her reply was fierce. "The baron is a *Norman*—a man who subjugates my people. He is also a butcher, and a thief." She continued haughtily, "I will deliver the report and nothing else."

"Yea, but he—"

"I will not discuss the matter any further with you." Rosamund's response was adamant, yet it was not as obdurate as the determination that raged inside Dagan as he turned away and went back to his work.

Feeling the weight of someone's stare, Dagan glanced up to see that the guard named Jacques eyed him with a half smile. Dagan held his temper with supreme effort, then turned to the supply wagon and snatched up another barrel. He ignored the stitch in his chest, feeling a gram of satisfaction as he tossed the barrel to the ground. Were his position different, he would have pulled that guard from his mount to dispense the penalty the fellow had earned by silently inferring that he and Rosamund were . . . that he was . . .

Dagan halted at that thought. He admired Rosamund's spirit as well as her versatile talents, and how he felt about her was none of the guard's affair.

Dagan tossed another barrel out of the wagon. He watched as it bumped and rolled along the ground to the irritated mumblings of workers who jumped out of its way.

He admired Rosamund. That was all. That was all there could be, since Rosamund was Saxon to the core and he was a man she would ultimately despise.

The night was darkening outside the hut as Hadley worked at the table and Rosamund tended to Dagan's wounds. She had treated the deep penetration on his bared chest many times before, yet this time her hands trembled.

Rosamund looked up to see Dagan regarding her intently with eyes that glowed an amber gold. His masculine scent stirred her, and his nearness made her insides flutter with an emotion she was afraid to name. Even as she touched the healing wound, her fingers tingled at the contact with his flesh. Something had changed within her as Dagan's wounds had gradually healed, as the swelling of his face gradually lessened and his strong features emerged. She didn't like the feeling that their relationship was changing, and that despite his debilities, their roles were reversing without her power to stop it.

It occurred to her as she glanced up at him that she wasn't actually certain what Dagan's eventual appearance would be. She only knew that his hair was thick and black, and that the thrashing he had sustained had compromised his strong profile and marked his cheeks with cuts and bruises. She had learned only when he had smiled briefly in the barn, baring teeth that were white and straight, that although his lips had been cut and swollen, they were unaffected. She recalled that his smile had transformed hard features that she suspected were no stranger to pain. Then she wondered why he had never smiled at her.

A moment later, the answer to that question became clear in her mind. The truth was that he had little to smile about.

She had seen the scars of previous battles that marked his flesh. His muscular arms and chest had indicated a life of labor. Yet she had been somehow unprepared for the supreme power he exuded when he stood up to tower over her with his great height and muscular form. His piercing, amber gaze had regarded her soberly, just as it did now when she realized that although he listened intently to all that was said, he made little comment.

Rosamund took a spontaneous step back. Chiding herself for her reaction a moment later, she concluded her ministrations hurriedly and said, "Your wounds are all but healed except for the deep one in your chest, which will take a little longer."

"Where I was stabbed."

"That memory is clear?"

"Clear enough."

Rosamund commented, "Some memories are to be stored for another time and never forgotten."

"Yea, some are, but others are not." Forestalling her reply, Dagan asked abruptly, "You and Hadley have finished your report?"

"We have conferred and I have confirmed Hadley's observations. We have outlined every portion of the foundation that must be reset."

"You intend to deliver the report to the baron tomorrow?"

"The baron has so directed."

Dagan's reaction to her reply was an almost imperceptible twitch of his lips . . . well-shaped lips that now held an appeal that Rosamund did not quite understand.

Annoyed at her reaction, Rosamund turned to clear away the soiled bandage. When she turned back, Dagan had lain down on his mattress and closed his eyes.

Their conversation had ended.

Speaking a few more words to Hadley, and noting that the old man had begun moving toward his mattress, Rosamund banked the fire and lay down on her own as the flames sputtered and the hut darkened. She closed her eyes, seeking sleep, aware that despite her bravado she was uncertain what the next day would bring.

The hut was silent in the darkness of night. Opening his eyes, Dagan saw that the old man had fallen asleep from sheer exhaustion as soon as he had lain down on his mattress. Although equally tired, Rosamund had twisted and turned before slumber prevailed.

He was still awake.

Rosamund's mattress was so close. Presently sleeping,

her back was partially turned toward him. If he reached out, he could easily touch her. If he did, would her pale hair feel silky to the touch? Would he discover the softness of flawless skin? Would he learn that those slender lips moving slightly in sleep tasted like a rich wine, and that she would—

When his body reinforced the direction of his thoughts, Dagan cursed softly and forced himself to close his eyes. He was determined to think no more.

Chapter Six

𝕯awn overwhelmed the darkness slowly. The overcast sky appeared reluctant to admit morning—almost as reluctant to surrender to the new day as the three approaching the site in silence. Activity had already begun despite the early hour as men arrived and went directly to work.

Rosamund turned toward Hadley and said, "I will take the report we have prepared to the baron now, Father. I will do it immediately, so he will have the full day to review its contents." Making an attempt to hide her hopefulness, she added, "He may not yet be awake, but I will leave it with the kitchen help so it may be delivered to him as soon as he awakens."

Rosamund's expression fell when Hadley responded, "You need not concern yourself in that regard. The baron will be awake. Even if he is not, you may be assured that he has instructed his people to awaken him when you arrive. For that reason, I will go with you."

"Nay, Father! The baron specifically stated that he does not want you to accompany me."

"I do not care what the baron said. I—"

"But *I* care . . ."

Turning toward Dagan when he interrupted their conversation, Rosamund replied haughtily, "*You* care?"

"I would have you follow the baron's orders."

Rosamund's lips tightened before she replied, "You surprise me. I would have thought the baron did not inspire your acquiescence."

His expression sober, Dagan advanced toward her as he said, "The baron does not want Hadley to accompany you, but he made no other restriction, did he? I will accompany you."

Startled by his reply, Rosamund shook her head. "Nay, I do not want you to become part of my problems."

"I am already a part of them."

"I will handle the baron myself."

"The baron has proved that he is one of William's most brilliant tacticians, but that he is ruthless as well. He will not be *handled* as easily as you think."

"There was no honor in defeating poorly armed peasants, if that is what you refer to as a demonstration of the baron's brilliant tactics; and although Hendsmille has learned that the baron is indeed ruthless, he may be handled by one who is more intelligent than he."

"And that person is you?"

"Perhaps."

"I will not depend on *perhaps*."

Struck with unexplained dread, Rosamund commanded, "I order you to stay here."

Taking a step closer, the scent of his breath warm on her face, his voice lowered to a soul-shaking timbre, Dagan looked directly into her eyes as he said softly, "I am in your debt, but I will not take your orders."

Rosamund swallowed and then raised her chin. Outwardly defiant despite the havoc the brief, unexpected intimacy had wrought inside her, she retorted, "Do what you want, then."

Rosamund turned toward the keep without speaking another word—only too conscious of Dagan's steady step behind her.

"My name is Ross Wedge. I am here to deliver the master mason's report to the baron."

Hyacinthe stared at the young fellow who stood resolutely in the kitchen doorway. She maintained her silence, noting that Edythe and Winifred appeared also at a loss for words. She paid no attention to the few men-at-arms who had risen from their mattresses in the next room, where they slept, to watch the exchange silently. Hyacinthe's breathing grew rough as she regarded the slender youth slowly. He was of medium height, but he was thin, with little muscle tone, and his features were small. He was effeminate in so many ways, with features too delicate to be male despite his attempts to deepen his voice and to walk with a swagger. Hyacinthe knew the baron's likes and dislikes, and she was well acquainted with his sexual appetite. She had catered to it over the years and had indulged every whim, yet she saw nothing in this young person that would raise desire in the man she loved.

Hyacinthe gasped at the unexpected appearance of the man who stepped into the doorway behind the youth. Taller than the young man by far, he was also well muscled, his back straight, and his chest full as he stood protectively close to him. His hair was dark and thick, his gaze under black brows drawn together intently was a peculiar shade of gold, and his appearance was formidable despite his common clothing and the yellow bruises visible on his face and body. She had no doubt that the ragged trousers he wore covered long legs that were similarly fortified by hard muscle. The fellow exuded masculinity. She suspected that his manhood served him well and at every opportunity. She also suspected that his presence beside the young man did not portend well for the baron's intentions.

Speaking up hesitantly, Edythe replied, "The baron expected you, but I admit that I did not. I had not thought . . . I did not believe . . ." She took a breath and continued, "The baron told me to send you upstairs to his chamber as soon as you arrived."

Hyacinthe's head jerked toward the old woman. The cook's face reddened as Hyacinthe interjected, "The baron is abed!"

"The baron was adamant that I should not allow the young man to leave without seeing him, whatever time he came." Flustered, the old woman added, "I do as I am ordered. Take the staircase in the corner of the hallway."

The young man replied unexpectedly, "I would leave the report with you rather than awaken him."

"The baron's instructions were clear."

The old woman's cheek ticked nervously. Seeing it, Ross mumbled, "All right, if that is what he ordered."

Hyacinthe watched as the young fellow turned toward the stairs.

"Wait!" The cook's voice rang out as the tall man behind Ross started to follow him. Addressing the larger man, she said harshly, "You cannot go upstairs.

The baron did not give permission for anyone else to enter his chambers."

"Permission is not necessary."

The aura of command in the big man's voice silenced the nervous cook, and Hyacinthe almost laughed. So, Guilbert had a surprise coming. It appeared that another had previous rights over the man of his choice, and he would not succeed as easily in his seduction as he believed.

Hyacinthe's tendency toward laughter faded when she envisioned the baron's displeasure. Someone would pay.

Slinking back into the corner of the kitchen, Hyacinthe watched the young fellow and his companion progress toward the stairs with a single thought.

Happily, it would not be she.

Rosamund paused at the top of the staircase. She glanced at Dagan where he stood on the staircase behind her and instructed, "Remain here while I deliver the report. You may rest assured that I will not allow the baron to sate his sexual fantasies."

Dagan did not reply.

"I will not allow you to involve yourself in my problems!"

"I have already stated that it is too late for that."

Uncertain what Dagan meant, Rosamund insisted, "I would not have you place yourself in danger for me, Dagan. You are not yet well. Your wounds have not yet healed."

"I am well enough."

"Dagan . . . please . . ."

Rosamund saw the light that entered Dagan's eyes at her plea. His expression softened. He was about to respond when the baron's shout came from the interior chamber. "Who approaches? Is that Ross I hear?"

Turning back toward the voice, Rosamund responded, "Yea, it is I."

"Enter. I have been waiting for you."

Her heart pounding, aware that the planes of Dagan's face had tightened into hard lines at the sound of the baron's voice, she turned deliberately and stepped into the vast bedchamber. She took a breath at what she saw. High ceilings and rough furniture covered a large space where fur rugs were thrown carelessly on the floor. The door to the garderobe was at the far corner. Candelabras and lanterns covered marked tables, and tattered chairs stood beside a great fireplace. Dusty tapestries of obvious value covered the walls; yet standing pristine and clean, overpowering the entire space with its presence, was a bed with finely carved posts supporting a canopy of rich fabric. Draperies of matching material hung from the wooden pillars where silk sheets and a lavish coverlet presently lay in disarray.

Refusing to blink, refusing to think of the many who had lain with the baron in that bed, as well as the plans he had for her future there, Rosamund heard the sound of Dagan's steady step behind her.

She stilled.

She did not have to wait long for the baron's reaction.

"What is *he* doing here?"

"Dagan accompanies me while I come to deliver the report on the progress of your cathedral."

Fully dressed in expensive garments, the baron approached with an expression steeped in fury. "I specifically told you that I wanted you to deliver the report alone."

Rosamund responded boldly. "Those were not your instructions, my lord. You said you wanted me to deliver the report *personally,* and I am here to comply."

The baron thundered, "I do not intend to play word games with you! That fellow may wait if he wishes, but he will remain in the kitchen where he belongs while you and I discuss . . . the construction of my cathedral."

"Nay, my lord." Speaking up for the first time, his voice matching the baron's in depth and purpose, Dagan responded with equal boldness, "I owe a debt of gratitude to Ross for his care. I have already determined that my payment will be to protect him from all manners of threat."

De Silva's handsome face flushed a deep red as he advanced to stand eye-to-eye to Dagan and responded, "Do you dare to suggest that my attention . . . to detail . . . indicates a threat to this young man?"

"I only repeat that I am Ross's guardian for as long as I remain at the site."

"Then it seems my only recourse will be to see that you are forcibly ejected from his side."

His anger obvious only in the tightening of his jaw and in the slight balling of his fists, Dagan replied, "If that is your only alternative, my lord . . ."

"My lord . . ." Interrupting the near violence of the exchange, Rosamund said tightly, "I asked Dagan not to accompany me. I told him I would be safe here, but he insisted. He has attached himself to my side since recuperating. He feels it is his duty to be my guard."

"You need no guard here."

"I told him that, but he—"

"I tire of this exchange." Turning back toward Dagan, the baron ordered, "This is my last warning. Leave this chamber now, or you will suffer my wrath."

About to reply, Dagan was interrupted by a heavy step at the doorway and Martin Venoir's unexpected appearance there as he announced, "You have a visitor, my lord. Sir Emile DuPree and his entourage have arrived to execute a mission for William that has kept them en route the year long. He is anxious to add the final details you may provide so they may return to court *rapidement*."

"I am otherwise engaged!"

Venoir's jaw firmed. "The gentleman stipulated that there was to be no delay."

Breathing deeply in an attempt to subdue his anger, the baron took a backward step and said gruffly, "We will continue this conversation at a more opportune time. Meanwhile, you may leave your report, Ross, with the assurance that we will discuss it in detail later. As for you—"

Turning to Dagan, he instructed tightly, "I suggest that you consider what I have said and review your actions carefully."

Allowing no time for Dagan's response, de Silva dismissed both Rosamund and Dagan with a glance and started toward the stairs. His descending step echoed against the high ceilings of the chamber as Rosamund turned toward Dagan and said quietly, "We must leave quickly, before he changes his mind."

"I do not fear the baron."

"Then Horstede's fate has taught you nothing, for the baron will not hesitate to serve everyone in Hendsmille a similar fate if he is displeased!"

"I will not allow the baron to take what he believes to be his due. The battle is long over. Assets that have not been awarded are no longer his by right."

Rosamund stared at Dagan. Noting that resolve had turned his gaze from amber to pure gold, she replied just as determinedly, "I have never been anyone's reward. Nor do I intend to allow anyone to exercise his right over me."

Rosamund turned toward the staircase without waiting for his reply. She emerged below and was about take her leave when she saw the baron speaking to an older gentleman whose garments, although obviously costly, appeared as trail-weary as he did himself. Standing behind the elderly gentleman were several others who appeared equally exhausted.

The baron turned toward her unexpectedly and directed coldly, "Now that you have delivered your report, you and your *guard* may return to work."

Dismissing her, the baron turned back to the elderly man. Rosamund looked over her shoulder, only to realize that Dagan had slipped out through the doorway and was waiting outside. Grateful for the unexpected reprieve, she returned to the construction site with Dagan close behind her.

Martin Venoir frowned as Hyacinthe emerged from the corner of the kitchen in which she had been hiding. Her eyes tight on de Silva's figure, she moved silently to the table, where she nodded silently at Edythe's commands. It had angered him to see her cowering like a dog in the corner, in obvious fear that the baron might choose to take out on her any anger that his latest paramour caused him. He wondered why a woman such as she had chosen to seek out a household where leftovers were her only prospect.

Martin stared at Hyacinthe for long moments. He had tried to make her see that the inner beauty she kept hidden was as tempting as her considerable outer fairness. In truth, he had never seen hair as thick and dark as hers. Nor had he ever seen black eyes as wide and as heavily lashed, or a body as voluptuously full and feminine. He had heard others speak of her antics with men in the past, but he was more keenly aware than most that her actions had not been those of a loose woman obsessed with sexual pleasure, but with the specific purpose of being able to maintain de Silva's interest. In any case, that time was long past.

Hyacinthe had always loved only one man. It did not seem to matter to her that the distance between them was wide and would keep them forever separated, or that the baron neither respected nor valued her in any way. It amazed him that she could delude herself into believing otherwise. That delusion was a point of ridicule that escaped no one, most especially the two women with whom she worked on a daily basis in the kitchen.

Martin silently lamented that Hyacinthe's efforts were a waste of youth and beauty that might be presented as a gift to another who would cherish it . . . that she wasted true emotion on one who had not a scrap of emotional truth in him . . . that she squandered all that she was when another might make her happy at last.

Martin straightened up the powerful shoulders that he had earned through difficult toil. Aware that he was not as handsome as the baron, that his scarred cheek caused some women to dismiss his obvious youth and vigor, he also knew that there were many woman who enjoyed each and every one of his scars. But like Hyacinthe, he was now interested in only one person . . .

Martin heard the sharpness in Edythe's tone when she spoke to Hyacinthe. The woman hated her, but he did not.

Yea . . . unfortunately for him, he could not.

With that thought darkening his countenance, Martin turned toward the outer yard and walked swiftly out of sight.

Dagan followed Rosamund silently as they made their way back to the work grounds. He was keenly aware that his true identity had almost been discovered. He had no doubt that Sir Emile DuPree would recognize him, no matter his present degree of battered dishevelment.

Unlike de Silva, who had seen Dagan only in his youth, Emile was one of William's trusted advisers. They had had an almost daily exchange at William's court, and they had true affection for each other. In truth, he had not realized that the mission on which William had dispatched Emile almost a year earlier would bring him to the shire at this time. The arrival could have been disastrous to his own mission—for an untimely identification was not in his plans.

Yet . . . what were his plans?

He had been injured, nursed back to health, and had been exposed to a side of the baron that he had not wished to see. It was a side that he still hoped did not reflect other liberties taken in William's name.

He was also obsessed by the driven nature of his feelings for Rosamund. But what exactly were those feelings? Why did the sight of her graceful profile set his heart pounding? Why did the sweet scent of her body set him afire? Why did her touch—platonic in every way—ignite a hunger inside him that drove all other thoughts from his mind?

The pain in his chest stirred and Dagan winced. He recalled the rumors that had caused William to send him here. The taking of victor's rights in the heat of a battle's aftermath was common, even if he had never found that indulgence to be necessary; yet the time for the taking of such rights was past. William had made that clear to his nobles.

Dagan looked at Rosamund as she turned back toward him. His mouth went dry and his heart lurched at her innate appeal. Confusion ruled his thoughts, but one thing was acutely clear: He needed to leave this place as soon as possible if he was to escape a conflict that he had no desire to face.

"Why did you do that? Why did you challenge the baron so openly?"

Turning to face Dagan squarely when they reached a secluded portion of the site and would not be overheard, Rosamund continued with obvious agitation, "You know he has superior forces to back him that you do not."

"I do not fear the baron's *superior forces,*" Dagan replied coldly.

"It would be wise if you did."

"I have not often been accused of being wise, but I have always been accused of being—"

"I know, I know." Rosamund was not amused by his response. "I will not be cajoled by your attempt to dismiss your unwise actions."

"My actions were not unwise."

"Were they not? What did you expect would happen if the baron's knight had not taken that moment to interrupt your exchange with him?"

"I told you, I do not fear the baron in any way."

"If you do not, you are a fool!" Her face flushed and her patience exhausted, Rosamund responded, "Now is not the time for confrontation! That time *will* come, but in the interim we must use our wits instead of our tongues."

"Spoken by one who guards his responses wisely."

Rosamund's color darkened at his sarcasm. "I use my tongue as a weapon because I have no other."

"We all use the weapons at our command."

"Why do you not listen to me?" Rosamund demanded. "Why do you chance wasting the time I took treating your wounds by risking your life so unwisely?"

"I do not risk my life unwisely. I told you that I would not allow the baron to visit his perversions on you."

"And I told you that I would not allow it, either."

"You were stepping into his web."

"I was progressing thoughtfully, using the weapons at my command."

"Excuses for unwise conduct!"

"Any unwise conduct was your own!"

"I do not agree. I was your own—"

Halting abruptly as he looked up into the distance, Dagan frowned and stepped back to say, "I do not wish to discuss this any longer. What's done is done. I must return to work."

"Go! Go then, and forget your foolishness, but remember that I will not allow you to provoke the baron again—under any circumstances!"

Dagan's amber-eyed gaze went cold. "We will see."

He startled her by turning his back and walking away. Rosamund gasped. The fool! Did he not see . . . was he not aware . . .

Rosamund stared at Dagan's broad back. She swallowed as tears unexpectedly filled her eyes and tightened her throat. Why did she care if he chose to disregard her warnings? Why did the thought of Dagan spending even a moment in the dark dungeon from which so few emerged frighten her more than she had ever been frightened for herself? And why did she want to beg him . . . yea, *beg him* . . . to allow her to handle the baron lest he suffer in her stead?

Rosamund paused in response to that question because the answer was suddenly clear.

Fighting the tears so close to falling, Rosamund whispered under her breath, "Damn him for his stubbornness! Damn him to hell!"

"Emile . . ." Dagan saw the exhausted, elderly gentleman turn at the sound of his name. He had not expected to be able to talk to the older man so soon, but he had snatched the opportunity when he saw Emile emerge from the keep in the distance while he was talking to Rosamund.

Dagan waited as Sir Emile approached across the brief lawn behind the keep. He smiled and shook the fellow's hand when he stood opposite him. The knight showed no surprise at his appearance when Dagan began, "I was startled to see you here, Emile. I had forgotten that you were due to arrive back at court from William's mission, and that this would most likely be the last of the places you would visit."

"I was surprised to see you here, too, Dagan." Dwarfed by Dagan's muscular stature and his eyes half-lidded with exhaustion, Emile continued, "I saw you when you and that other young man came down from de Silva's quarters, you know. I admit to being momentarily taken aback at the conditions you seem to be living under, but I knew immediately when you slipped from sight that you wished to conceal your true identity for some reason, and that it would be un-wise for me to speak to you."

"And I thought I had been so clever."

"You have obviously been clever if you've managed to maintain this disguise." His lips twitched. "And who is this young man you guard?"

"That young man saved my life when I was at-tacked and nearly expired from my wounds."

Emile shook his head. "That accounts for your bruises, but it does not explain your disguise as one of the workers here."

"No, it does not, and I do not have the time to make a full explanation to you, for I will soon be missed. I can only say that I came to Hendsmille on an errand for William, and that circumstances have proved to me that this disguise is necessary if I am to complete the task William has assigned me."

Emile's lined face grew grim. "I admit that I was sus-picious of duplicity when I spoke briefly to de Silva and realized that he knew nothing about the role you have assumed. Rest assured that I will keep your secret and report on the situation to William when I return to court."

"Thank you, Emile."

"Do not thank me. I am simply performing my duty as sworn to William. I admit that after all my traveling, it is my pleasure to speak to one who admires William as much as I."

"However this affair ends, that truth will never change." Dagan hesitated. He looked around himself and said urgently, "I must go now."

"May the good Lord guide your step, Dagan." The

old man smiled. "I will only be here a day or so longer, for most of my mapping is finished. I need only to define the forested area designated for William's hunting grounds. Remember not to take any risks that will endanger you."

"My life has been dedicated to William's service. I will take any risk necessary to accomplish my purpose here."

Emile's lined face drew into a smile. "I will be sure to tell William that as well."

Familiar warmth welled inside Dagan. He had always liked the old man. He had accomplished one necessary task by explaining the situation to him, yet a far more difficult one lay before him.

Back at the site, Dagan looked at Rosamund where she worked at Hadley's side. She had been angered at their earlier exchange, and now it was time to seek her out when she was alone and explain his harsh response as best he could.

Dagan sat quietly as Rosamund went about her evening tasks. The workday had come to a close. They had eaten their humble meal of pottage and ale, the daily fare for those who labored at the baron's command and who were forbidden to hunt in the abundant forests surrounding them. Dagan's stomach growled as he thought of the elaborate menus at court. He made a mental note to speak to William about the deprivations the common man suffered in Hendsmille.

The unnatural silence in the hut continued. Hadley had had a difficult day. He had struggled to see the plans for the cathedral clearly, and he was frustrated by his handicap. Rosamund was still angry at Dagan. He had not had an opportunity to speak to her alone, and he wondered when he would. The necessity grew more urgent with each hour that passed.

As if reading his thoughts, Rosamund turned to Hadley and said, "I need to retrieve more water from the stream. I will be back shortly."

Hadley grunted in response, engaged in his own pursuits. It had become Dagan's practice to visit the barn each day, and he knew it would not seem strange when he left the hut shortly after Rosamund did. He walked as swiftly as possible toward the stream where water was gathered each day. Dagan realized he might not find Rosamund alone there and one glance proved his expectations correct. Workers' wives knelt by the bank with buckets in hand. There was only one thing he could do.

Slipping into the foliage, where he would not be seen, Dagan prepared to wait. Only a few minutes passed before he saw Rosamund returning from the stream carrying a full bucket. He paused until she was opposite him before sliding his hand over her mouth and pulling her into the forest. Rosamund struggled wildly, spilling the contents of her bucket in the act, but Dagan drew her backward relentlessly.

Satisfied at last that they were deep enough into the forested glade to have achieved complete privacy, Dagan ordered, "Stop struggling!"

At the sound of his voice, Rosamund went still. She glared up at him as he said softly, "Do not scream when I remove my hand. I only wish to speak to you in private."

Her indignation obvious when he removed his hand, Rosamund asked, "Was that necessary?"

Dagan almost smiled at her anger. "It was necessary if I wished to speak to you alone."

Her eyebrows raised, Rosamund inquired tightly in return, "Why was it necessary to speak to me alone?"

"It was necessary if I felt the need to apologize."

Rosamund went still. "You wish to apologize to me?"

"You did not neglect my wounds when we returned to the hut this evening, but I confess I was uncomfortable with the situation between us. I realize the fault is partially mine, and I—"

Dagan halted abruptly, his brows gathering in a frown when Rosamund's glorious eyes unexpectedly filled with tears. He demanded incredulously, "Are you crying?"

"Nay." Her tone defensive, Rosamund replied, "What you see is my reaction to the frustration you caused me."

"Frustration?"

"I am certain the baron will take steps against you because of me. It is only a matter of time until he does. Your only recourse now is to leave this place."

Dagan's expression went cold. "I told you, I do not fear de Silva."

"That is the reason I am frustrated .... and frightened! I do not want to see you killed or imprisoned. I do not want to see that happen to you."

"It will not."

"Yea, it will if you persist in your attitude."

"Why do you care how my attitude affects the baron?"

135

"Why?" Retreating into her male persona, Rosamund replied, "No man should be made to suffer when he has wronged no one, but de Silva does not make that distinction when he is angry. And he is very angry with you."

"Because he wants you."

Rosamund took a breath. "Yea, there can be no denying that he does at the moment, but he will soon find another to tease his passions—a maiden perhaps. I have only to avoid his attentions until that moment comes."

Aware that he could no longer participate in this farce, Dagan whispered, "It will do no good to pretend with me any longer . . . Rosamund."

"Rosamund!" She gasped. "My name is Ross!"

"I have known from the moment my senses returned fully that there was no way you could be other than a woman, Rosamund."

"But . . ."

"Surely you did not believe you deceived me with your disguise? Even in your male garb, you are feminine and beautiful. It was not difficult for me to see that the male mannerisms you assumed when away from the hut were feigned. I can only assume that you and Hadley chose such a disguise with de Silva in mind. Fool that he is, de Silva has not yet seen through it. Instead, the potential perversion intrigues him." Dagan's expression hardened. "But you may rest assured that I will not allow the baron to harm you."

Dagan clutched Rosamund closer at that thought, his protective instincts overwhelming him as he continued hoarsely, "Nay, you are meant for more than de

Silva's crude intentions. You are too intelligent . . . too beautiful . . . too womanly . . . too worthwhile in both body and spirit for a man who has the reputation of having used so many, only to discard them when his interest waned."

Intoxicated by her scent, by the feminine warmth of her, Dagan stroked Rosamund's hair. He marveled that the pale tresses were as silken as he had imagined and whispered, "Your hair glows despite its cut, you know. Although my vision was impaired when you first tended my wounds, I recall that your hair was akin to a halo surrounding delicate features that I struggled to see. As I recovered, I spent hours imagining how it would feel to stroke those gleaming tresses . . . to feel them slip through my fingers. I longed to smooth the flawlessness of your cheek . . . to follow the contours of your ears with my tongue . . . to follow a course that could only lead to your lips. I wondered . . . I *ached* with a need to know if they were as sweet to the taste as they seemed, and if . . . if . . ."

Words slipped away as Dagan touched his lips to Rosamund's. He pressed his mouth deeper, inwardly reveling when Rosamund's lips parted to accept his kiss. He heard her gasp become a groan when he quickly adjusted her clothing and then his own. He held her close, feeling her womanly softness yield to his masculinity, and marveled at the way she fit in his arms . . . so close . . . so perfect.

His senses reeled as his lips found the soft mounds of her breasts at last. The taste of her filled him . . . lifted him high on a plane that he had never reached before.

The sweet intensity . . . the bliss . . . the awe . . .

And when he slipped inside her, the world went still.

Rosamund gasped as Dagan slid himself inside her. She did not recall the exact moment when his ministrations drove all thought but his touch from her mind. She knew only that his lips on hers had been sweet and right . . . that she had cried out at his kiss and the sensations he evoked when he pressed his heated kisses against her suddenly naked breasts. She recalled holding him tight against her when he found the roseate crests at last and suckled them fervently. Her passions rapidly escalating, she accepted his loving ministrations with an ever-growing need of her own, until she curved her arms around his neck, then waited breathlessly when he laid her down at last and thrust himself inside her.

Dagan stilled, his gold eyes touching hers in a silent question. Rosamund searched his gaze and saw an emotion there that matched her own. It was powerful beyond her wildest dreams, and joy welled inside her. This was what she had sensed, what she had wanted so desperately. Drawing him down upon her, she welcomed his lovemaking. She met his thrusts instinctively as they grew more rapid, steeling herself against the wonder he raised inside her. Ecstasy deepened, a vista of incredible colors that grew brighter, more brilliant, until—

The moment came in a burst of glory, with Dagan throbbing to fulfillment inside her as her own pleasure winged free at last.

All movement halted. Dagan lay full upon her, the heat of their mutual passion fusing them as one.

A breathless silence reigned. The sky was darkening. The traffic to the stream had all but ceased, and they were alone in the lengthening shadows. His gaze holding hers, Dagan whispered as he searched her expression, "I didn't intend this when I came to find you, Rosamund. I wanted only to apologize . . . to explain that I knew . . . to tell you that—"

Sliding her hand across his lips, Rosamund whispered, "You need not attempt to explain an emotion that I understand too well. This was meant to be between us, Dagan. I know that in my heart now—I suppose I knew it from the first moment I saw you. You were dear to me from that first instant. My heart beat wildly each time our gazes met, and I felt an emotion that I did not understand. I realize now that this time together is a gift that we will remember when it is long past and other things are forgotten."

"Remember? Other things?" Dagan shook his head. "I don't understand."

Unexpected tears filled Rosamund's eyes as she replied, "Is it so difficult to understand, Dagan, that if I deemed it necessary to conceal my gender from all who did not know me, that I might also conceal another secret as well?"

Dagan stared. "Rosamund . . ."

Rosamund curved her palm around his cheek, tears slipping silently into the fair hair at her temples. "It grows dark. Hadley will wonder where we are. I do not want him to attempt to look for either of us."

"Rosamund, I do not understand."

Rosamund pressed a finger against his lips. "There is beauty in this moment, Dagan. I would not have the world intrude."

Rosamund's eyes held his. In her gaze, Dagan saw an unanticipated strength . . . and a secret that still went untold.

A secret.

Momentarily angry that Rosamund should keep a secret from him, Dagan rationalized that he kept one from her as well—a secret that could easily turn her against him when the truth was out.

Frowning with confused uncertainty at that thought, Dagan helped Rosamund to her feet. He straightened his clothing as she adjusted hers, until she was a youth once more.

Abruptly giving vent to need, to the passions surging hotly inside him, Dagan crushed Rosamund close and claimed her lips in a kiss. He was uncertain of the complications the future might bring, but of one thing he was sure: Whether she realized it or not, he had claimed Rosamund for his own, and no one would take her from him.

"Come . . . we must hurry."

His introspection interrupted by Rosamund's urging, Dagan frowned and followed her out onto the trail. He filled the bucket once more and walked beside her until the danger of being seen parted them. Allowing her to return to the hut ahead of him, he watched her slender figure in the doorway, etched in dark relief by the light from within until she disappeared from sight.

Dagan's heart lurched at the temporary deprivation. He vowed into the silence, "Whoever she is, whatever her secret, Rosamund is mine."

Chapter Seven

Sounds of feasting filled the great hall of the keep as night fell. Annoyed, de Silva barely withheld a sneer when he observed the tables loaded with delicacies: swine that had been dressed and cooked with great care, shellfish and meat pies touched with herbs, puddings, all manner of cooked and baked fruit, nuts, figs, and honey cakes. All was washed down liberally with his good ale, so strong that it left some of his men tipsy.

De Silva raised his chin. He did not normally deem it necessary to feed all the men who remained ready to fight at his beck and call through the years. Rather, he fed only the knights who were unattached and demanded that those of his men who lived in nearby huts with their women should share their food. Yet he had decided that it would be wise to allow DuPree to see the full number of knights in service to him.

De Silva observed that Martin Venoir sat among his fellow knights rather than at his side, while visitors and soldiers alike enjoyed the banquet he had ordered in the hope of distracting DuPree from his mission. He did not like it, but he admitted to himself that Martin's decision was a wise one that would endear him to the men. It occurred to the baron that Martin was far cleverer than he had realized.

De Silva's smile concealed his annoyance that such abundance now would render his own meals and those of the knights he allowed at his table wanting later in the season.

"Damn the old man!" de Silva whispered heatedly in Champlain's ear. "He rested after arriving this morning and appears to be unnaturally rejuvenated, considering his age. I had expected to be allowed some time, but he wants to see William's hunting preserve tomorrow. He claims he can map it for William no other way, and he does not want to waste any time in getting back to London because William is anxious to return to Normandy."

Champlain shook his head, his dark brows furrowing. "DuPree will be too tired to observe the perimeters of the preserve after this merrymaking. You will still be able to arrange matters so you will not be discovered."

"Discovered?"

"He might otherwise determine that you have been clearing the land of Saxon huts and declaring their land William's hunting preserves only to usurp it as your own."

"Usurp . . . *usurp*?" Blood rising to his face, de Silva spewed, "Unlike the Bastard, royal blood flows through my veins! That land is mine, won in battle from a pretender to the throne—a throne that I will take rightfully from another pretender when the time is ripe!" Suddenly aware that his haughty response and loss of temper might have been overheard, de Silva glanced at the table around him where his guests and knights still supped. Satisfied that the din of merrymaking had masked his words, de Silva turned back toward Champlain and whispered impatiently, "DuPree is determined to obey William's charge. Nothing will deter him from the course he has been set upon. He has William's ear. I dare not do anything that might raise suspicions about the plot to overthrow William."

"William is still in England. Your allies dare not make a move until he leaves."

"I am not sure they are prepared to wait. In any case, his residence is temporary. He but awaits Emile's return and will then return to Normandy as soon as he is able. Everyone knows of William's preference for his native land and language." De Silva snickered. "I have used that argument often against him."

"Yea, but—"

De Silva's expression hardened as he interrupted. "Since the plan has not been set into motion and I am not yet ready to declare myself to William, I have no choice but to offer DuPree a hunt. Hopefully, I can distract him from too close an observance of the lands by filling his mind with the quality of my falcons and hounds, and perhaps by his participation in the argument that inevitably erupts between huntsmen and falconers over which form of hunting suits nobles best."

Champlain nodded. "Observing the construction of the cathedral underway should sway him favorably."

"Yea . . ." De Silva responded, but he was no longer listening. Instead, his eyes were on the youths who scurried back and forth, bringing food to the tables.

Champlain nudged, "Guilbert . . ."

"It amazes me that I feel no attraction to any of the youths who serve my tables. They would be easy sport."

"Unlike Hadley's apprentice . . ."

"Yea, unlike Hadley's apprentice." Turning back to his friend, de Silva said darkly, "The lad avoids me. He even had the gall to bring that big fellow to protect him when I called him to my room."

A rare smile quirked at Champlain's mouth. "So I heard."

"The young fellow does not seem to realize how greatly an affiliation with me might benefit him. I have invited him to follow the hunt tomorrow."

All trace of Champlain's smile disappeared as he responded, "Do you think that is wise? He probably doesn't even know how to ride."

"He will learn, and that is what I have commanded." He added, "Commanded, do you hear? Ross did not dare challenge me." He sneered and added, "I have ordered that one of my finest hunting mounts be furnished for his use. During the hunt, he will see that the hounds are treated more gently than children, and that the falcons receive similar attention. When I have properly impressed him with the stables at my command—with the well-trained horses, birds, and dogs, with the freedom I am allowed on the hunting grounds, and with the outstanding ability of my men and myself, most especially—I will call him to my room again. He will not hesitate a second time."

"Guilbert . . . the man who claims to be his guard . . ."

"I have ordered that he not accompany Ross to the hunt or to my quarters. He will not dare disobey a direct command."

Champlain hesitated, and then said, "Have you

considered that he may have a previous claim to the youth?"

De Silva's nostrils quivered as he suppressed his anger and ordered, "Do not speak to me of that again, do you hear? I care not about previous claims. There is only one claim that I consider valid, and that is mine!"

Champlain hesitated, then replied darkly, "As you wish."

De Silva maintained his silence as Champlain turned back to the feast without another word, but the damage had been done. Champlain had spoken aloud the thought that gnawed at him, the very real possibility that the big man called Dagan might be exercising a previous claim on the one he desired.

Nay, he would not acknowledge any such thing! He had already stated the simple truth that the only valid claim was his own.

That determination in mind, de Silva turned back to garner the attention of DuPree, his favored guest. His smile belied the dark resolve in his heart.

Hyacinthe moved amid the group of young men tending the invited throng in the great hall. With a provocative step, she tread the fresh rushes scattered for the occasion and managed a sultry dip of her shoulders that allowed for a view of her ample bosom as she served the baron's men. She had taken particular care with the dark hair that hung against her shoulders in curling profusion, and had used the hand mirror that de Silva had given her in a generous moment to peruse her features. She had made sure to pinch her cheeks for color, to make sure her smile glowed. Yet as she glanced up at the head table, she saw that contrary to the jealousy and desire she had hoped to inspire, de Silva appeared totally unaffected and was too deep in his conversation with Champlain to pay her any mind at all.

She shrugged off men with a smile, and was about to dislodge another unwanted touch on her arm when Martin Venoir stayed her and said, "You look lovely tonight, Hyacinthe."

A glance at Martin's expression revealed his sincerity. Hyacinthe replied with a twitch of her lips, "Do I? It does not seem that my appearance has garnered any notice."

"Yea, it has . . . from me, and from many others. It just has not garnered the notice of the man you hoped to impress."

Suddenly angry, Hyacinthe hissed, "Why did you not tell me of Guilbert's new penchant for perversion?"

"It was not my place."

"A poor excuse."

"Would you have believed me if I had spoken?"

"Perhaps not, but—"

Martin's smile fell as he continued, "I had hoped de Silva's decision for tomorrow's festivities would not affect you unfavorably, but—"

"His decision?" Hyacinthe's heart began a slow pounding. "You are speaking of the planned hunt, are you not? Why should I be affected?"

"Then you do not know."

"Know what?"

"That the baron has invited the youth . . . Ross Wedge . . . to attend the hunt."

Hyacinthe paled. "I do not believe you! Guilbert would not make so obvious an attempt to impress anyone. Besides not having the proper equipment, the boy probably has no idea what is involved in a hunt."

"The baron has given the order to supply all that he might need . . . even one of the best horses in his stable."

Hyacinthe stared up at Martin incredulously. She had thought he was one of the few knights she had served that night who was not far into his cups. But why else would he make so outrageous a statement?

Raising her voice over the din surrounding them, she replied, "You must be wrong. Guilbert would not invite one as common as his master mason's apprentice to the hunt for any reason. He would not make so open a gesture."

"He has commanded the young man to attend and ordered that a horse and equipment be sent for his use tomorrow morning. He has commanded that the youth take a place at the rear of the procession, but it is my thought that once the mayhem of the hunt begins, the baron will see to it that he does not remain there."

"What do you mean?"

"I mean, the baron desires the young man. He obviously hopes to impress him. He will probably take him under his wing.

"*Take him under his wing . . .*"

Hyacinthe was beginning to tremble. Observing her disquiet, Martin rose abruptly and took her arm. He drew her outside, away from the din in the interior hall. Once in the darkened hallway, he whispered

sincerely, "I'm sorry, Hyacinthe. I know this is difficult for you."

Breathless, Hyacinthe pressed, "By taking him under his wing, you mean that Guilbert will—"

"I mean only that I believe the baron will take the
opportunity to attempt to impress the boy with his
prowess."

"But . . . but the hunt is meant to impress DuPree,
not the youth."

"I fear . . ." Martin hesitated. His strong features
tightened as he continued, "I fear the baron is more
concerned with impressing the youth, than he is in
distracting DuPree."

"But Guilbert knows DuPree could complicate
everything he has achieved. He knows how important
the hunt can be."

"He knows, but I suspect his emotions are too involved for him to make a wise decision."

"His emotions . . ." Hyacinthe whispered, "Does
Guilbert not realize that I love him?"

When Martin did not reply, Hyacinthe pressed,
"Does he not?"

"I fear . . ." Martin took a breath before continuing
resolutely, "I fear he knows but does not care."

Hyacinthe went still. There was no doubting Martin's sincerity. There was no doubting that somehow . . . somewhere through their long acquaintance,
Martin had become a true friend who would tell her
the truth as he saw it. But he was wrong! Damn it all,
he was wrong!

Sobbing wildly, Hyacinthe was not aware of the

moment when Martin's arms closed around her, when he drew her against his strong chest and held her tightly in consolation. She did not hear the soft reassurances he whispered, so great was her heartbreak.

Martin held Hyacinthe protectively. He wished that he had the power to ease her pain but he knew he did not.

Martin drew Hyacinthe closer. She was sobbing uncontrollably. She did not hear when he whispered that she was beautiful and womanly, that any man would be fortunate to have her love him. She did not notice when he said that the baron was an aberration . . . a man consumed with self . . . a man who sought to be king and would never take a common woman to wife.

Martin knew instinctively what Hyacinthe wanted. She wanted to be wife to the baron. She wanted to bear his children and to spend the rest of her life serving him in any way he wished. She would not accept the reality that even with all she had to offer—true beauty, deep love, incredible devotion, and everlasting loyalty—de Silva did not consider her good enough for him and never would.

Martin drew her closer. He held her tighter as her sobs continued. But she was good enough for him . . . too good for a man who had made his way in the world by the wanton shedding of the blood of strangers. If she only knew . . . if he could only tell her that truth . . . But she loved de Silva, and he had become her friend.

Her friend . . .

By accepting that reality, Martin feared he would never have more.

The sun was rising and the morning air was crisp as Rosamund rode at the rear of the procession. The hunt had begun, but Rosamund's mind was occupied, recalling Hadley and Dagan's dark expressions of disapproval when a messenger had appeared at the hut the previous evening to inform her that de Silva had invited Ross to attend the hunt the following day. Their expressions had darkened even further that morning when a silent servant delivered the horse and the necessary apparel.

Rosamund winced as she recalled the conversation that had ensued the moment the *invitation* was issued.

"I do not want you to accept the baron's invitation. His intentions are obvious, and I would not have you suffer at his hands because of me," Hadley had said.

"Father, the baron has commanded that I attend. I dare not refuse outright without incurring his wrath. But you need not fear; I will be wary of his attentions," she had responded pleadingly.

Hadley had remained unconvinced. The argument had resumed as dawn crept over the horizon and a mount and the equipment and apparel necessary for the hunt were delivered to her door. Only too aware that Dagan had maintained his silence throughout, Rosamund had faced down Hadley's objections. "Please try to understand that I have no choice but to accommodate the baron temporarily. But your concerns are for naught. He will be too busy with the contingent from William to bother with me. I intend to remain at the end of the procession, out of his sight."

"He will not allow you to remain there."

Rosamund had turned sharply toward Dagan when he made his first comment. She was about to protest when he continued, "Your father is right. De Silva is using this opportunity to attempt to impress you."

She had replied heatedly, "He cannot impress me with the power he commands in this shire because of the Saxon blood that he has shed, or with the wealth he stole from the farmers that he conquered so easily. He never will!"

"He is not aware of the extent of your loyalty. He believes he may awe you with his prowess."

"Prowess? I know of no prowess. Even the most common Saxon farmer could hunt as well as he does if he were allowed to do so without fear."

Hadley had insisted. "I will find an excuse so that you will not attend the hunt. I will tell the baron that I need you, that another day will hinder—"

A sound outside the hut had halted Hadley's response the moment before a uniformed soldier had appeared in the doorway to say, "The baron has commanded that I escort you to the keep, where you will join those preparing for the hunt."

"Tell the baron I will not allow Ross to come, that I—"

Stepping forward, Rosamund had interrupted Hadley to say, "I will follow you."

Mounting up on the steed waiting outside the hunt,

Rosamund had followed the uniformed soldier without another word, leaving the two men standing silently behind them.

Though she still rode at the rear of the procession now, Rosamund's positive thoughts wavered. She had not had the opportunity to tell Hadley that Dagan was aware of her true gender. Nor had Dagan spoken a word after the first messenger arrived. They had slept on their separate mattresses, only inches from each other, yet they had not touched. With the memory of Dagan's strong arms around her, of lying close to him, of the unexpected wonder he had evoked, she had felt a deprivation unlike any she had experienced before.

Rosamund glanced at the hunters surrounding her. The baron's knights practiced fighting whenever the weather permitted so they might be available on an instant's notice when the baron summoned their expertise. When springtime came, however, they spent their time in the woods and fields, hunting with the hounds and hawks in order to maintain their form. She had had no trouble keeping up with them while they sang and made music as they traversed the wooded glade and waited for the hounds to pick up the scent, but that would change once the hunt began in earnest.

Through all the pomp and ceremony of the hunt, she had watched the faces of the peasants as hunters had wantonly trampled their fields and crops and forced them to supply refreshments from their small supplies of food. She had pretended not to notice the peasants who had been "poaching" on land that had once been their own and who hid from the unannounced hunting procession, obviously terrified of being discovered and punished.

The hunting horn sounded unexpectedly, breaking into Rosamund's somber thoughts as the hounds surged forward in wild pursuit of game. The horses followed instinctively, and the hunters leaned forward to accommodate their mounts' sudden burst of speed as they leaped obstacles and chased at a pace that set her heart to pounding.

Rosamund gripped her mount's reins tightly as it responded spontaneously to the increased heat of the chase. The animal nearly unseated her several times as it followed the rabid throng over hill and dale, through dense forest and brambles that tore at her borrowed hunting clothing and slapped at her face.

She gasped when she saw the mounts in front of her leap as one over a muddy ditch. Determined not to be defeated by the challenge, she gripped her mount's reins tightly, only to hear the unexpected sound of a snap a moment before the reins broke, throwing her high into the air for long seconds before she hit the damp, leafy ground with a loud crack.

A darkness filled with the dwindling sound of the hunt enveloped her. She strained to open her eyes, hardly conscious of the deep, male voice in her ear . . . a familiar, well-loved voice . . . calling her back. Rosamund looked up into Dagan's tight expression. He stroked her cheek and whispered words she could not quite understand, concern creasing his face as he gently probed her muddied scalp for signs of injury. Finding none, he systematically searched her body for broken bones.

When his gaze returned to her face at last, he whispered, "It appears you have no injuries. I was afraid that—" He hesitated, then continued hoarsely, "You shouldn't have attempted to keep up with the other hunters. They are practiced at this sport. They know its rigors. They have—"

"Get away from him!"

Dagan's head jerked up at the baron's command. He did not move from her side as de Silva drew his mount to a sliding halt and dismounted with several men at his heels. "Leave him alone so he may mount his horse! He will continue with the hunt."

Standing, Dagan faced de Silva coldly. "The equipment you provided for Ross was faulty. The reins broke, causing his fall. As a result, not only is Ross incapacitated, but his mount is unable to continue on. I will assist him back to his hut."

"He is fine!" De Silva ordered harshly, "Get up, Ross. Show this man that contrary to his assessment, you are ready to mount up and continue on."

Still disoriented but unwilling to allow the baron's anger to fall on Dagan, Rosamund attempted to rise. She grunted as she stumbled back to the ground again.

Enraged, de Silva repeated, "Get up, I said!"

Immediately kneeling at her side, Dagan responded harshly, "He cannot get up. Neither he nor his equipment is equal to the chase. I will take him back to his hut so he may recover fully."

Dagan attempted to help Rosamund to her feet, only to stiffen when de Silva rasped, "I told you to take your hands off him. What are you doing here, anyway? I did not invite you to attend the hunt. To the contrary, I stipulated that Ross should attend alone."

"Ross obeyed your command. However, you did not say that I could not follow him. In light of his inexperience, I was fearful that he might have an accident. I wanted to be there to tend to him."

"Nay, you will not *tend to him.* Nor will you take him back to his hut. Instead, I will—"

"What is wrong here?"

De Silva turned abruptly toward Emile DuPree as the old man drew his mount to a halt beside them with unexpected skill. The baron responded, "I did not expect you to interrupt your hunt for so inconsequential a matter as a young man's fall."

Emile frowned at de Silva's glance, responding, "When you disappeared, I came to find you. The hounds seem to have lost the scent anyway, so it did not matter."

De Silva nodded. "Then it will be no difficult matter for the young man to catch up."

"So, what is the problem?"

De Silva turned as Dagan helped Rosamund to her feet. He frowned when he noted her unsteady state and responded to Emile, "The youth fell from his horse at a jump, and this man claims the boy is done for the day. I do not ascribe to that defeatist attitude. It is my thought that he should remount and continue on."

Emile replied impatiently, "This young fellow has obviously had a hard fall and is unsteady on his feet. I cannot imagine why he was invited to participate in the hunt, since he is obviously a novice, but this other man is willing to help him return to his quarters. Since my time is limited and I am awaiting your direction to observe the perimeters of this hunting preserve, Guilbert, I would say this situation has an easy solution."

De Silva lips tightened before he responded, "Of course, you are correct." He turned toward Dagan to say, "Take the young man back to his hut, then. I will check on him when the hunt is over. In the meantime, I charge you with his safety." He added more softly, "His *safety*, do you hear?"

When Dagan nodded and motioned Conqueror toward him, de Silva's gaze narrowed. "This mount is yours?"

His expression wary, Dagan responded, "Yea, it is mine."

"The animal has the look of a warhorse . . . certainly no mount for a common man."

"I found him abandoned and near death on the field of battle. I nursed him back to health, and his loyalty to me has been unsurpassed ever since."

Hesitating at Dagan's response, de Silva turned back to Emile. "On with the hunt, then."

Still standing unsteadily in the curve of Dagan's arm, Rosamund held her breath until the mounted entourage slipped from sight. Then she looked up at Dagan and said stiffly, "I would not have fallen if my mount's reins had not snapped."

"I know."

"I am a good rider. My father made sure of that. I could have made it to the end of the day."

"I know."

"I would not have allowed the baron to believe he could best me in any way."

His light eyes tight on hers, Dagan replied, "The baron did not best you. The equipment was at fault. In any case, you have other abilities that I suspect the baron could never appreciate . . . abilities that I value above all, and that I intend to help you develop."

Color flooded Rosamund's cheeks.

Dagan lifted Rosamund onto Conqueror's back without another word. He attached a lead to her mount's saddle so that the horse followed them and mounted up behind her. Leaning back against the broad wall of his chest, safe and content at last, Rosamund was somehow glad when he remained silent, because she realized there was no way she could respond at all.

Concealed in a heavy copse a little distance away, Martin watched as Dagan and Ross rode off. The object of de Silva's attentions appeared to be only too content in the arms of his friend.

Martin had listened intently to their conversation after de Silva left. Ross's voice had risen to a womanly pitch when he did not believe he would be overhead, and Dagan's expression had been revealing. The way they had looked at each other . . . Somehow, Dagan did not seem to be the type to respond to a man's appeal.

Brows furrowed, Martin considered the scene he had witnessed. He wondered . . .

The hunting horn sounded again, and Martin's head snapped up toward the sound. The hounds had regained the scent.

Turning his horse, Martin galloped in the direction

of the sound, the puzzling events he had witnessed temporarily thrust from his mind.

"I am fine, I tell you."

Having regained her senses after a silent trip back to her hut, Rosamund protested as Dagan attempted to help her down from Conqueror. She slipped to the ground, ignoring her aching muscles as she walked inside. Acutely aware that Dagan's gaze followed her, she refused to limp. Each step was a test of her resolve, but she would not be coddled.

"You are stubborn." His expression tightened as he followed her inside. "You have yet to learn that you are human and suffer the same weaknesses as others."

"I have no weaknesses!"

Dagan considered Rosamund's adamant statement silently before replying, "Yea, I stand corrected. You do not. Still, there is no shame in feeling sore after a hard fall."

"I need only wash the dirt and debris from my body and I will be as good as new."

"Perhaps."

Fighting the desire to surrender to her aches and pains, Rosamund stated flatly, "I will go to the stream. No one will be there at this time of day, and I will wash away all trace of my mishap. I will change back into my own clothing and take my place at Hadley's side as if the fall never occurred."

"If that is what you want."

Fighting a desire to cry as her soreness increased, Rosamund snapped, "I appreciate your concern, but that is what I want. In the meantime, you may return to your own work. I am sure you have been missed."

Taking up a cloth and a precious piece of soap, Rosamund started toward the stream. Satisfied that she was finally out of Dagan's sight when she rounded a bend in the trail, she limped to the stream's edge. After a glimpse around her, she shed the muddied hunting clothes with which she had been provided and walked naked into the shallow stream.

The cool water reached only to her knees, so Rosamund knelt to wash the debris from her hair. She splashed away the remainder of the soapy residue from her scalp and skin before attempting to stand.

Her sore muscles refused to respond. Rosamund tried again. It appeared that standing was more easily said than done.

She tried again to stand, and then again. She realized with a start of disbelief that her injured muscles had become frozen—that she was unable to move! She was stuck there, naked and helpless. She had guarded her gender so carefully, yet it was now visible to even the most casual eye.

Rosamund thrust back a heavy lock of fair hair from her forehead and again attempted to stand. She closed her eyes as the tears she had steadfastly withheld slid past her closed lids. Her eye snapped open again with a start when she was swept unexpectedly from the water and found herself held against Dagan's broad chest as he waded back to the bank with her in his arms.

"Put me down!" Protesting hotly despite the tears

she had not yet wiped from her cheeks, Rosamund ordered, "I can walk."

"All right, I will put you down."

Dagan placed her on a coverlet stretched out on the stream's bank and kneeled beside her. She frowned when he picked up a familiar bottle and poured some liquid into his hand.

"What are you doing?"

"You know what I am doing."

"If I did, I would not have asked."

Dagan's mouth twitched with amusement as he replied, "This salve is your own. You used it on me when I needed it, and I will now use it on you."

"That substance is precious. It is not to be wasted."

"It will not be wasted."

"I do not need it. I am fine."

"Are you?"

Aware that her nakedness did not support her assertion, Rosamund raised her chin. "Yea, I am."

"Stand up."

Rosamund did not respond.

"Stand up . . . if you can."

Rosamund raised her chin higher. "I am naked. I choose not to stand."

Dagan whispered, "I have seen you naked before." Rosamund flushed as he repeated, "Stand up."

Her chin thrust even higher, Rosamund finally replied, "I cannot."

Dagan's amber eyes flashed at her admission and he replied hoarsely, "Lie back, then. I will massage away your aches and you will be as good as new again."

"Nay, I—"

Dagan interrupted softly, "Rosamund, I did not balk when I was injured and you tended most intimately to me. I ask only to be allowed to repay the service."

Her throat tight, Rosamund nodded. She turned onto her stomach with great effort and closed her eyes.

The torment began.

Perspiration dotted Dagan's brow as Rosamund turned laboriously onto her stomach and he straddled her motionless form. Fearing for her safety, yet unwilling to argue with her determination, he had hidden and observed her as she bathed. Naked, her skin shining and her hair glowing, she had kneeled in the rippling water of the stream, a goddess in an eternal spring—bright, faultless, untouchable. His heart had pounded at the fallacy there, knowing that despite her appearance, she was human and she was his, intimately claimed and more honestly adored than he had ever intended.

But she was in pain.

Dagan tilted the bottle of medicinal liquid he had taken from the hut and poured it into his palm. He smoothed it against her skin, marveling at the womanly perfection Rosamund had kept concealed under her male garb—the graceful contours of her slender back, her incredibly narrow waist, and her smooth, rounded buttocks. He frowned at the bruises gradually darkening that perfection, aware even as he did that no temporary discoloration could compromise her feminine beauty.

Dagan kneaded Rosamund's cramped muscles patiently until they relaxed under his touch at last. Aware that his breathing had roughened at the effort, he sat back and ordered gruffly, "Turn onto your back."

Obeying his command, Rosamund turned over, and Dagan stilled at the beauty exposed to him. High cheekbones, a long, graceful neck, firm and gently rounded breasts, and feminine curves that culminated in a small patch of hair nestled between her thighs, long slender legs . . . His gaze returned unconsciously to the patch of fair hair between her thighs, and Dagan sucked in his breath. Refusing to meet her gaze, he poured more of the precious liquid into his palm and continued.

Torture.

Rosamund closed her eyes as Dagan poured the liquid onto her shoulders and rubbed it in gently. His hands lowered to the rounded globes of her breasts to massage them tenderly. She swallowed when his touch moved on to her ribs as he paused briefly there before massaging her waist and the curve of her hips. Her eyes fluttered shut when his fingers slid past the lightly furred triangle at the juncture of her thighs to smooth the muscles of her legs. Uncertain, she only knew that the torment was unlike any she had ever known. His touch moved to her inner thighs, then slid into the warm crevice wet with wanting him. She was breathing as heavily as he then, and whatever stiffness remained was forgotten when he entered her at last and she welcomed him with a desire that surged between them.

Opening her eyes when Dagan suddenly stilled inside her, Rosamund saw a spark of regret in his gaze as he whispered, "I did not intend this when I came here, Rosamund . . . truly."

"I know."

"I but wanted to provide you with relief from your pain."

"I know."

"I was determined to just—"

Rosamund interrupted breathlessly, "I was determined to resist you, Dagan, but my arms welcomed you just as I welcome you now." Drawing his mouth down to hers, Rosamund kissed him with all the hunger that she had suppressed, separating her lips to allow him deeper intimacy before drawing back to whisper, "I have no other recourse but to repeat the words that you once said to me, that between us at this moment, this was meant to be." She urged softly, "Finish what you have started. And know that whatever you feel, I feel . . . whatever you want, I want, and that whatever—"

Rosamund's statement went unfinished when Dagan thrust himself deep inside her again, and with a few breathtaking movements, brought them to mutual, ecstatic fulfillment.

Breathless in its wake, Rosamund clutched Dagan close against her. Her heart pounding, her emotions unbridled, she was grateful that he had brought them to swift culmination because she knew they could not chance being seen. Still clutching him tightly, aware that their precious time together would be limited at best, she silently cursed the cruel fate that had brought him to her at a time when she must think of her people and ignore her heart.

Rosamund was unaware that tears had slipped from underneath her closed eyelids until Dagan drew back and brushed them away with a gentle touch. He whispered, "Why do you cry, Rosamund? Did I press you too hard? Did I hurt you?"

"Nay." Aware that Dagan had withdrawn from her, Rosamund drew strength from the warmth of his strong body still pressed against her. She said hesitantly, "I need to explain some things to you now . . . difficult things that I hope you will understand."

"You need not explain anything."

"Yea, I must, so that you may understand the reason for the priorities that I must set." Rosamund took a breath and began slowly, "I am not an ordinary Saxon maid, as I would have everyone believe."

"I have never believed you to be ordinary."

"Nay, Dagan. The meaning of my words goes far deeper." The clear blue of her gaze was intent as she continued, "Although the affection between Hadley and myself is sincere, he is not my father. The truth is that I am the daughter of the true Lord of Hendsmille, the true heir to the land that the baron was awarded for spilling my father's blood."

Momentarily silent, his expression unrevealing despite her disclosure, Dagan insisted, "You need make no explanations to me, Rosamund. I—"

"Nay, please allow me to continue, Dagan. It is important that I make this revelation to you now . . . so you may understand." When Dagan did not respond, she continued, "I was but a child of eight when the Norman invasion came. Hadley's daughter was my best friend, and I was visiting her when the raiders attacked.

My friend died during the raid. I, too, would have been slain had not Hadley appeared to save me. He took me as his own daughter at my father's dying request. True to his word Hadley buried his daughter in secret and claimed me as his own. It was not a difficult task to be accepted in my friend's place at a time when such confusion reigned. In the years since, Hadley has raised me and treated me as his own while allowing me to maintain my real identity as well. As a child, I knew somehow that there was a reason I had been spared during that time of slaughter. As my knowledge grew, I realized that because of my heritage, I alone possessed the key to restoring the pride of Hendesmille. That responsibility resonates deep inside me, Dagan. Because of it, I have maintained contact with northern military forces. I hope to unite my people with them in the near future. If I am successful is this area, I can inspire others to fight for that which was, and that which will be again. Although I am unsure what the future holds for me, I am certain that my destiny is to fulfill that quest. I will never desert my people. You see, I am their last hope."

Dagan remained silent. His gaze inscrutable, he looked down at her. His grip tightened, yet he did not speak.

A nudge of uncertainty growing, Rosamund whispered, "I await your response, Dagan." When he did not reply, her uneasiness swelled and she asked, "Is it the baron you fear . . . that he will discover who I am, and that he will—"

"It is not the baron I fear."

"Yet I see your uncertainty."

"Yea, I am uncertain."

Her heart beginning a slow pounding, Rosamund whispered, "You want to say something, yet you hold it back. Tell me."

Dagan's gaze darkened as he scrutinized Rosamund's expression closely. She was correct. He had not expected the true depth of the secret she concealed. Nor had he expected the true depth of her determination. Yet he knew that her whispered confidence made his own secret more difficult to reveal.

Looking at her, aware of what he risked, Dagan hesitated before whispering, "Is this the time for confession then, Rosamund?"

Dagan felt Rosamond slowly stiffen as she replied, "Yea, it is the time."

"Then I hope you will understand when I tell you—when I confide in you a secret that could cost me my life should de Silva discover it before I am ready. Rosamund . . ." Dagan hesitated again. His voice deepened as he disclosed, "I am not fully Saxon, as I claimed. Nor was I a resident of Horstede at the time of the invasion. I am a knight in William's service . . . a knight who played an important role in the invasion. I am also William's trusted friend. He sent me here to investigate rumors that abound about the baron. On the way, I was set upon by thieves, not Norman soldiers as you believed. I was saved from death when Conqueror returned to carry me here, where you assumed my care."

"But . . . but your name?"

"My mother was English, my father French. My full name is Sir Dagan Waterford de Lance."

Dagan felt the chill that shook Rosamund as she whispered, "Then you are Norman."

"Yea, that is so."

Thrusting him away from her, Rosamund said incredulously, "You were a part of the force that subdued Saxons and made them slaves!"

"If that is the way you wish to view all that transpired."

Her face growing hot, Rosamund fully separated herself from Dagan and stood. She reached for her clothing when he stood up as well and said, "You are no better than your Viking forebears!"

"Were that true, no one in Hendsmille would have been left standing after the revolt, and William would not have sent me to discover whether the rumors about the shire were true."

"You slaughter indiscriminately."

"William had no choice in what he did. Saxons received only what was due them for accepting a monarch like Harold, who did not belong on the throne."

"William does not belong on the throne. He cares naught about our people. He cares only for Normandy."

"That is untrue."

"It is true for every Saxon who has lived and died under William's ruthless rule."

"William is not a ruthless man—nor is his rule ruthless. Once the baron's tactics in this shire have been reported, you will see William's true worth, and the time for healing will begin."

"There will be no healing for a people whose liberty has been stolen from them."

"Saxon peasants have no liberty now because the

baron oppresses them in William's name. I need to investigate further and make a full report to William. The baron's unjust practices will then be curtailed."

Rosamund scoffed.

"I am not your enemy! To the contrary, I am—"

"Stop!" Standing opposite Dagan, fully dressed at last, Rosamund turned toward him, her smile bitter. "Do you think I am a complete fool? I may briefly have been deceived, but I know now who my enemies are." Pausing, Rosamund added, "Do what you want with what I have disclosed to you, but for us, it ends here. The die has been cast."

Turning, Rosamund started back up the path. Unrelenting, she left Dagan speechless where he stood on the bank of the stream, watching as she walked away.

Chapter Eight

He has gone to his room to rest. I am free of him for a while." De Silva turned back toward Champlain with a relieved expression after DuPree and his entourage returned to their respective quarters. Together, he and Champlain walked toward the great hall, silent in the aftermath of the long day spent hunting from first light. Concealing his stress with a smile, de Silva had strained to hide the true perimeters of the hunting preserve reserved for William from DuPree's watchful eye, but the effort had been exhausting. The hunters had returned victoriously with their spoils as the sun made its slow descent toward the horizon. Openly fatigued, DuPree had nevertheless announced his decision to write the last addition to his report that night so he might return to London where William awaited him, the following day.

De Silva snorted unconsciously at that thought. DuPree's estimation of his importance was doubtless exaggerated. William would not wait for him or any man to arrive back at the castle when he chose to return to his beloved Normandy.

Ever present in the back of de Silva's mind as he had striven to impress DuPree, was the importance of presenting a loyal appearance while the exact timing of Cnut's planned invasion was still in flux. It was a waiting game—a game with which he was fast becoming impatient.

Events from earlier that morning returned to haunt him. Had it not been for his desire to impress DuPree, the situation would not have turned out the way it had when Ross was thrown from his horse. He would not have left Ross behind in the hands of the big man who had declared himself Ross's guardian. Instead, when he realized Ross was unable to remount, he would have seen to it that he returned to *his* quarters in the castle keep so he might recuperate there. He would have earned the youth's gratitude—a gratitude that would have served de Silva well.

De Silva snorted again. Gratitude. He would have preferred to stir a far more powerful emotion in Ross. He still did not quite understand why the young man had become so important to him, why he was drawn to him even more strongly than he had ever been drawn to a woman before him, why every moment spent in his presence seemed to affect his libido even more, and why all else paled in comparison to this relentless craving.

De Silva glanced at the gradually waning light shining through the narrow window of the keep. He squinted thoughtfully. Hadley and the rest of the workers would not have returned to their huts yet. If he did not miss his guess, Ross's injuries were such that he would not have been able to return to work that day, despite Hadley's need for him. He frowned at the thought that the big man would probably have remained at his side, but he pushed that discomfort aside. He would visit Ross and explain his lapse of temper earlier, and he would see to it that the fellow called Dagan left them alone when he did. He would do that before the workers returned for the day so they would not see him and think him weak. By doing so, he would impress upon Ross unconsciously that Dagan was subject to his command, as was Ross himself.

With that thought in mind, de Silva turned abruptly toward the door.

"Where are you going?"

Rounding on Champlain, de Silva raised a haughty brow at the inquiry. "You are welcome to enjoy all that I have earned in this place, but you are *not* welcome to question my actions in any way.

Champlain's jaded gaze narrowed. "So you go to visit the young man. Remember," he cautioned, "the big fellow may still be with him."

"I am not concerned with that man. He will obey me or he will suffer the consequences."

"Methinks he will suffer the consequences more easily than he will obey you."

"We will see."

With those words, de Silva turned on his heel and headed for the door.

Dagan drew Conqueror's lead behind him as he approached the barn. The loyal animal had carried Rosamund and him back to the hut with ease and then waited patiently at his command as he had covertly followed Rosamund to the stream and had fruitlessly attempted to talk to her in the hut they shared afterward. Dagan was still uncertain what she intended to do about his revelation; but he had already decided that he would not compromise Rosamund's disguise in any way.

Aware that it was time to settle Conqueror back in the barn after the difficult day, Dagan also hoped that in allowing Rosamund privacy to think, she might come to a decision in his favor. Despite the information that she had shared—a reality that he understood more than she realized—he hoped she might put aside the thought of joining any incursions as a figurehead against William.

He was certain it would be a grave mistake.

Dagan entered the barn and allowed Conqueror to slip free of his saddle and bridle. He placed them nearby as the great gray whinnied his appreciation and waited patiently while Dagan filled buckets with water and food. At his command, the great warhorse dipped his head to eat hungrily. Watching him eat, Dagan recalled hearing somewhere that all wounds healed in time. He hoped that would prove true for Rosamund, yet he knew her ties to her heritage were strong.

Dagan sighed. In any event, he was powerless at present. All he could do was wait.

De Silva walked cautiously toward the hut where Ross resided. He was well aware that although he would react favorably to a visit from him as opposed to a command to report to the castle, it would not do to be seen there.

Frowning when the master mason's hut came into view, de Silva scanned the vicinity before approaching. The area was temporarily deserted, as he had expected. He approached the hut cautiously and paused at a window to peer inside. He was only too aware of the unspoken bond existing between Ross and the big man he had nursed back to health. He hoped it merely reflected Dagan's appreciation for Ross's care, but his suspicions were rife.

Unseen, he looked into the meager quarters, and then gawked.

Preoccupied by her thoughts, Rosamund brushed as much mud as possible from the hunting attire she had been provided and prepared to slip on Ross's shirt. Her shoulders ached from her fall—the same ache that had temporarily disappeared under Dagan's patient ministrations. Aware that Dagan was tending to Conqueror and that the others were not yet due to return, Rosamund walked to the mirror that Hadley had provided. Bare to the waist, she scrutinized her back. Considering the size of the bruise, it was surprising that Dagan had been able to eliminate her pain even temporarily. Yet she was not truly surprised. It was his touch . . . so gentle and loving.

Suddenly succumbing to the emotion that had threatened throughout the day, Rosamund covered her face and allowed tears to fall. Why had she not suspected that Dagan concealed a secret? The truth that he was a knight who had fought Saxons in William's name had struck her like a blow. They had made love—an intimacy that she had allowed no other man. She had been truthful with him while he had maintained his disguise. Would Dagan have confided the truth of his mission if she had not spoken first? And . . . would her true identity remain a secret now?

Her partial nakedness forgotten, Rosamund sobbed at the collapse of a dream she had not been aware she had even briefly entertained. She wished she could put aside her bitterness at William's theft of Saxon life and liberty. She wished she were no more than a common maid, with none of the responsibilities inherent in her heritage. She wished she had the power to change the destiny posed by that heritage . . . and she ultimately wished with all her heart that she did not love the man who had revealed himself as the personification of all she despised.

But in the end she knew that wishing did not make it so.

And the realization was almost more than she could bear.

De Silva swallowed. He stared, not quite believing his eyes. He held in a bark of pure delight.

He understood now why he had felt no attraction to the young men who served his tables and who would have been easy sport. He knew why thoughts of Ross had allowed him no respite from the driving need within him.

He had simply responded unconsciously to the female aura that Ross projected!

He had become obsessed with Ross without even realizing that . . . Ross was a woman!

De Silva briefly closed his eyes as pure glee overwhelmed him. She had sought to deceive him, doubtless hoping to evade his attentions, yet he had somehow sensed the deception. Now her secret was out!

De Silva's expression changed as he briefly indulged

visions of the ways he would make her pay for the torment she had caused him.

He envisioned forcing Ross to stand naked in front
of him until she acknowledged at last the supreme
power he held over her; of freely observing . . .
touching . . . stroking the female glory exposed to his
gaze while she attempted to halt his searching probes;
of exploring her female flesh intimately in his great
bed until she begged him to stop; of hearing her cry
out with a joy mixed with pain when he entered her at
last—all of which she would not dare deny him for
fear of the punishment he would threaten to mete out
on her elderly and equally deceitful father.

Yet de Silva was only momentarily satisfied by his
thoughts. The fellow Dagan remained a complication.
Who was he? Why did he stand so diligently at her
side? He had not believed Dagan's tale about finding,
rescuing, and securing the fealty of the great animal
he commanded. There was more to that story than the
man had divulged.

The sound of footsteps in the distance turned de
Silva abruptly in its direction and he gasped. The workers were returning. He could not be seen there. He
needed time and anonymity so he might fit the final
pieces of the puzzle into place.

With that thought in mind, de Silva avoided discovery by slipping silently into the lengthening shadows

He moved stealthily to the barn that housed the
draft animals. He told himself he had a small window
of time before they would be returned for a night's
rest . . . a brief period when he might find the answers
to the questions inundating his mind.

Halting his approach abruptly, de Silva stepped back into the shadows as Dagan emerged from the barn and closed the doors behind him. He cursed at his near blunder and waited while Dagan walked back toward the hut with a determined step. He waited only a moment longer before opening the doors of the barn and slipping inside. De Silva turned, unprepared for the angry snorting and prancing that faced him.

"Back . . . back!" murmuring desperate commands under his breath, de Silva sought to avoid the great gray's flying hooves as the animal reared and whinnied at his appearance. When the animal refused to obey him, he grasped a whip hanging nearby and cracked it mercilessly against the animal's hide. The great steed's eyes bulged under his assault. It charged, almost knocking him to the ground. Forced into a corner of a stall, de Silva shielded himself from the animal's angry hooves before managing to reach the stall gate behind him and slam it shut, locking them both inside. He scrambled over the partition, barely escaping the angry destrier as he jumped down into freedom on the other side.

Jubilant, de Silva stared at the great animal as he snorted and stamped helplessly. He searched for the whip he had dropped, but his eye fell instead on the bridle that had been removed from the animal and put aside. Surprised at its obvious quality, he picked it up and scrutinized the fine tooled leather carefully. Turning it this way and that, he realized that the subtle decoration was a masterpiece of design, then went still when he saw the familiar mark it bore. It was William's mark, placed on all gifts he had bestowed in gratitude for loyal service during the invasion.

Loyal service!

De Silva's eyes widened. The reason for Dagan Waterford's great stature and muscle tone, as well as his lack of fear when facing him down at every opportunity, was suddenly clear. Dagan Waterford was a knight in William's service! The only reason for his disguise as a commoner had to be that William had heard the rumors and had sent Dagan to spy on him.

As abruptly clear to him then was a cold truth he could no longer deny—that due to the living arrangements that Ross had afforded the fellow while recuperating, Dagan had probably known all along that the object of both their affections was not male, and was instead a desirable woman.

Hatred, rage, and a driving hunger for revenge rose within de Silva. They had thought to deceive him, make a fool of him, and report their findings to William! Well, he would see about that!

De Silva breathed deeply. He would get his revenge. He would make both of them pay in ways they had never envisioned, but he needed to bide his time.

Yea . . . bide his time.

That thought held little appeal as de Silva slipped silently back the way he had come.

"I leave now because I know William awaits me, but I admit that I am not truly satisfied with my findings here."

Dagan faced Emile DuPree in the early morning shadows of the keep. DuPree said, "My entourage leaves in less than an hour, but I must admit that the hunt de Silva organized yesterday was a spark of genius. In the mayhem that transpired, I became truly uncertain as to the boundaries of the hunting preserve we traversed. I needed to take his word for its dimensions for the most part . . . a sad commentary indeed, considering my silent opinion of the man's honesty." He sighed. "Since I am satisfied with what I have learned elsewhere, I suppose it will now be up to you to determine whether the baron has taken advantage of his position here or is really the man William hopes he is." DuPree smiled. "I admit to being undecided about de Silva, but there is one thing I know for sure—if I had any doubts at all about who Ross really is, your actions yesterday settled them." Pausing, he added with an unexpected twinkle in his eye, "What I do not know is how you became involved with *her.*"

"Rosamund . . ."

"Yea, if that is her true name. I was not deceived very long by her disguise, you know." He snickered. "I am not *that* old."

"Rosamund and her father were well aware of de Silva's reputation for exploiting women. Among other considerations, they hoped to avoid his attentions with her charade. They expected that it would protect her from de Silva's interest. However it did not, and because Rosamund has shown a preference for my company, de Silva bears a dangerous antipathy for me."

"He is jealous of her obvious affection for you."

Dagan responded, "Rosamund nursed me back to health after an attack that nearly killed me—that is the truth. I allowed the people here to believe that I was Saxon because it allowed me a unique opportunity to gauge the truth of the rumors that abounded about de Silva. Rosamund held my life in her hands while I recuperated, and she holds it there still."

DuPree frowned. "You told her who you are and why you are here, then?"

"She knows I am Norman and sent here by William, but I do not know if either of us is certain of the lengths to which de Silva will go to protect himself if he finds me out before I am ready."

DuPree's eyebrows rose at Dagan's reply. "I suppose we shall have to wait for your final assessment, then." Extending his hand, DuPree said, "Godspeed in that regard, Dagan. I will return to William with my report, and I will tell him to await yours."

Dagan clasped the old man's hand. With a final smile of farewell, he slipped back into the shadows.

De Silva watched as DuPree's entourage slipped from sight on the narrow trail. He grunted and glanced at the morning sky impatiently as the sun made its gradual ascent. It had been a torment untold to wait while DuPree's cavalcade slowly assembled in the shadows of early morning and made ready to depart. Through the long night past, he had planned his next moves so carefully that he had not allowed himself more than a few hours' sleep despite his exhaustion. He was anxious to put them into effect, although he was aware of the importance of presenting a smiling exterior to DuPree before his departure.

Waiting only minutes longer to make sure DuPree's cavalcade was gone, de Silva turned abruptly toward

Champlain, who stood beside him. He asked abruptly, "Where is Martin? His place is at your side."

"Methinks Martin's thoughts are presently elsewhere." Champlain shrugged with obvious annoyance. "On a woman. But he will be easy enough to call to task if it becomes necessary."

De Silva gritted his teeth. "Not even a temporary preoccupation is excusable at this time."

"Do not concern yourself. I will handle the situation without him." Champlain's response was cold.

Still holding his gaze intently, de Silva whispered heatedly, "I will depend on that, but for now . . . we begin."

Dagan glanced up at the hot morning sun and then paused to wipe the perspiration from his brow. It was unusually warm and he had slept poorly the previous night; yet had arisen before dawn so he might contact Emile before he left. Hadley had come back from the cathedral before he had returned to the hut the previous evening, forestalling any further conversation between Rosamund and Dagan. Through the night, Rosamund had lain on her mattress only inches away, but she had not spoken a word to him. He knew Hadley had sensed the discomfort between them, but he was also sure that Rosamund had not revealed his true identity to the old man. He was not certain how long her silence would last but had decided that he owed it to her to allow her to make the first move.

Owed it to her.

Dagan was inwardly amused at the phrase he had chosen. Yea, he owed Rosamund his life. That was ironic; without conscious volition, he had decided that he wanted to spend the life that her care had granted him with her . . . always.

If only she still felt the same as he.

Dagan's expression grew pained. The truth was that he could not seem to get enough of her: the taste of her lips, her sweet scent. The touch of her flesh, warm against his, sent tremors of ecstasy coursing mindlessly through him. Nothing, not even her present loathing for the man he had confessed to being, had altered his love for her. He had seen the gleam in de Silva's eyes when he looked at Rosamund and knew now, just as he had sensed from that first moment, that de Silva and he would be at odds. Strangely enough, he had started out wanting to protect Rosamund from de Silva, a man who was one of William's honored knights like him. Yet in his wildest dreams, he had never expected that Rosamund would come to despise them both.

Dagan pushed back the heavy dark hair that had fallen onto his forehead in the heat of the day. He needed time to convince Rosamund that she had made a mistake in maintaining communication with the remaining few men in the north who plotted against William. He needed to explain that any action they might take was doomed to failure because a man such as William would never accept defeat. He needed to make her understand that William was a good man who would right whatever inequity existed as a result of de Silva's governing—yet in order to find out to what extent that inequity prevailed, he needed to maintain his disguise as a common man a little longer. But most of all, he needed to make Rosamund believe in his love, and know that although the past was irrevocably gone as Saxons had known it, together they could make the future bright.

Dagan allowed his gaze to rest on Rosamund's slender figure where she stood beside Hadley in her male attire. Even so dressed, she was beautiful. Her platinum, awkwardly cut hair gleamed in the sunlight, the graceful line of her profile as she studied the drawings in Hadley's hands was matchless, and the heavily lashed, clear blue of her eyes as she glanced up briefly was more brilliant than the morning sky.

So entranced was he at that moment that he did not see a short fellow move cautiously out of the bushes toward him. He turned at a touch on his arm and accepted the note the man put into his hand with a furtive glance before slipping back out of sight as silently as he had come.

The note was addressed to Sir Dagan Waterford. Dagan frowned as he read:

> It has come to my attention that although you are presently functioning incognito in Hendsmille, you are in reality one of William's favored knights. Since I am also one of his loyal followers, I would like to meet with you so we may put aside all past differences and work together to accomplish whatever mission William has assigned to you. I do not wish to compromise your mission and have presently dismissed my men and all but the one loyal servant who brought you this note. You may rest assured that a visit to my quarters will not endanger your disguise. I hope you will honor this invitation.

I presently await you in my quarters.
Loyal in William's service, I remain,
Baron Guilbert Bernard de Silva.

Dagan looked up to see that the messenger had indeed not awaited his reply. So his disguise was no longer a secret from de Silva, despite Rosamund's silence; yet considering the tone of de Silva's note and the discretion involved, he wondered if the wily fellow was truly to be trusted.

Dagan pondered the situation silently. De Silva awaited him in his quarters. Uncertain how he had been discovered, Dagan realized that de Silva's overture would afford him the opportunity to talk to the baron face-to-face, as his equal in the brotherhood of knighthood.

Making a quick decision, Dagan laid down the shovel he had been handed upon arriving at the construction site. There was only one way to discover what de Silva had in mind. The new foundation for the cathedral that Hadley had deemed necessary would have to wait a little longer while he settled the situation with the baron once and for all.

"You made a mistake in sending Dagan that note, Guilbert. He is now aware that he no longer deceives you. He will be suspicious of your motives."

Standing beside Champlain in the silence of his quarters, de Silva replied, "Fool that you are, Champlain, you do not recognize the brilliance of my plan. Dagan will be intrigued. He will wonder how I became aware of the sham he practiced. He will meet with me because he is obviously not yet ready to declare himself, and he wonders what I am planning."

"You take a chance, Guilbert. You assume that the fellow trusts you."

"Since I have proved myself one of William's *loyal* supporters, there is no reason he should not."

"What is he doing here, then? Surely William sent him because he has heard rumors regarding your allegiance. Perhaps he knows of your communications with Cnut and of your intentions to join the invasion."

"That is foolishness! If he did, William would already have imprisoned me."

"Perhaps he is suspicious, then."

"Perhaps . . . perhaps . . ." His patience short, de Silva snapped, "I do not deal with possibilities. I choose to act rather than assume."

Champlain took a step toward him and said darkly, "This all has to do with that fellow Ross, hasn't it?"

"That *fellow*?" De Silva's laughter was harsh. "You were deceived by her pretense also, then."

"*Her* pretense?"

"Her name is Rosamund, not Ross. She is beautiful, desirable, and intelligent. Strangely, I admit to admiring her for her craftiness in deceiving me, and find myself more determined than ever to see that she occupies my bed for as long as my desire for her remains."

"But how can you be sure that you will win the consent you have deemed so necessary in her case?"

"I will obtain her consent in my own way, and she will bow to me as she bowed to no other. Yet a better question would be, how I could have been fooled by her charade as long as I was?" De Silva's lips tightened at that admission. He continued tightly, "But that is over and done now. Some covert investigation this morning revealed two very important facts—Rosamund's true name, and the fact that she is a virgin."

"A virgin?" Champlain raised his heavy brows. "Even if that were once true, I venture to say it is no longer, considering her guard's proprietary manner."

His face flushing, de Silva ordered, "Cease your useless prattling and take your place as ordered! Dagan Waterford—or whatever his true name is—will arrive here soon because William's mission demands it."

"You are wrong, Guilbert."

His jaw tightening, de Silva replied, "We shall see then, shall we not?"

A step at the door snapped the attention of both men in its direction before a small servant entered timorously to announce, "A messenger, my lord. He has come a long way. He says he brings news of great import from London."

"I have no interest—"

Responding in his stead, Champlain ordered, "Send the man in."

A trail-weary messenger approached de Silva to hand him a note bearing the royal seal. He opened it cautiously when he saw it came from William and was addressed to Baron Guilbert Bernard de Silva, Loyal Knight in William's Service.

An invasion by Cnut, son of King Swein of Denmark, has been efficiently routed despite his successful ventures in York. His invasion followed a northern route and was successful in destroying St. Peter's min-

*ster and absconding with much of its treasure. When
faced with impossible opposition, Cnut retreated to
his fleet and left the country, leaving all of his fellow
conspirators in England to perish. Included in that
number were the son of Earl Haken and those who
had joined with him.*

*The country is again safe and your aid will not
be necessary at this time."*

Reading over de Silva's shoulder, Champlain whispered, "Cnut did not inform you when he landed his fleet?"

"The fool obviously did not, though I suppose I will never know why." De Silva raised his chin. "But I made the necessary provisions in the event the scheme I brokered with him failed."

Choosing that moment to turn back to the messenger, de Silva instructed in a voice that rang in the silence of the room. "Go to the stable and see to your horse while the kitchen help prepares a repast for you. You will then return to London with a message from me to be delivered directly to William. Listen closely to me, because I want you to speak my reply to him personally and with deep conviction. Say to him simply, '*I am your loyal servant.*'"

Waiting only until the weary fellow had left, Champlain turned to de Silva and said, "So Cnut is not the man you had supposed him to be, and your elaborate plans goes awry."

"My plans . . ." De Silva laughed unexpectedly. "I care not what news the messenger brought. All my hopes did not rest on that foreigner to our shores.

William will receive my message supporting my placement here. He will receive DuPree's report and learn that the construction of the cathedral is underway, and he will begin doubting the rumors he heard, especially when there is no one to confirm them."

"No one to confirm them? By that you mean—"

"I mean, I will effectively eliminate two birds with one stone."

De Silva looked up at the sound of a second step on the staircase. He smiled when Dagan's broad form filled the doorway.

De Silva was smiling.

Dagan stood in the doorway of de Silva's quarters. He glanced around to see that the suite was vacant except for Franchot Champlain, de Silva's man. True to his word, de Silva had dismissed all other knights and servants.

Hesitant, Dagan remained in the doorway until de Silva urged, "Enter, please. I ordered my servants to provide a repast before they left."

Still uncertain, Dagan glanced around himself. He didn't like this. De Silva's expression was almost victorious, which did not bode well. His discomfort growing, Dagan replied, "I did not come here to eat your food. Instead, I would have some plain talk between us, as should be the course for two who have shared the rigors of victory in William's service."

"That is also my intention." De Silva offered hospitably, "Enter, please. It is time to end all hard feelings between us, and we can do that in only one way."

"Which way is that?"

A heavy blow from behind was de Silva's unexpected response to Dagan's question. Lurching forward, Dagan fell heavily to the floor. The last words he heard before unconsciousness took him was de Silva's fading reply, "Your question has been answered."

The day had turned humid and the sun was unusually hot as the noon hour approached. Aware that the workers would soon break for their meager midday meal, Rosamund glanced around her. She had been intensely aware of Dagan's presence all morning—so aware that when she turned to find him no longer visible to her eye, she became strangely unnerved.

Rosamund muttered a few words to Hadley and started toward the spot where she had last seen Dagan. Unable to find him there, she halted, uncertain whether he had taken the opportunity to declare himself to de Silva. She was well aware that should he betray her identity, de Silva would doubtless kill her, and with her, any remaining Saxon hopes.

Those thoughts were heavy on her mind when two knights approached her. Rosamund stilled when an armed, bearded fellow with eyes cold as ice addressed her. "The baron summons you."

With no other recourse, she accompanied them without a reply.

Hyacinthe watched as Ross entered the kitchen with two knights at her side. He was silent, his skin colorless as they ushered him up the stairs toward the baron's quarters. Hyacinthe's gaze narrowed when both knights descended the stairs moments later and disappeared from sight.

"You do well to observe closely." Obviously desiring to teach the French whore a lesson, Edythe approached. "The baron ordered a repast to be delivered to his quarters before he ordered us all out of the keep this morning. Why do you suppose that was? When his friend obviously did not appear for their assignation as he expected, he sent two of his knights to bring him forcibly to his quarters."

"You are wrong, old woman! The baron but needed to question the fellow, who obviously protested."

"Oh, he protested."

"Witch! You are wrong in your assumptions." Ignoring the frightened expression of Winifred, who cowered in the corner of the kitchen, Hyacinthe stood adamant and warned, "I will speak to Guilbert about your behavior and you will suffer for it."

"*Guilbert,* is it?" Strands of graying hair escaped confinement to sway against her rounded shoulders as Edythe laughed heartily. "Use the baron's given name in his presence and he will flay you within an inch of your life."

"Again you are wrong! I use the baron's given name openly when I share his bed."

"Which you have not done for a longer period than you wish to admit. You are nothing more to him than a French trollop who followed him from his precious Normandy, and who is allowed into his bed only when he is desperate for company—which he will not be now that his new playmate is firmly established in his quarters."

"You lie! You wish it to be so."

"I know it to be so, and so does everyone else who knows the baron as well as I. Everyone else . . . except you, that is."

"I will prove to you that Guilbert has no desire for the young man who was escorted to his quarters. I will prove to you that he but hopes for . . . for information that only that young man may provide to him."

"Balderdash!"

"Is it? I will demonstrate to you and to everyone else who doubts the baron's affection for me that he prefers me, especially to that young man. I will be the one to remain with the baron long after that other is removed this morning!"

Enraged, Hyacinthe started toward the stairs, her dark eyes flashing. She laughed aloud at Edythe's gasp and Winifred's low moan of disquiet as she ascended toward the baron's quarters. Guilbert would want her again. Guilbert would prefer her to the thin, poorly muscled, effeminate male who had entered his rooms.

He had to.

Her throat tight, Hyacinthe climbed the stairs with tearful determination.

"You have no choice but to submit, my dear."

"But I do have a choice." Rosamund faced the baron boldly as she continued, "And it will never be you."

His smile fading, de Silva advanced toward Rosamund slowly. Standing only a hairsbreadth away, he said softly, "You will regret those words."

"I will not."

"You will . . . Rosamund."

Her color fading at the use of her true name, Rosamund maintained her silence, and de Silva's smile returned. "You are wondering how I became aware of your charade while I am wondering why I did not see through it sooner. I can only think that the aura you projected drew me in, my love, and that I desired you intensely in spite of your pretended sex."

"*My love.*" Rosamund sneered. "You do not know the meaning of the word *love*. Nor will you ever have me—not willingly."

"You err." Ignoring Champlain's presence in the room, de Silva continued softly, "You see, I have the key to your acceptance."

"There is no key!"

"Yea, there is. His name is Dagan."

"Dagan!" Rosamund's eyes widened. "Where is he?"

"You do not know?" De Silva laughed again. "I wager that no one else knows either. You see, I have discovered his true identity. I know William sent him here. I dismissed my knights and servants for a few hours and then sent a loyal servant to surreptitiously deliver a note to him. Dagan came here wondering what I had in mind because I indicated that I had found him out and hoped to work with him. He came, but he did not expect the reception he received."

Rosamund despised the trembling in her voice as she inquired, "What reception was that?"

"What do you suppose it was?"

"You dared to attack William's envoy?"

"I dare much, which is how I achieve much. In any case, Champlain, here, and the loyal servant I referred to earlier, carried your friend down to the dungeon below the castle keep before the servants returned."

Rosamund whitened.

"That is correct, Rosamund . . . the dungeon. My jailors tend to him even now. Their ways are a well-kept secret in this shire, and I need not tell you how few manage to live through their attentions."

"William will rise up against you for this!"

"It is strange to hear you speak up in William's behalf, since I assume you are his enemy. William will never discover how his favored knight disappeared or where he is. DuPree recognized Dagan, I am sure of that now, but his report will be inconclusive except to say that Dagan pretended to be a peasant in order to complete the mission William assigned him. I will be most sincere when explaining that I know nothing about what happened to him because I did not know of his identity. Because of my superior previous service and loyalty to him, and with no one to refute my fidelity, William will eventually assume Dagan was found out and executed by angry Saxons, who resented his duplicity. Perhaps when I mention his name, William might even suspect . . . Hadley."

"Nay!"

"Does that bother you, Rosamund? How does it feel to be trapped by someone wilier than you?"

Her composure barely maintained, Rosamund asked, "What do you wish?"

"Need you even ask?"

"My compliance with your demand."

"That is all that will allow Dagan to continue drawing breath."

Rosamund shook her head bitterly. "Surely my compliance is not necessary. It was not necessary with others who came before me."

"But you are different, Rosamund." De Silva stroked her cheek as he whispered, "I prefer complete surrender from you so that my possession will be complete."

"So you may then toss me aside as you have done with others!"

"Perhaps." De Silva shrugged. "My position is such that I need not make any promises to anyone."

"That is where you are wrong."

De Silva's smile was triumphant. "Am I?"

Rosamund raised her chin higher. "You say you hold the key to my compliance, but it is I who hold the key to all you desire here."

"You? You hold yourself in too high esteem, my love."

"Does the daughter of the Saxon Lord of Hendsmille—the Saxon heir to this shire, where you will never be recognized as the true lord without her acceptance—hold herself in too high esteem? As the true Saxon heir, is not my approval of your position here the solution to all the problems that beset you?"

"You are Hadley Wedge's daughter!"

"Hadley's daughter was killed in the invasion. He raised me in her stead while I awaited the right moment to declare myself."

"No one will believe your claim!"

"Saxons have long memories. They respect Hadley and will recall that he was my father's friend when he stands beside me in affirmation of all I claim. They will also remember the ring my father wore that bore the family crest. It was passed down from father to son, but he gave it to his only living heir before going into battle. I have kept that ring and cherished it these many years, knowing it would identify me when I chose to declare myself."

"I wish to see this ring!"

"Do you think me a complete fool? Nay, it is well hidden and will remain so until I choose to bring it to light. You may ask Hadley if you wish. He will confirm its existence."

"You wish to bargain with this ring, perhaps?" Ignoring Champlain's presence, de Silva whispered, "You know my desire for you, but you do not realize that with your revelation, you have provided me with yet another means of accomplishing my plans. You see, once we are married, my position here will be sealed forever—the old with the new, Saxon and Norman united forever!"

"Married! I will never marry you!"

"Will you not?"

"Unless—"

De Silva's gaze grew cold. "And so the bargaining begins."

"Unless I may see for myself that Dagan lives, that he is well cared for wherever he is being held."

"I guarantee nothing about the future!"

"Nor do I!"

De Silva grew wary. "Meaning?"

"Meaning, if I may see for myself that Dagan is alive and well, if I may ascertain that you do not allow the ghouls in your dungeons to torture him, I will agree to a union between us. If you do not grant my condition, I will find a way to escape you, even if it causes my death."

"Your death, eh? Nay, that would be a waste." De Silva paused. "If I agree, you will agree to a union between us and all it entails?"

Rosamund swallowed her revulsion and nodded.

Forcing her unexpectedly tight against him, de Silva ground his mouth into hers, dissatisfied until the taste of her blood filled his mouth. Obviously enjoying the pain he caused, he drew back breathlessly, wiped his mouth, and sneered. "Our pact is sealed in blood, then. I will take you personally to the dungeon to see Dagan and confirm all I have said, and I will then announce your true identity to the shire—confirmed by Hadley—and tell them that you have consented to become my wife."

Rosamund's skin blanched. Aware that Dagan's life was at stake, she nodded her acquiescence. The baron smiled in triumph and crushed his mouth against hers. Yet none within were prepared for the gasping exclamation that echoed from the doorway where Hyacinthe suddenly appeared. "Stop!"

De Silva's face turned hot with anger as Hyacinthe stood boldly in the doorway of his quarters. He ordered, "Leave! I did not invite kitchen help here."

"Kitchen help? Is that what I am to you now?" Hyacinthe advanced into the room. Her skin colorless and her ample breasts heaving, she said incredulously, "That is not what you said when you took me as a child and told me that you could not resist my beauty . . . or when you returned to Normandy *and me* after each incursion with William and proved your manhood through long days and nights in your bed. That is not what you whispered when you again held me tight on your silken sheets here, where I pleasured you, fulfilling your every whim while anticipating more. That is not what you sighed when I used every technique I knew to titillate your senses and did not cease until you were sated at last."

"You are a whore, and I treated you as one."

"You said you loved me!"

"Did I? I loved what you did for me at the time, but I am no longer interested in your practiced wiles."

"Wiles that I practiced to maintain your interest!"

"That is as good an excuse as any for your wonton behavior with any male who would have you."

"That is not true!"

"It is true. Get out!"

"I . . . I have been your lover since I was a child. You cannot throw me away."

"What did you expect of me?" De Silva walked toward Hyacinthe with a heavy step. "A permanent relationship?"

"I expected you to marry to me!"

"You!" De Silva was convulsed with laughter. "I would never have soiled my name by joining it with a woman of your caliber. You are an unworthy commoner and a dreamer if you entertained that thought for even a moment."

"Nay, do not say that." Throwing herself against him in desperation, Hyacinthe begged as she raised her tear-streaked face to his. "Tell me again that you love me . . . that you want me."

"Let me go." When Hyacinthe still clung to him, de Silva raised his closed fist and struck her mightily. Thrust backward by the strength of his blow, Hyacinthe staggered to the floor. Blood streamed from her nose as she slowly drew herself to her feet, and de Silva ordered, "Get out now, and leave this keep! I do not wish to set eyes on you again."

"But—"

Hyacinthe drew back instinctively when de Silva advanced toward her again. Without another word, she fled down the stairs.

Turning back toward Rosamund, de Silva shook off his rage with disturbing ease as he said, "Come, my love. It is time for our rendezvous."

The smell of mold and decay grew stronger as Rosamund descended the stairs to the dungeons established below the castle keep. The baron walked beside her as she looked at the pitch torches that hung in a haphazard fashion from walls dripping with moisture and other suspicious substances. The torches cast wavering shadows that confused the eye and emitted a thick smoke that added to the overwhelming stench of the place.

When de Silva stopped, she stood silently, awaiting his direction through the dank tunnels. A jailor emerged unexpectedly from the semidarkness. The man smelled of human waste and death, and wore an unholy smile as he motioned them forward. Unable to do else, Rosamund followed stiffly when he led them to a door bearing a single window to illuminate the darkness of the cell beyond. The jailor unlocked the cell with a key he took from his belt.

"Are you ready for what you will find on the other side, Rosamund?" De Silva's question broke the silence with its gleeful tone. "I expect that it will not be what you hoped for, but I suspect it will suffice."

Refusing to respond, Rosamund waited until the jailor pulled the door open wide for them to enter. The stench of urine and feces struck her like a blow when she walked inside and took a moment to acclimate to the almost lightless interior. She swallowed tightly as a tall figure stood up from the bench against the wall and walked unsteadily toward her.

"Stop there or I will direct the jailor to stop you!" De Silva's command rang in the silence when Dagan came into view.

Rosamund refused to react to Dagan's appearance— the wound on his head, his sullied clothing, and the filth caked on his skin. Noting the flicker in Dagan's gaze, she said imperiously, "I wish to talk to Dagan alone."

"I did not agree to that."

Turning toward de Silva, Rosamund replied, "Whether you agreed to that particular point is not significant. You agreed to allow me to see Dagan and ascertain that he was well."

De Silva's gaze narrowed. "I agreed to that, did I?"

"You did, and since I can only judge Dagan's condition honestly without you at my side, I ask that you leave." When de Silva did not move, she said coolly, "Or do I assume that our agreement is void?"

Rosamund maintained her stability with true strength of will as de Silva considered her demand. She released a silent sigh of relief when he said at last, "I will allow you a few moments with the prisoner. I am sure you will have had enough of this place by then. I will arrange for us both to bathe when we leave here."

When Dagan took a threatening step toward him, de Silva said snidely, "I beg you to attempt what you cannot hope to achieve, sir knight, so I may defend myself and end this farce once and for all."

Dagan halted where he stood, and Rosamund turned back to de Silva to say in an emotionless voice, "I ask that you keep the terms of our agreement foremost in your mind. If you do, I will honor it in the same way you honor yours."

De Silva smiled abruptly. "I rely on your word, my love."

The door clicked closed behind him and the key turned in the lock, sending a chill down her spine.

Rosamund turned back toward Dagan. Hesitating only a moment, she moved instinctively into his arms.

Suddenly aware that Dagan did not return her embrace, Rosamund drew back. She realized with a start that the chains binding his wrists and ankles did not extend farther than the spot where he stood. Touching the manacles that bound his wrists, she looked up at him and murmered, "Dagan . . ."

"Do not judge from appearances, Rosamund. I am well."

"Well?" Noting the determination in Dagan's voice, Rosamund whispered, "Do you not realize where you are? Do you not realize the potential for disaster here?"

"I will find a way to escape this cell, Rosamund. The jailors are a sorry lot. They are dim of mind. Only their penchant for delivering torture and for the privilege of keeping the keys to these enclosures allow them a reason for existence. They are easily outwitted."

"Are they?" Rosamund shook her head. "Do you think I am unaware of what you are attempting to do with these words, Dagan? Do you believe I do not realize that you wish to send me away from here with false hope?"

"Rosamund, please . . ."

"I cannot leave you here this way!" Rosamund took a breath and continued softly, "Your confession shocked me. I made myself believe that I could never take a man such as you into my heart. Yet in quiet moments afterward, I questioned why you were brought to me at death's door; why I should have tended to you day and night; why I should have wished desperately for your recovery; why I should have come to revere the man you showed yourself to be before learning of your alliance with William. When the baron told me that he had confined you here, I realized that for better or worse, you had become a part of me, and that no amount of words could change that truth. Oh, Dagan, I did not realize until then how much I loved you."

Rosamund attempted to slide her arms around him again, but Dagan stepped back. "Nay, do not come any closer. I am unclean. I smell of this place . . ."

"I do not care about your appearance!" Briefly closing her eyes, Rosamund whispered, "I am sorry, Dagan. I was deliberately cruel the last time I spoke to you. I turned my back on you and would not allow you to speak of what caused you to join William's camp, or of how your fealty to him grew. I only know that your loyalty is as strong as mine, but that you could never be one such as the . . ."

Rosamund's words were cut short by the sudden heat of Dagan's mouth against hers. She felt the warmth of him . . . the taste of him. She made a soft sound of protest when he drew back reluctantly and whispered, "Forgive me. I could not resist."

"You did not *take* a kiss, Dagan. I gave it gladly."

Ignoring her response, Dagan continued resolutely, "Speak no more of your guilt to me, for I bear a fair share in all that transpired between us." Glancing up at the door, Dagan whispered, "We have so little time to say so much, so you must listen carefully to me when I say I love you, Rosamund. I tell you now that I will escape from this place, and I will hold you in my arms again, and whatever transpires, I will never allow de Silva to claim what is mine."

Pausing, pinning her with his gaze, Dagan said simply, "Do you believe me?"

Rosamund's throat was tight as she responded, "I believe you, Dagan."

His gaze reflecting all that went unsaid, Dagan whispered, "Tell me now, how does de Silva come to call you Rosamund?"

"When he summoned me to his quarters, he knew."

"Did you tell him all . . . your true name as heir to this shire?"

"I did."

"He wishes to use it against you?"

"Nay, I used that secret as a bartering tool."

Dagan went still before whispering, "Barter . . . for my life."

"Barter to keep you alive until—"

The sound of a key turning in the lock interrupted their exchange and Dagan whispered, "Step back. Do not allow the baron to see that we have touched. And do not despair. I will escape before—"

"It is time to leave here, my love." The baron walked boldly into the cell and took Rosamund's arm.

Freeing herself, Rosamund walked back toward the door. "I will accompany you out of this place. However, I ask you to remember, my lord, that as you keep your bargain, I will keep mine."

"My name is Guilbert." The baron halted unexpectedly in the doorway. "I would hear my name on your lips, Rosamund."

Rosamund heard restless movement from behind her. She knew Dagan inwardly raged. Hoping to alleviate his distress, she said simply, "We are not friends. I will not use your given name until our agreement comes to fruition."

"Our agreement . . . meaning the moment when we take our vows and become one." De Silva snickered. "I suppose I can wait a little longer."

Rosamund briefly closed her eyes when the cell door closed behind her and they started back down the passageway. The baron continued a warm dialogue, but with one thought in mind, Rosamund heard little.

Dagan was alive, but he would not remain alive very long under the harsh conditions of the dungeon.

Blinking back tears, Rosamund raised her chin resolutely. She had no time for weakness. Dagan depended on her.

Chapter Nine

The door of Dagan's cell snapped closed and his frustration rose. He listened to the sound of Rosamund's retreating footsteps and heard the heavier sound of de Silva's tread beside hers. He glanced down at the manacles on his wrists and ankles and at the dark, dank cell in which he was confined, intensely aware of his helplessness. He had awakened in this place with chains binding him but he had no memory of being moved. Despite de Silva's previous actions, Dagan had not expected such treachery when summoned to speak with him. It was now evident that he had made a mistake, that de Silva was neither honest nor trustworthy, and that he felt no loyalty to William or to the knights who had fought in the King's name.

Dagan choked on the stench of his cell. He was only too aware of the chance Rosamund had taken in revealing her heritage to de Silva. She could have paid with her life if de Silva had decided that Rosamund's true identity as the Saxon heir to the shire endangered his position. Instead, because he was obsessed with her, because he presently desired her and was determined to have her despite her antipathy for him, and because he wanted to prove to her that he had won in the end, de Silva had decided to use it against her.

Dagan recalled Rosamund's kiss. Despite the manner of their last parting, she had spoken to him lovingly without allowing herself to react to the odor or to the conditions of his imprisonment; yet he had heard the desperation in her voice after de Silva left them. He had promised her that he would escape and he was determined that he would.

Dagan took a breath. Rosamund's future—the future she was willing to sacrifice for him, the same bright future he had silently hoped they would spend together—depended on him as it never had before.

He loved Rosamund in a way he had never loved a woman—with his heart, with his body, and with a commitment as lasting as time. He wanted the opportunity to prove his love for her each and every day until she no longer retained any doubts about their future together, or about the future of all she cherished.

Dagan looked up at the sound of the jailor's dragging footsteps in the passageway. He listened as they hesitated at his door and then moved on.

With new determination, and aware that his time was limited, he began formulating a plan.

The afternoon grew surprisingly hot as Martin approached the keep. He frowned and wiped his brow with the back of his arm, aware as he straightened to his full height that his clothing was stained with perspiration and with the marks of riotous play. Time spent in the kennels had become his only respite of late from the constant training expected of knights of his caliber. He enjoyed the time he spent with the friendly animals there, and was particularly fond of several of them; yet he resented the fact that for the most part, the hounds were treated with more consideration than the Saxon children of the shire. The baron had made sure of it by forbidding the inhabitants of the shire to hunt, by keeping them poor, and by encouraging their fear.

Martin did not hold the superior treatment the agreeable hounds received against them. He knew that de Silva had no personal attachment to them, and that like his hunting falcons, they were simply a symbol to him that marked how far he had come in his quest for prominence.

Martin silently acknowledged that although de Silva's word was considered law as long as it did not contradict William's in any way, de Silva wanted still more.

More . . . when all he had to do was to enjoy what was his.

Unsettling thoughts continued to trouble Martin as he walked toward the keep. The truth was that he was tired of the life he presently led. Making war on the enemy, constant training for incursions, and watching as innocent peasants suffered the idiosyncrasies of the master, wasn't his way.

A familiar resentment stirred. He was younger than de Silva and Champlain, and his ways were not set in stone as were theirs. He had tired of taking women to satisfy his animal needs. He wanted more to show for his life. He had saved his pay frugally and could now afford a home of his own away from the lifestyle that grew more abhorrent to him with each day that passed. Yet he knew that resigning his post would not be easy.

Martin's step stilled when a familiar sound reached

his ears as he approached the keep. He scanned the yard, his gaze finally coming to rest on a towering pile of logs that had been cut to size so they might easily feed the great fireplace. He approached the log pile slowly.

There was no need to wonder who had hidden herself away from all who might revel in her distress.

Martin peered behind the woodpile. His thoughts were confirmed when he saw the woman crouched mournfully there. He asked softly, "What is wrong, Hyacinthe?"

Hyacinthe started with surprise when she looked up at him. Ashamed, she looked away, attempting to conceal the blood that trailed from her nose and the swelling cheek that bore the mark of a brutal hand. She shrunk back from him as he crouched beside her and whispered incredulously, "What happened to you?"

"Need you ask?" she responded hoarsely. "Guilbert has replaced me with another. It was my misfortune to see his lover being escorted to his quarters by two of his knights. I followed them and saw them embracing. I begged Guilbert to turn the young man away, but he refused. He laughed when I said I had believed him when he said he loved me. He said his words had been expedient, that he only loved what I *did* for him. He called me a whore and said he had not for a moment considered a lasting commitment with a woman of my *caliber*."

"Hyacinthe . . ."

"I begged him to take me back, Martin. I threw myself against him . . . crawled on my knees. When I would not release him as he demanded, he struck me."

"He struck you . . ."

"Yet his words caused me more pain than the blow because he said . . ." Hyacinthe took a breath. "He ordered me out of his quarters and demanded that I leave the castle keep so he would never set eyes on me again!"

Suffering at her torment, Martin drew Hyacinthe close. He felt her trembling when she whispered, "He doesn't love me, Martin. He never loved me."

"Hyacinthe . . . I told you . . . the baron doesn't know how to love."

"Yet he knows desire and was only too happy to allow me to sate it." Red-faced at her admission, Hyacinthe drew back to look up at Martin. "But that isn't true anymore. He wants Ross now, and he's throwing me away just as he did all the others."

"He . . . he didn't mean what he said." Forcing the words past his lips in an effort to console her, Martin whispered, "The baron will tire of this Ross. When the emotion of the moment passes, he will forget he ever said those things to you."

Hyacinthe raised her chin. "He may forget what he said, but I will never forget it."

"Hyacinthe . . . please. You are too young and beautiful for bitter thoughts. You will meet a young man someday whom you will love, and he will return your love."

"Nay . . ."

"You are beautiful . . . desirable . . . a woman with so much to offer a man. Surely you know that. Surely you realize that I would not be able to say these things if I did not hold the hope in my heart that someday—"

Hyacinthe interrupted him as if he had not spoken. "I have wasted the greater part of my life entertaining a worthless dream, Martin. I believed all that Guilbert said . . . all that he promised me. I told myself he was not yet ready to settle down, but when he did . . ." Momentarily unable to go on, Hyacinthe rasped, "Guilbert will suffer for his transgression."

A chill moved down Martin's spine at Hyacinthe's vow. He replied softly, "It is senseless to speak of vengeance. There is no way a simple woman will be able to wreak revenge on a man as powerful as the baron."

"Yea, there is a way. There has to be a way."

"Listen to me!" Giving her a gentle shake in an attempt to gain her attention, Martin rasped, "You will do nothing but bring about your own demise if you attempt retribution.

"I will find a way."

Realizing the hopelessness of that tact, Martin tried again. "You cannot remain here. The baron told you to leave the keep, never to return."

"He will never see me in the kitchen. I am invisible to him there. He will forget what he said in a few days. You said so yourself."

"I but hoped to encourage you with those words."

Her eyes taking on a sudden, softer hue, Hyacinthe looked at Martin silently for long moments. She said wistfully, "You are a handsome man, Martin. You are brave and strong, yet you are a gentle person—everything a woman could want. Unlike me, someone with nothing left to offer . . . someone whose future has been stolen from her."

"Your future is your own!"

"Nay, *your* future is your own. Do not allow Guilbert's ruthlessness to infect you. Get away from him. Find yourself a position where you will be valued for the man you are, and find a maiden who appreciates you."

"You value me, do you not?"

"I value you greatly. You are the only friend I have in this foreign place where all who have come in contact with me hate me."

"That is untrue!"

"Nay, it is more true than I have allowed myself to believe. I have sought nothing but Guilbert's love, and I have not cared if I earned hatred from others with my immoral ways."

"You are not immoral."

"It is true that I did not think of myself as immoral. I thought of myself as a woman in love who fought to win the man she cherished. As shocking as they were to me, Guilbert's words allowed me to see myself as others see me . . . as a poor, depraved woman who sought the attentions of a man who would never love her."

"Not all those whom you have come into contact with here hate you, Hyacinthe. I . . . I love you."

"And I love you." Suddenly hugging him close, Hyacinthe whispered against his chest, "I value your friendship more than you know, Martin, but your friendship does not satisfy the need within me."

Friendship . . .

Martin went cold. He remained silent when Hyacinthe drew back and wiped the trickling blood from her face with the hem of her dress. She raised her chin and said earnestly, "Thank you, Martin. You have given me hope."

"You must leave this place."

"Nay, I will stay."

"Why? So you may suffer more at the baron's hands?"

Hyacinthe smiled. She drew herself to her feet and brushed off her clothing. She watched as Martin stood beside her. "Do not worry about me. I have suffered worse than this bruise."

"Think what you are doing, Hyacinthe. You cannot win."

"Yea, I will, for retribution against all that the baron has taken from me is all I have left."

Hyacinthe pressed a chaste, fleeting kiss against Martin's lips before heading for the kitchen.

He watched as she slipped inside with her chin held high. Still feeling the warmth of her lips against his own, he took a step, and then halted. Hyacinthe was determined to exact revenge. He only hoped he could find a way to save her.

"Why did the baron force you away from your work when he knew I needed you, Ross?" Hadley spoke with a halting breath as Rosamund urged him to a more private spot, with the baron close behind her. Suspicion entered his voice at the man's possessive manner, and he continued determinedly, "What is so urgent that you and the baron must speak to me now when I am otherwise involved in his project?"

When Rosamund hesitated to respond, Hadley

strained to see her clearly through eyes that beheld little more than shadows, his trepidation burgeoning. The late afternoon sun beat on his head, raising beads of perspiration as he prompted, "I await your response, Ross."

The baron's lips twitched and his arrogant expression tightened. "You need no longer maintain the deception, Hadley. I know all."

"Ross?"

"Do not pretend ignorance! I am weary of your lies! I know the truth of Rosamund's sex, just as I know her true name. It galls me still that I allowed myself to be so deceived. My only consolation is that I sensed the truth despite her attempt to mislead me."

Hadley glanced at Rosamund warily. He saw the whitening of her countenance as the baron continued, "Rosamund also informed me of the truth of her birth. I admit to being delighted to learn that she is the former heir to this shire, especially since she has consented to wed me."

"To wed you!"

"Why do you seem surprised, old man?" His feigned benevolence slipping, de Silva grated, "Did you believe you would be able to continue with your deception? That I would never come to know who and what Rosamund is? Or is it simply that you did not believe Rosamund would ever consent to become my bride?"

Momentarily at a loss, Hadley did not respond. Taking advantage of the opportunity, the baron slid his arm around Rosamund's shoulders. He pretended not to notice that she shrunk from his touch as he declared, "Rosamund thought you should be the first to be informed that she has consented to wear the ring her father left her when she becomes my wife."

"I . . . I do not understand."

His composure slipping further, de Silva advanced threateningly toward Hadley. "What is so difficult to understand, old man? If I did not feel it would be worth my while to have you present at our marriage, I would take my vengeance on you for your duplicity. Instead, I have decided to enjoy your discomfort at the ceremony. I will notify William of the coming nuptials, of course. He will be delighted that I am to settle down at last, especially with someone who will bring a sense of unity to the godforsaken shire he has awarded me. He may even desire to attend the ceremony, which would doubtless add to your discomfort, while I will use it as a stepping stone to my true aspirations at court."

"But . . ."

"Fool! After your attempt to trick me, you should feel privileged that Rosamund and I came here to announce our nuptials to you."

When Rosamund continued to maintain her silence, Hadley questioned softly, "Is all this true, Rosamund?"

Rosamund raised her chin. "It is true, Father."

"He is not your father, and I would not have you address him that way!" De Silva snapped.

"He is the only father I have known since my own sire died defending this shire. I will call him father openly now, whether it pleases you or not!"

De Silva forced a smile and replied, "As you wish, my dear . . . for the time being, anyway. At any rate, I will leave you now so I may prepare a missive to William announcing our troth. The dressmakers will arrive soon to prepare your gown for the ceremony. Hadley needs you here, and I know you will not stray far."

Rosamund responded tightly, "Nay, I will not stray."

Appearing unable to conceal his smile, de Silva turned and walked back in the direction of the keep. He was out of earshot when Hadley said, "What happened, Rosamund? Why did you consent to this?"

"Dagan."

Stunned, Hadley took a backward step. "Dagan disappeared shortly before you did. Where is he now?"

"Dagan is a prisoner in the dungeon and the baron holds the key to his survival." Rosamund took a breath and then said flatly, "Dagan is Norman, Father. He is one of William's knights and was active in his victory here. William sent him to investigate rumors about de Silva's spurious activities, but thieves robbed him and left him for dead. That is why he came here in a commoner's garb."

Hadley nodded. "I feared something like that was true." At Rosamund's surprise, he continued, "Dagan's stature, his silent endurance, and the intelligence he exhibited—all made me suspect that he was not what he seemed. The loyal warhorse only added to my suspicion."

"Yet you said nothing."

"He was helpless while you tended to his wounds, and you were so concerned about his welfare. In any case, my suspicions were allayed when he chose to labor as if he were a common man. Yet his protective attitude toward you in the face of de Silva's arrogance led me to observe him rather than accuse him."

"You did not tell me of your suspicions, although you knew I believed him an innocent victim of circumstance and never questioned his allegiance."

"I knew you were blinded by emotion."

"So . . . so you know . . ."

"That you love Dagan? Yea, I know. I also knew when Dagan kept our secret that whoever he was, he loved you, too."

A tear slid from the corner of Rosamund's eye. "So you know I must wed the baron or he will act against Dagan."

"I know only that you must temporarily agree to all the baron says."

"The baron took me down to the cell where Dagan is chained hand and foot. No one can survive there, Father! Dagan told me not to fear because he would escape, but in my heart I know that any attempt he might make is doomed to failure. Meanwhile, the jailors slaver at the thought of the torture they could inflict on him. They only await the baron's word. If I do not agree to his demands, the baron will arrange for Dagan to die slowly there. I have thought of carrying my tale to William himself, but I know what the outcome would be. If I were even granted an opportunity to speak to him, William would never believe me—a Saxon whose father was killed in the attack he ordered—as opposed to a knight who has fought loyally for him. It would not matter how many rumors abound about the baron; without verification from one William trusts, the rumors mean nothing. The baron would see to it that Dagan simply disappeared, which would not be inconceivable in a forest filled with hungry, angry men."

"Do not allow yourself to panic, Rosamund."

"Panic? I had hoped to gain more time by announcing my true status to the baron and declaring that he could claim acceptance if we were wed legally in the eyes of the shire—but gain time to do what? The bitter truth is that I would rather die than allow the baron to touch me."

"Do not speak such words! You can leave. Dagan would gladly sacrifice his life if it meant your freedom."

"But I do not want him to sacrifice his life for me!"

"Rosamund . . ."

"I tell you now, Father . . . I would rather die."

"Oh, you come here to celebrate with us, I suppose." Edythe's sagging face wrinkled in a smile as Hyacinthe entered the kitchen. She eyed Hyacinthe's swollen face and commented, "I see that you have already registered your objection to the baron's plans."

"The baron has nothing to do with these bruises. I fell on the steps when I came down from his quarters."

"Yea . . . you fell."

Refusing to react to Edythe's comment, and aware that Winifred and several of the younger kitchen helpers kept on with their chores while watching her covertly, Hyacinthe asked, "What do you celebrate?"

"The baron's intended nuptials, of course."

Hyacinthe gasped. Aware that both women watched her closely, she strained for composure as she asked, "What is the name of the woman he is to wed?"

"You do not know? You met her when you went upstairs. Am I to believe that the baron did not inform you of Ross's deceit?"

"Deceit?" Losing patience with Edythe, Hyacinthe demanded, "Out with it, woman, unless you want me to beat it out of you!"

"Do not threaten me, whore! You no longer have the weight of the baron's favor on your side. He is to wed Rosamund Wedge . . . *Ross* as she was previously known."

Hyacinthe shook her head, incredulous, as she asked, "You are saying . . ."

"I am saying that Ross's name is really Rosamund, and that she is a woman who hid her identity because she has proof that she is the true heir to the land that William awarded to the baron for his victory."

"She is a woman?"

"Are you not listening? She is not *a* woman. She is *the* woman who is key to the baron's acceptance here, to the possible forgiveness of all his former ills, and to his possible admission to a place at William's court . . . perhaps even to a place at William's side."

"Nay . . ."

"It will do you no good to attempt to deny the truth."

"I do not believe you! How do you know all this?"

"I have big ears and I listen well."

"You have always had *big ears,* but they have not done you any good in the past."

"I also have a steady hand at the cookstove."

"Meaning?"

"Meaning that the baron depends on me to provide food for those in the dungeons below."

Uncertain of Edythe's meaning, Hyacinthe did not respond.

Obviously regretting her outburst, Edythe turned back toward the table in front of her and said abruptly, "I have said enough. I will say no more."

"Speak, woman!"

Grasping a knife, Edythe turned toward Hyacinthe and said hoarsely, "I told you that I will say no more, do you understand? Get back to work and ask no more questions or I will see to it that the baron sends you away for good."

Hyacinthe did not bother to respond. Instead, she took up the basket in the corner of the kitchen and strode out to the woodpile to fill it. She smiled bitterly as she stepped out of sight. It was not necessary for Edythe to say more. Guilbert had decided to marry a Saxon wench. She obviously would not have consented if the baron had pressured her in some way.

Hyacinthe reached the woodpile and began filling the basket. Yea, Edythe, hotheaded fool that she was, had said enough. The answer to all her questions lay in the dungeon below the keep. . . .

At the sound of voices, Dagan looked up and then struggled to move closer to the door of his filthy cell so he might hear the conversation. Restrained by the chains that bound him, he strove to hear the feminine voice that replied coyly to the slurred tones of his jailor, who seemed only too eager to begin the same treatment that all previous inhabitants of his cell had suffered. He knew only one thing held the jailor back—de Silva's orders—and he relied on the frustration that order caused him. He hoped that under the present circumstances, with resentment burgeoning, his jailor would not be thinking clearly. He knew that contacting Rosamund was impossible since de Silva's guards would undoubtedly be watching her closely, but he hoped to find a way to convince the dim-witted jailor to approach Hadley with the message that Dagan wanted to speak with him.

Dagan could only hope that the jailor would fall in with his plans for one reason or another, but that portion of his plan remained uncertain. He was sure, however, that Hadley would respond to his summons. He believed Hadley had suspected he was not what he had claimed to be from the first day he arrived, and he was prepared to convince the man to help him by telling him that he loved Rosamund, that his greatest wish was to see that the promise she saw for their people's future was realized under William's rule. The Saxons would be oppressed no longer, but would regain their pride under the man he considered the true heir to the throne. Dagan believed that Hadley knew as well as he that de Silva had no integrity, that marriage to Rosamund would negate any promises made to her. Once they were legally bound, Rosamund's sacrifice would be for naught.

Whatever Hadley's response, he could not allow that to happen.

The purring conversation in the corridor halted abruptly at the unexpected turning of his lock and the entrance of a female figure into his cell.

"Do not worry. The prisoner is chained. He cannot advance any farther than a few feet from the wall."

"That is good," the woman responded. "My desire

to see the object of the baron's animosity is overwhelming. I believe it will bring me pleasure as well, since I am a Norman."

"Yea . . . a beautiful Norman."

The jailor's voice revealed his intoxication with the woman's wiles. Turning toward the man with a sultry gaze, the woman caressed his cheek before saying, "You will leave us alone, won't you, so I may get my fill of the pleasure the prisoner gives me?"

"Yea . . . I will do that."

"You will not listen, will you? There are some things I would not have anyone know about my visit here."

"Anything for you, Hyacinthe."

Hyacinthe.

Dagan frowned, remembering the servant who had followed de Silva from Normandy. Yea, he had seen her before, but he had not recognized her immediately with her face grossly swollen as it was. He wondered at the jailor's bemusement, and then realized that she was nevertheless beautiful to him.

The door closed behind Hyacinthe, and Dagan kept his silence as she listened to the jailor's departing footsteps, making certain that the fellow had left the corridor before advancing toward him to say, "So you are the reason why Rosamund agreed to marry the baron!"

Dagan replied coldly, "And you are his lover."

"His *former* lover. My face bear the marks of the baron's displeasure."

"Is that why you come?" Irritated by the woman's appearance, confused by her dedication to a man who had so little to offer her, he asked tightly, "Do you come to indulge dreams of vengeance against the man who struck you, or do you come to share the baron's delight at seeing me so confined?"

"I come with the former desire in mind."

"Are you sure you are not here to enjoy the supposed agony of one of William's knights at the hand of the baron?"

Momentarily silent, Hyacinthe responded incredulously, "You are one of William's knights?"

"Do you doubt my word?"

"Nay." Hyacinthe shook her head. "It is suddenly clear to me why you are so confined, and why the baron is so anxious for William to see him married to a Saxon heiress."

"De Silva is a traitor who is not worthy of William's regard! Neither is he worthy of knighthood, despite his former campaigns in William's name, and he knows I would tell William that truth if I escaped this place."

"The campaigns that the baron conducted over the years were in his own name, not in William's," Hyacinthe stated boldly. "I know. I listened to the baron's railing against William after each successive return to Normandy from William's incursions. The baron did not believe in William. He believed him a pretender with common blood who had no right to the throne despite the weight his name carried. He claimed that royal blood ran in his own veins and his fealty to William was temporary until *he* could assume the throne."

"That day will never come," Dagan replied tightly.

"I agree, and I am here to assure that outcome."

Dagan halted at Hyacinthe's statement. He did not trust her. He needed more time for his plans to free Rosamund, but he was suddenly uncertain if this was his final opportunity to accomplish that goal. Staring at Hyacinthe in the flickering torchlight, he asked flatly, "Why do you come here?"

Hyacinthe responded as coldly as he. "The baron is not the man either of us believed him to be. I have spent years of my life in pursuit of a dream that will never come to fruition . . . worshipping a man who did not exist." Drawing herself up proudly despite her temporary disfigurement, Hyacinthe proclaimed softly, "I expect him to pay and pay heavily for the years I wasted loving a man who lied to me and cheated me of all I could otherwise have been."

Dagan squinted into the semidarkness. He saw the set of the woman's shoulders and the prideful tilt of her head and asked, "How far are you prepared to go to achieve your ends?"

Hyacinthe responded with a deep breath, "I will do what I must."

Dagan hesitated, feeling the pressure of his situation. Should he trust this woman who had loved the baron for years? Should he believe her when she said she was through with him and wanted revenge for the years she had lost? Or should he set his hopes on a dim-witted jailor who looked at him with clear thoughts of enjoying the torture he would eventually inflict on him?

As Dagan hesitated, a small amount of blood oozed

from Hyacinthe's swollen nose. It trickled onto her equally swollen lips, lips that the baron had most likely kissed freely when the situation suited him— lips that he had then struck without remorse, uncaring that the blow caused more than physical damage to a woman who had loved him.

Suddenly tasting the bitterness of her own blood, Hyacinthe brushed the narrow stream away with obvious embarrassment. Her eyes brimmed with tears she refused to shed as she continued to face him squarely, revealing clearly to Dagan for the first time the agony that had brought her to his squalid cell.

Dagan glanced at the cell door and then whispered, "We have little time if you speak truthfully and are willing to help me."

Hyacinthe raised her chin a fraction higher. "Yea, that is why I have come here."

"Then there is one thing I would ask of you."

The shuffling sound of footsteps in the corridor announced the jailor's return in time for Hyacinthe to listen intently and nod before feigning loud laughter for the jailor's benefit as she said, "So here you are at the baron's mercy. Fie on you!"

Hyacinthe turned toward the door with a smile when the jailor opened it. She walked toward the slovenly fellow where he stood in the opening. Standing at eye-level with him, she said, "Thank you for allowing me the time to gloat at what is to come. I will not forget you for it."

Pressing a brief kiss against the jailor's drooling lips, Hyacinthe disappeared from sight.

The door of the cell slammed closed. The key turned

in the lock. Silent, alone again, and suddenly uncertain, Dagan listened to the subtle sounds of shuffling in the dark corners behind him.

He had taken a chance. The rest was up to Hyacinthe.

Chapter Ten

Shaken awake although it was still dark, Rosamund blinked at the knights standing over her in the small hut that Hadley and she shared. Momentarily confused, she sat up and asked, "What are you doing here? What do you want?" She glanced at the gradually brightening dawn outside the doorway and said, "It is not yet time for work to start."

"The baron has commanded that you be brought to the castle keep . . . to the room awaiting you there."

"What?"

Rosamund glanced at Hadley where he stood flanked by knights. She responded, "My father needs me. The baron assured me that I may remain here with him until the wedding."

"He has changed his mind."

"I don't understand."

Urged to her feet, Rosamund realized that it made no difference whether she understood or not . . . until she stood facing the baron in the silence of the keep and said defiantly, "You broke your word. You assured me that I could remain free to work with my father until our wedding."

"You may work with him." The baron dismissed his knights with a nod. He waited until they had taken their place outside his doorway to continue, "I have no objection to your helping Hadley." The baron's statement was accompanied by his most appealing smile. Yea, he was brutishly handsome, but Rosamund had no intention of becoming one of the women who succumbed to his practiced charm.

With a sudden flush, Rosamund recalled the moment when Dagan took her into his arms in that dank cell. The warmth of him, the wonder of being in his arms, the sweet taste of his mouth, and the realization that she had nearly lost him in her anger, had been almost more than she could bear. She had realized then that despite the differences that had previously forced them apart, their love was strong enough to overcome all.

As for the baron's attempt to charm her, he was wasting his time. She had seen the other side of his smile, and she would never forget it.

With those thoughts in mind, Rosamund did not respond to the baron's entreaties, forcing him to continue, "All I presently demand is that you stay here, in the room that I have had prepared for you, until we are wed."

She responded again, "You said I could remain with my father until—"

"I did not say that. I said that nothing would change for you until the day we take our vows. Other than this, nothing will. I do not intend to violate your privacy." His smile stiffened. "There will be time for intimacy after William witnesses our nuptials."

"You said—"

"I said nothing else would change!" His smile

disappearing as his patience waned, the baron took an aggressive step and then halted before he continued, "You only assumed that I would allow you to remain at that meager hut you shared with Hadley. I could not do that. It would not appear seemly to William if I allowed my betrothed to live under such circumstances."

"Those *circumstances* were sufficient when you believed I was Ross, Hadley's assistant."

"But you are not Ross, are you?" The baron took another step that brought him so close to Rosamund that she could see a vein it his temple throbbing with suppressed anger. Yet she was startled when he curled his hand in her shorn locks, effectively holding her captive as he purred, "You have beautiful hair. It is so thick and blonde . . . so *Saxon*. But I enjoy women with long hair. It is a pity you cut yours."

"I could not be happier that my hair is short since it is not my desire to afford you pleasure of any kind."

Twisting his grip in her hair until the pain caused Rosamund's eyes to water, de Silva whispered, "But you will give me pleasure, won't you? That is the responsibility of a wife. And you *will* be a wife to me, Rosamund, with all that title entails."

De Silva released her so abruptly that Rosamund stumbled a few steps backward. He smiled again and said, "I will not go against my word. As a matter of fact, I will have my knights see to it that you aid Hadley's efforts in constructing the cathedral, if that is your wish. The only demand I will make of you is that you make yourself available for fittings when dressmakers arrive to fashion your new wardrobe . . . and your wedding dress."

"I do not need dressmakers. I have enough clothes."

"Dresses . . . I would have you wear dresses . . . gowns as befit a woman of your social standing!"

"My own clothing is suitable enough."

"Not for me!" His former conciliatory expression disappearing in an instant, de Silva towered threateningly over Rosamund and ordered, "You will obey my command. If you do not, I will have no qualms about allowing your dear Dagan an hour with his jailor."

Trembling, Rosamund stated, "You prove the veracity of the name Saxons have given you."

"The Saxon name for me? Pray tell me what that might be."

"They call you the Butcher of Hendsmille."

"I do not feel that I deserve such a name as yet, but perhaps I will attempt to live up to it . . . with you at my side."

"I will never stand at your side!"

"You will if you hope to see your dear Dagan live beyond this day! I will have my men show you to your room, where you may rest until it is time for you to go to Hadley. As promised, I will not interfere with your work there. If you are tempted to interfere in my plans in any way, however, I would caution you to keep in mind that *you* will not be the one to suffer."

Allowing a moment for his statement to register, de Silva jerked Rosamund toward him and pressed another kiss against her lips. He released her, laughed, and whispered, "Do not bother to ask for more, for no more will be forthcoming until the day we speak our vows."

Shaken, but incensed at the baron's words, Rosamund rubbed her mouth to remove all trace of his kiss. She turned abruptly toward the doorway and the knights awaiting her there as de Silva ordered, "Take her to her room and wait there until she changes into the dress delivered to her hut. Only when she is dressed to reflect her true sex will you allow her to go advise Hadley." In a softer tone, he warned, "Watch her carefully. See that she behaves as befits a betrothed woman of standing, and do not leave her side."

Rosamund left the baron's quarters with his warnings ringing in her ears.

"You must listen to me and you must believe what I say." Hyacinthe faced Hadley in a private area of the cathedral grounds. Aware that he had just arrived there with Horace's help, and that Rosamund had been delivered to the keep only minutes earlier, she addressed Hadley with continued vehemence. "Dagan is confined in the dungeon below the keep. I entered by a hidden stairway and saw him there last night. I talked to him. He asked me to tell you it is urgent that he speak to you."

"I know where Dagan is." His expression stern, Hadley said as he strained to see her more clearly, "Your name is Hyacinthe, is it not? Your accent betrays all that you are—a Norman who has no place in this shire."

"Yea, I am a Norman, and was always proud to be so until I came here and circumstances changed."

"Circumstances changed . . ." Hadley's smile was bitter. "You are referring to the recent discovery your lover made, that Ross is in reality Rosamund, a woman and true heiress to this shire, and that the baron intends to marry her in order to strengthen his position with William."

"Yea, that is so." Making no attempt to deceive him, Hyacinthe continued coldly, "But my motives should not concern you at present, since I am the only person who can help you weather this debacle."

"Why should I believe you?"

"Why should you not? What would I have to gain by speaking to you? You know the intimacies the baron and I shared . . . intimacies he now scorns as he scorns me. You see the marks of the baron's heavy hand on my face. What you do not know is that as painful as his blow was, it was the words he spoke accompanying it that caused me to steal down into the dungeon to ascertain for myself the reason for Rosamund's sudden acquiescence to marriage. When I saw Dagan there, I realized that the baron held Dagan's welfare over her head."

Hadley stared at Hyacinthe, attempting to gauge her sincerity. He said abruptly, "I still see no reason to trust you."

"I will only respond by saying that Dagan trusted me to bring you this message as soon as the day dawned. He awaits you in his cell . . . and I do not believe he has much time left."

"Dagan, who is a Norman as you are."

"Yea, I am aware that he is a Norman, that he is actually one of William's knights, but I am also aware that strong feelings exist between Dagan and Rosamund."

"How do you know that?"

"For what other reason would Rosamund—a Saxon and the heir to this shire—be willing to sacrifice her heritage to save one of William's men? Yea, Dagan is Norman, but the only thing that he and I have in common is the desire to see that the baron receives that which he deserves."

His lined face hardening at Hyacinthe's words, Hadley replied, "Even should I trust you, there is no way I will be able to go down into the dungeon to speak to Dagan and still expect to return."

"I have visited him there, and I have returned."

Hadley maintained his silence.

Hyacinthe sneered, "You are correct in what you are thinking . . . that I used my feminine wiles on a feeble-minded jailor. What you do not realize is that I am not above doing so again. I will do whatever I must in order to achieve my ends."

"Meaning . . . ?"

"Meaning, if you decided to absent yourself now, your friend would be able to conceal your disappearance. I would see to it that you are allowed entrance to the dungeon and exit when you are finished there."

"I am practically blind."

"I would guide your way."

"Both in and out?"

Hyacinthe nodded. She drew back into the bushes when one of the baron's men strolled past. She whispered when the soldier was out of hearing, "I do not intend to risk my safety by speaking to you again."

Hadley hesitated. He called Horace to him and whispered a few words into his ear. Then he slipped into the foliage beside Hyacinthe and allowed her to lead him forward.

The sun slipped behind black clouds as Hadley and Hyacinthe reached the concealed entrance to the dungeon. The rough stairs were almost invisible to Hadley as Hyacinthe led him forward cautiously. He started when a hulking form appeared in the shadows at the bottom of the steps and motioned another guard back into a winding corridor. The odors of decay and death assaulted his nose as they continued on.

Releasing his arm unexpectedly, Hyacinthe walked toward the smiling jailor and whispered familiarly in his ear as he began to maul her breasts. Hadley tightened his lips. Hyacinthe barely controlled her revulsion when she turned back toward him and motioned him forward. It was then that he realized that she had spoken honestly when she said she would do what she must to accomplish her ends.

The jailor led the way as Hyacinthe took Hadley's arm and followed him. The fellow halted in front of a cell door, unlocked it, and waited. Waving Hadley forward, Hyacinthe whispered that she would return for him as soon as she was able.

Hadley stepped into the dim cell in front of him. The rancid smell of the small enclosure swept his senses as the lock clicked behind him. Repulsed, Hadley scrutinized the cell. He went silent at first sight of the man chained there.

Hadley stood silently just inside the entrance of the cell, and Dagan felt again the frustration of being chained. The old man had proven his worth by responding to his summons and fearlessly descending into a dungeon from which it was reputed that no one returned. He silently vowed not to forget Hadley's courage.

Dagan listened intently as Hadley started their conversation by saying gruffly, "I know now that you are Norman, Dagan, and that you fought in William's name, yet it pains me to see you confined in this place."

Hadley's unexpected greeting settled deep within Dagan as he responded honestly, "I started out for Hendsmille on an errand for William, whom I know as few others do and for whom I feel the greatest respect and loyalty. Despite the charge he gave me, I did not expect to be confined in a dungeon by one of William's own knights. If given the time and the opportunity, I would be able to outsmart a feeble-minded jailor. Yet time is not on my side. I cannot allow Rosamund to believe she is saving my life by sacrificing her future. Only I, as one of William's trusted knights, will be able to convince William of de Silva's treachery. Only I will be able to make him believe that nuptials between Rosamund and de Silva represent only the first step in de Silva's true aspirations."

"The first step . . ."

"You do not truly believe de Silva will honor his word and allow me to live once his marriage to Rosamund takes place, do you? He will dispense with me as soon as it is convenient. Then he will threaten Rosamund into further silence, perhaps even using you as a weapon against her."

"What can I do? I have been ineffective in thwarting him thus far."

"I do not ask you to thwart him. You need only help me to shed these chains and escape. I have fought all my life to protect William. You may rest assured that I will fight with even greater vigilance to protect the woman who has captured my heart."

"Captured your heart . . ."

"Rosamund is *mine*. She will be wife to no man but me, and I will have no man gain influence over her in any way." His expression hardening with resolution, his voice deep and gruff, Dagan declared, "I love Rosamund. I have never met a woman her equal. I grew to cherish her courage as well as her skill while recuperating from my wounds. I discovered in her an innate honesty that went beyond the sham she was forced to live in order to avoid de Silva's attentions. I love her for the person she is—strong but giving, relentlessly determined but loving. I would not change her in any way, and I will not allow de Silva to attempt to claim all that she offers."

Pausing, Dagan continued more softly, "I want to show Rosamund that she need not overthrow William's rule in order to achieve her ends. I hope to prove to her that unlike de Silva, William's integrity has worth. I want the chance to explain to her that although I would never fail William, she is my life—a life I would share with no one but her."

Momentarily silent, Hadley responded, "I believe you speak from the heart, but I am old and nearly blind. What can I do?"

"Age and wisdom have earned you the respect of all within the shire. Your work on the cathedral has earned you the esteem of the workers there. In the short time that I labored there, I made valued friends among the workers. I ask that you use the respect you have earned to enlist a few who are willing to risk their lives to free me from this cell."

"They may not believe that Rosamund is the heiress of the shire."

"They will believe you if you show them the ring."

"The ring? What do you know about that?"

"Rosamund told me that the crest would identify her. I know she does not carry it with her, but I assume it is never far from her sight. I assume as well that you know where she keeps it."

"Yea, I do, but even should I be able to convince some to do as you say, de Silva has well-armed knights who fight diligently in his name. Any force I might raise would be ineffective against them."

"After freeing me, they need not linger, for I will take care of the rest."

Dagan watched as Hadley hesitated again, and then said, "I was asked to trust a Norman woman when Hyacinthe came to me. I am now asked to trust a Norman prisoner."

"Hyacinthe asked me to trust her as well. I admit to hesitating because she was formerly close to de Silva. Yet she has not betrayed me, and I will not betray you."

"She has not betrayed me either . . . *yet*."

Aware that Hadley's reservations remained, Dagan whispered, "Did I not work tirelessly for you while seeking to discover the truth of the situation here, instead of going directly to de Silva when I was well enough to declare myself? Did I not keep silent about Rosamund's true sex until de Silva inadvertently discovered it?"

"Yea, that is so."

"I ask you, Norman though I am and Norman that I will always be—do you honestly believe that I would now betray either Rosamund or you, or that I would allow anyone else to betray her?"

"Nay, I do not," Hadley admitted. "But the danger to Rosamund is even greater now that her secret is out. If the baron cannot marry her, he will doubtlessly attempt to kill her."

Dagan replied doggedly, "I will not allow that to happen. On my life, I give you that solemn promise."

The sound of footsteps in the corridor beyond the door brought a premature end to their conversation. Hadley turned as the door opened and Hyacinthe stepped into the doorway with the jailor behind her. She said with a forced smile, "We must leave before you are missed, Hadley."

"Yea . . . it is time."

Turning back toward Dagan briefly, Hadley whispered, "I will see what I can do."

"What did he say?" Hyacinthe's expression was tight when they emerged from the dungeon. They stepped out into the castle yard and slipped into the shadows, surprised by the rain that pelted them relentlessly. Her hair and clothing adhering to her body, Hyacinthe urged an equally soaked Hadley forward as she demanded, "Tell me what transpired."

"Dagan wants me to raise a force to free him."

Hyacinthe took a breath. "What was your answer?"

"I was uncertain. Most Saxons here have learned to value safety above honor."

"Until they are pushed too far. Although I have little else in common with them, I know that we all have limits." Her expression unyielding, Hyacinthe declared, "If you will do your part, I will do mine."

Hadley turned toward her to adjudge her sincerity as well as her meaning. Hyacinthe grimaced and said, "I have won a favored place with the jailor. Fool that he is, he trusts me because of the few intimacies I have allowed him. He does not realize that I left him wanting with a purpose in mind, so that I might aid whatever effort you devise. You have only to find a few men to help."

"A few men who are expected to overcome the jailor's crew, as well as de Silva's knights?"

"Surprise is a weapon that may prove effective."

"The jailor is dim-witted. He commands only a small force, but they are determined to the point of death not to surrender their underground kingdom."

"I will take care of the jailor. His men are but sheep who will be lost without their leader."

Hadley stood silently as the rain beat a relentless tattoo against the ground around them, turning a formerly hard-packed terrain into mud. He responded, "We must work quickly then. I fear for Rosamund."

"I fear for her as well."

Hadley's response was cold. "Pretense does not suit you. You do not care about Rosamund. You care only for vengeance."

"You are wrong. I have learned a valuable lesson. I will not allow the baron to turn one who has resisted him with all her strength into someone like me, who trusted and was betrayed. I do not know Rosamund, but I respect her as I do not respect myself."

Hadley offered gruffly, "You are too hard on yourself, Hyacinthe."

Her eyes brimming with sudden moisture, Hyacinthe responded, "You would not have said those words a few days ago."

"Perhaps not." Changing the subject, Hadley strained to see more clearly as the downpour continued. "Work at the site will have been curtailed by the storm. Take me back to my hut."

Hyacinthe rejoined, "I must warn you that the need for haste is paramount. The baron will work swiftly to secure his position here in William's eyes. He has already sent a messenger to the king with notification of his intention to wed Rosamund. He intends to accomplish all as quickly as possible so that Rosamund will not find time to thwart him."

"I will do the best I can."

"And you will allow me to help you?"

"Yea; in fact, I will depend on your help."

The silence that prevailed until they reached Hadley's hut was broken when Hyacinthe said unexpectedly, "Thank you."

"Why do you thank me?" Hadley frowned. "It is I who should thank you."

"I thank you because you have allowed me to make recompense for the wrongs I have done since I came here."

Silent for long moments, Hadley responded, "You are welcome."

He was still staring in her direction when Hyacinthe disappeared into the pounding rain.

"I will take her food to her." Aware that the supper hour was over but a tray had not yet been taken to the room Rosamund occupied, Hyacinthe offered, "She has not eaten yet. She will be hungry."

Evening shadows overwhelmed the kitchen as Edythe raised her wiry brows at Hyacinthe's offer and said, "It was not oversight on my part that delayed her tray. The baron commanded that she wait for her meals. Doubtless, it is his means of reminding her that she relies on him." She shook her head. "As for your offer to bring her tray . . . nay, I think not. I will take it instead."

Hyacinthe snickered under her breath, aware that the act would irritate Edythe as she responded, "*You* will take the baron's betrothed her tray this evening? You are jesting, are you not? Winifred has gone home for the day and you forget that there are many stairs to climb—narrow stairs that will make climbing difficult for a woman of your size and weight, even without the long day that you have spent on your feet."

Edythe sniffed. "I could do it if I wanted to, but perhaps I will have one of the servant lads take her food to her instead."

"One of the servant lads . . . true Saxons all. Can you trust that they will not respond to whatever wiles she chooses to use?"

"One of the baron's knights, then," Edythe countered stiffly.

"All of whom will not look very kindly on taking orders from you."

Edythe's face flushed a hot red as she snapped, "The baron's men do not resent me. I am considered a loyal Norman now."

"Not by them."

Edythe's gaze narrowed as she asked, "Why are you so determined to bring the baron's betrothed her supper tonight . . . so determined that you are willing to risk my displeasure in order to do it? What is your intention? Serving the woman who has displaced you, no matter how absurd the dreams that you cherished for so many years, cannot be a pleasant duty."

"On the contrary, I would enjoy seeing for myself a woman stupid enough to believe the baron's promises . . . a woman other than myself, that is."

Edythe scoffed at Hyacinthe's unexpected self-deprecation. She looked at Hyacinthe's bruises and said haughtily, "So you have learned a valuable lesson—obviously well taught."

"I admit my new attitude is partially due to the baron's teaching methods."

"And you would attempt to teach the baron's betrothed in the same manner."

"Nay, I but wish to see her . . . to feast my eyes on a true Saxon who will suffer the baron's faithlessness while bound to him in a way that I never was."

Edythe looked around her. She noted that the boys in the kitchen watched her out of the corners of their eyes in the obvious hope that they would be chosen to replace Winifred in delivering the evening meal. Nay, she could not trust them. She had seen the baron's betrothed in her female attire and knew they would be easily duped, not only because she was so fair, but by the fact that she was Saxon as they were. They would believe whatever she chose to tell them.

Making her decision, Edythe said, "All right; you may take the baron's betrothed her tray, but remember, you must not upset her or the baron will take his anger out on both of us."

"I will not upset her in any way."

Edythe's small eyes narrowed. "I trust you only because you are too smart to offend a man in the baron's position."

"And because the staircase is narrow, because your legs are tired from supporting your great weight throughout the day, and because—"

"That is enough!" Annoyed by Hyacinthe's repetition of her shortcomings, Edythe said, "Take this tray that I have prepared before the food grows even colder, but I warn you: Do not take the opportunity to go to the baron's quarters, for you will only receive more of the same from him if you do."

"I do not doubt that."

Snatching up the tray, Hyacinthe headed for the staircase. The broad smile that had curved her lips fell the moment she was out of sight.

Rosamund paused when she heard a step on the stairs beyond her door. She did not immediately recognize it, but the guard's voice was clear as he said, "Halt! The baron has ordered that no one is to enter his betrothed's room."

"Surely he did not mean me. I bring his darling her nightly repast."

Rosamund did not recognize the female voice as the guard responded laughingly, "*His darling?* Perhaps you call her that because the baron used that name for you . . . at certain times."

"Nay, at those times he called me his wench."

The guard's laughter rang again before he added, "But it appears all that is in the past, since your face bears the mark of his hand."

"Perhaps it is . . . but the baron has claimed to be finished with me before."

The guard responded lasciviously, "Why do you waste your time on dreams that will never come to fruition when a man such as I could do more for you than the baron ever could, Hyacinthe?"

Rosamund gasped. The guard had called the woman Hyacinthe. He was speaking to the servant who had followed the baron from Normandy.

Rosamund listened more closely as Hyacinthe responded with typical flirtatiousness. "Perhaps I will yet experience what you have to offer, but I have been assigned another task this evening, and this food grows cold."

"Cold food . . . long hours between paltry meals . . . solitude relieved only by his presence . . . the baron knows how to break a woman's resistance down slowly."

"Is that what he is doing?" Hyacinthe questioned. "I wondered."

"Did you really wonder, Hyacinthe?" The sudden interruption of a familiar voice startled Rosamund. She did not have to see the baron to know that he had appeared unexpectedly in the hallway.

De Silva's voice grew gruff as he said, "I thought I recognized your voice, Hyacinthe. Did I not order you from this keep? Did I not say I no longer wanted to set eyes upon you?"

"You said that, my lord," Hyacinthe returned flatly, "But you have said similar things to me before. I hoped to outwait your dismissal."

"Perhaps my blow was not convincing enough? Perhaps I should strike harder."

Hyacinthe replied, "Whatever you wish. I am your servant, my lord. I but await your pleasure."

The unexpectedness of Hyacinthe's reply was reflected in the baron's response when he ordered, "Begone! I will take my betrothed's tray in to her."

"That menial a task is beneath you, my lord," Hyacinthe replied adamantly.

"But it allows me quiet time with my betrothed."

Hyacinthe's voice hardened when she replied as unexpectedly as before, "You never needed an excuse to see me."

"That is true. But you were never a challenge to me and I became bored with you. Now, begone!"

Rosamund heard the rattling of a tray and the retreat of light footsteps. Then she heard the baron speak to the guard in a whisper before the door opened and he entered, bearing the tray.

Rosamund realized at that moment that she had never despised a man more.

Hyacinthe slowed her pace on the stairs just before reaching the kitchen. Pride caused her to wipe away the tears that the baron's words had raised before she entered with her head high.

Edythe could not hide her gleefulness when she asked, "What happened? Did the baron's betrothed throw you out of the room that he prepared for her?"

"Nay, I changed my mind and left the tray with her handsome guard."

"*Handsome,* eh? You are already casting your eyes for a replacement of the baron?"

"Perhaps." Shrugging, pretending that the knot inside her was not twisting tighter with every word, she asked, "Speaking of handsome men, where is Martin?"

"Are you referring to Sir Martin Venoir?"

"One and the same," Hyacinthe replied with a flippant shrug of her shoulders that she did not feel.

"He is gone."

"Gone?" Hyacinthe went still. "Where?"

"I cannot say, except that he asked me to prepare food for him to take with him. I have noticed his discomfort with the baron's handling of the situation here before. I can only assume he went home to Normandy, where life will be more to his liking."

"Oh."

Quick to assess her response, Edythe said, "It's too late if you hoped to seduce that fellow. You missed out on him because of your obsession with the baron."

"Martin and I were just friends."

"A woman like you never has male friends."

"A woman like me . . ." Hyacinthe laughed harshly and turned toward the door. She walked out into the yard, disregarding the rain that pounded against her skin as a deep sadness enveloped her. Edythe was correct: She had hoped to warn Rosamund that she must remain alert because an attempt would be made to rescue the man she loved from the dungeon, but even that selfless act had been thwarted. She supposed *a woman like her* had no right to expect more. And a woman like her had no right to expect a man like Martin Venoir to . . . really care.

Chapter Eleven

At this moment my efficient jailor is bringing your beloved his nightly fare. Make no mistake, the food is not of the same quality that you see on the tray before you. Nor does it match the quantity, but it will suffice to keep him alive if he decides to eat it before the other occupants of his cell become aware that it is there."

Staring at de Silva in the silence of her room—a silence broken only by his low snicker of laughter—Rosamund did not immediately respond. The day following her confinement had passed slowly. It had marked two days that had passed since Dagan's confinement in the dungeon below her luxurious accommodations.

Aware of the effect of his visits, the baron had made sure to allow no one to enter the room. He had delivered all sustenance himself, and had instructed that all other necessities be left at the door when he was not present to deliver them to her. He had engineered a seclusion where she depended solely on him.

Unexpected torrents of rain continued to deluge the area, turning the outdoors into a swamp of mud that prohibited further work on the cathedral. Rosamund cursed at the unexpected complication. She had wanted to see Hadley, to speak to him and ascertain what and how much he knew of the situation as it presently stood. Aware that he would be her only contact with the outside world, she had hoped desperately that she could convince him to help Dagan in some way, if only to forestall the plans of her marriage.

The one exception to the baron's rule of seclusion was the dressmakers who had arrived that morning despite the weather and brought all manner of luxurious cloth to stitch a new wardrobe for her. Obviously instructed not to converse with her, the seamstresses had done their work quickly while asking questions related only to the attire being constructed. She had almost gasped at the beauty of the fabric to be used for an extravagant lace wedding gown, which would be adorned with countless pearls and sparkling stones. She had barely restrained her tears, knowing that the beauteous garment would mark her wedding to a man she abhorred.

Rosamund knew that she was helpless under the baron's watchful eye, that he waited for her to become desperate enough to agree to anything he offered. She maintained her determination with sheer strength of will. Still, she wondered and hoped—

"You could improve your beloved's fare and make it become more palatable. You have only to say the word."

"What word would that be, my lord?" Rosamund replied tightly.

The baron came closer to the spot where she stood beside the tray he had delivered moments earlier. Aware that despite her hunger she would refuse to touch the food until he left, he smiled. "Words have power. I promised that we would not become intimate until the day we wed, but I admit that I find you even more appealing in your female attire . . . so much so that I might be convinced to improve the aspects of Dagan's imprisonment . . ."

"Words have power . . . yea, I agree." Unwilling to allow him to continue, Rosamund said solemnly, "For that reason, I tell you now that I will hold you to your word to keep Dagan alive and well if I marry you. However, I will never consent to anything more."

"You are a fool, Rosamund!" the baron replied. "You cannot hope to win out over me! You will surrender in the end. You will become my wife and produce my heirs, and you will refuse to acknowledge any of my paramours simply because in doing so, you will keep your lover alive. With that in mind, I ask again for you to say the word."

Rosamund briefly closed her eyes in an effort to control the rage surging through her. The man was vile. It was his design to strip her of all self-respect so that he might grind her people and the last of their resistance under his heels when he did. She would never let that happen.

Opening her eyes again, she said in a voice that trembled with restrained fury, "So you may never ask again, I repeat that I will hold you to your word, that I will keep mine, but that I will never consent to more." She asked coldly, "Was *consent* the word you were hoping for, my lord? Because I know that you can just as easily take what you ask me to give. If that is true, I hope you will keep my response in mind before making a similarly useless request again."

The baron's face froze. Rosamund saw his fist

clench . . . saw the absolute control he practiced in holding his arm against his side when he desired to strike her refusal of him from her lips. Yet she knew that any sign of disfigurement when they were wed would be an indication of coercion to William.

Yet she waited.

The baron turned abruptly on his heel, words obviously beyond him as he stalked out of her room without responding.

Surprisingly shaken, Rosamund felt the heat of unexpected tears when the door closed behind him. Brushing them from her cheeks, she trailed her fingertips against her lips. She closed her eyes, feeling Dagan's lips touching hers. His kiss was so real . . . as if he were suddenly there to hold her close. Yet his situation was so abominable. She wondered whether he thought of her now, just as she thought of him. She wondered if he had shared that moment . . . that kiss.

Dagan's struggles to free himself stopped short at the unexpectedly vivid memory of Rosamund's lips against his. He experienced her warmth . . . tasted her mouth . . . felt her love sweep over him.

Spurred on by those thoughts, Dagan struggled even harder at the manacles that bound him. He halted when blood dripped from his chafed wrists, aware that the scent would attract the silent, skulking rodents inhabiting his cell.

He stared at the tray left within his reach by the arrogant jailor a few minutes earlier. He raised the chipped bowl to his lips and choked on the watery, tasteless gruel as he swallowed determinedly. He then bit off a piece of the moldy bread that lay beside it, resolved to maintain his strength for the battle to come.

The battle to come . . . Dagan frowned at the thought. Two days had passed and he had heard nothing from Hadley. His jailor had spoken to him for the first time that morning, tormenting him with the news that dressmakers had arrived to fashion Rosamund's gown for a wedding that would take place as soon as the gown was completed. The thought had nearly driven him mad. Tormenting him further was the fact that time was a mitigating factor in the plan he had forged with Hadley, yet he had had no communication from him. What was Hadley doing? Was the plan they had discussed underway, or had he been somehow thwarted?

Dagan felt his frustration soar. He was manacled hand and foot by chains that limited his movement; he was confined in a lightless, airless cell that defied description; he was helpless, with powerful friends unaware of his situation. Yet Rosamund, his love, was depending on him as he had once depended on her.

"I tried, but the attempt failed. I could not warn her."

Soaked to the skin, Hyacinthe spoke from the doorway of Hadley's hut. When another day passed and renewed efforts to speak to Rosamund were in vain, she had waited until her work in the kitchen was done for the day and had used the heavy rain as her shield as she raced to his hut to speak to him. She had hoped desperately that Hadley had fared better than she in his plans to aid Dagan, yet one look at the old man's haggard face was more revealing than words.

"What happened? Did you speak to those who might help you?"

"I did. I defied the rain with the help of my good friend, Horace, and visited the huts of the workers here. With the exception of a few, all refused me. Dagan is a Norman. There are few who are willing to risk their lives on his word."

"The ring . . . the crest that proves Rosamund's true identity . . ."

"The Saxons recognized the crest on the ring I took from Rosamund's hiding place. They believed what I had to say. Only they were willing to help, but they are few and it will take too long to raise an army of other believers from the surrounding countryside. Their help would come too late to halt the baron's marriage plans."

"How many workers at the construction site agreed to help?"

"Five, excluding myself and Horace."

"Five . . ."

"Five against a vicious crew of jailors who live in the dungeon quarters . . . five against an army of knights trained to fight on the baron's behalf."

Momentarily speechless, Hyacinthe raised her chin. "Five will be enough."

"Wha . . . what are you saying? Five brave men and two old men against a well-trained army?"

"Five brave men, two old men . . . and one woman." Hyacinthe raised her chin with determination. "I will disable the jailor and his crew. It will not be difficult; I have his trust."

"But how?"

"I make no explanations, but I will do it, I promise

you that. I will immobilize those men, but it will be up to your brave followers to help."

"Help . . . how? We have no weapons . . . no training."

"I can provide weapons. All your men need do is provide Dagan with the time he needs."

"Dagan needs more than time."

"Time that is not on his side, old man! Believe me when I say that the baron will dispense with him as soon as the vows between Rosamund and he are sanctioned. Dagan will die in that dungeon. He may yet die if he is freed, but at least this way he has a chance."

Hyacinthe felt Hadley's scrutiny. She held her breath awaiting his response.

"Tomorrow morning . . . I will arrange to raise the willing five to the task when it is once again light and we will have no trouble seeing our way. If it is still storming, surprise will be on our side, but even if it is not, work on the cathedral will not progress until the mud hardens underfoot."

Hyacinthe nodded. "Come to the staircase to the dungeon at dawn. I will tell you and your men when it is safe to enter."

"I tell you now that safe or not, the five are committed."

Committed. Hyacinthe smiled at that word. She had been *committed* to a relationship that had never existed. She had been *committed* to a man unworthy of her fealty. She had been *committed* to a life that had been promised in moments of passion but would never come to fruition.

She was now wiser, more determined . . . and she was still *committed*.

The word pleased her.

Dagan awoke slowly in the dank cell. Still manacled, he moved stiffly and stood up to flex shoulder muscles cramped by inactivity and stretch his legs as far as his chains allowed. He pushed back the heavy hair that had fallen forward on his forehead, noting that the chaffed skin beneath his manacles was still raw. No good could come of open wounds, and months spent in the dank cell would work as effectively on him as an opponent's sword.

Suddenly alert, Dagan heard a female voice in the corridor beyond his door. He stilled upon recognizing the woman's accent. It was Hyacinthe, de Silva's former lover. He strained to hear, only to be shocked when the cell door opened and the jailor entered bearing a heavily loaded tray. Hyacinthe was at his heels.

The jailor said with a hint of ridicule, "See the beautiful tray that Hyacinthe has prepared for me and the men here." The jailor waved the tray just out of his reach as he continued, "I know you are hungry. I volunteered to eat it all in front of you so that you might enjoy the repast with me, but Hyacinthe has other plans. She would rather that I shared what she brought with the other men in my crew so they might esteem her as much as I do." He paused, his smile falling as he glanced at her and said, "I have told Hyacinthe that I will share the food, but I will not share her."

Slipping her arm through his, Hyacinthe tossed her hair as she responded playfully, "I do not want you to share me, either. Come, I have had enough of this prisoner. There is another man I fancy instead."

Dagan watched as his two visitors left and then sat abruptly. His stomach was growling and he was holding his aching head in his hands some time later when he heard the key turn in the lock. He rose when Hyacinthe entered and approached him with the jailor's keys in her hand.

"The jailor and most of his crew ate the food I brought to break their fast, and they will bother us no longer. Five of Hadley's men will restrain the others." Hyacinthe handed him a sword and said, "The rest is up to you."

"Where did you get this weapon?"

"It is best that you do not know where I obtained this one or the others that Hadley's men bear."

Hyacinthe unlocked the manacles on his wrists and ankles. When he was free at last, Dagan said, "You may rest assured that I will not forget your bravery."

Hyacinthe retorted unexpectedly, "I am not brave. Bravery is a noble emotion felt by noble people . . . not by people like me. I have simply faced a difficult truth for the first time, and hope to make amends."

"However you wish to see it." Dagan frowned when he said, "I need to know where Rosamund is being held."

"She is in a special room the baron has had prepared for her in the keep. It will not be difficult to find. Merely climb the stairs and look for the door where knights stand guard."

"She will not be a prisoner much longer."

With those resolute words, Dagan walked through

the door of his cell. Close behind him, Hyacinthe directed him to the outside entrance to the dungeon through which he might emerge unseen, and Dagan climbed the stairs warily.

Hadley's loyal men still struggled with the jailors. Unwilling to wait for any help that might be forthcoming, Dagan stepped out alone into the pouring rain and stood there briefly. Ripping off his filthy shirt, he exposed the full breadth of his muscular chest to the elements and allowed the pounding raindrops to wash away all trace of his incarceration. Revived and restored at last, Dagan straightened up to his full height. He pushed back his hair, blinked away the water that clung to his dark lashes, and gripping his weapon, started forward.

Edythe gasped at the flurry of motion that ensued when the dungeon prisoner called Dagan appeared unexpectedly in the kitchen doorway. Stripped to the waist and brandishing his sword in the manner of a man accustomed to its weight, he halted the knights emerging from their room with a glance. He warned, "Think carefully before attempting to best a swordsman who has stood at William's back through many battles. Know that in attacking me, you attack him. Know that I do not delight in ending the life of any man who has fought for William because in our loyalty to him, we are brothers. Yet I am sworn to the use of my sword in his name, and I will use it in my own name as well. I will not hesitate to smite any man who becomes my enemy."

The charge that followed was unexpected. It sent

Edythe scurrying to the corner of the kitchen as Dagan dodged and feinted, swinging his sword without fear. Holding off his attackers, he isolated them from each other with his superior skill until he cut each of them down, one by one. Then Dagan turned to fix his gaze on other of de Silva's men who emerged into the kitchen. Edythe saw the men fall back in disbelief at the carnage that met their gaze while Dagan stood motionless and undaunted. They remained frozen when Dagan raced to the staircase and, within moments, had climbed out of sight.

"Why do you hesitate to eat the repast I brought for you, Rosamund?"

"A better question is, why are you here so early in the morn?" Rosamund's response was tight. She had not expected to be shaken awake by the baron. Nor had she been expecting that he would come bearing a full tray so early in the day, accustomed as she was to waiting for her food. Her suspicions raised, she asked bluntly, "What do you have in mind, my lord?"

De Silva responded with an attempt to lighten his response. "I have considered your reply to my offer yesterday and have come to the conclusion that the promises I first made to you were given under duress and should not be considered binding. Since we are now betrothed, I have also come to the conclusion that I should be allowed certain liberties."

"Promises . . . betrothed . . . *liberties?* Say what you mean, my lord."

Stepping closer, until he stood only a hairsbreadth from her, the baron said softly, "I am saying that you are a beautiful, desirable woman presently under my protection. I will soon take you to wife, but I intend to sample all you have to offer beforehand to ensure that you meet my expectations."

"Expectations?" Rosamund laughed aloud. "You gain the good will of William and of my people with this marriage, while I have only your word that Dagan will be allowed to live. If there is one who might be cheated by this marriage, it is I."

"You will not be cheated, Rosamund," the baron replied confidently. "You will be bound to a man who will exceed the one you protect in every way . . . *every way*."

Tensing, Rosamund replied, "I do not wish to discuss the merits of the agreement we have struck. I wish only—"

"You do not understand, Rosamund." Growing more aggressive, the baron clasped her close as he continued, "It is not a matter of what you wish any longer. I have been too easy with you. I will now show you the kind of man I am—and you will come begging!"

"Begging!" Enraged, Rosamund managed to free her arms. She scratched and clawed, fighting wildly as the baron attempted to subdue her. Aware that she was weakening, she was near panic when the sounds of struggle in the outer hallway caught the baron's attention. Releasing her, he grasped the sword at his waist and turned in time to see the door open. She saw the shock that rocked him when Dagan stepped into the opening.

Glaring, his bared chest heaving, and his sword dripping blood, Dagan said, "You made a mistake in challenging William's rule, de Silva, and you made a mistake in challenging me. Recant now and save your life."

"Recant?" Laughing aloud, the baron did not bother to say more as he charged forward, swinging his blade.

The clash of weapons rocked the room as Rosamund stood still, mesmerized by the heat of the deadly encounter. Sounds of heavy breathing, grunts, and crashing swords echoed in the silent space as the opponents bobbed and weaved, each avoiding his opponent's thrusts with practiced skill. Their bodies grew slick with perspiration and the blood that dripped freely from their wounds as the conflict raged on.

With a spontaneous intake of breath, Rosamund noted the exact moment when the baron appeared to weaken under Dagan's relentless assault. His expression grew frenzied and his breathing became labored as he lunged more wildly and less accurately, until the tide of battle began turning in Dagan's favor.

Unrelenting, Dagan allowed no quarter until with a deft, almost indiscernible thrust, he knocked the baron backward onto the floor and the man's sword went flying.

Rosamund swallowed as Dagan paused over his defenseless opponent, his chest heaving and his sword at the baron's throat. She saw blood trail from the tip of Dagan's sword and paused, realizing that the man she saw standing there with bloodlust in his eyes, with hatred in his heart, and without a trace of mercy in his expression, was a man she did not know. She recognized him as one of the many who had invaded their small shire and cut down those who had stood up in its defense.

He was a stranger.

Rosamund stepped back, ready to turn away. She was startled by the sound of Dagan's voice when he rasped, "Despite your many attempts to kill me, de Silva, I hesitate to take the life of a man who has served William well. I give you one last chance to relent, to renounce—"

Rosamund jumped with a start when Franchot Champlain appeared at Dagan's back and struck a blow that glanced off the side of his head, knocking him to the floor. Watching in horror as Champlain raised his sword again to deliver a fatal blow, she reacted instinctively by grasping a heavy poker lying nearby and swinging it heartily at Champlain.

Rosamund did not wait for the man to fall before moving to Dagan's side and crouching over him with her heart pounding. Blood streamed from the wound on his head, but she saw his eyelids flutter. He was alive, but still dazed, when the baron drew himself to his feet.

Swearing under his breath at the sight of Champlain lying unconscious nearby, de Silva looked at Dagan and gasped, "I will not kill you here. Instead, I will have my men return you to the dungeon, where I will see to it that you die slowly at the hands of the jailor who awaits you there."

Rosamund screamed, "Nay, you will not!"

She stood up as the baron raced toward the door. She followed him, fighting him every step of the way as he started to descend the stairs. Furious, he turned toward her, about to shout a command, when he lost his footing and tumbled head over heels onto the lower landing—where he hit with a crack.

All movement within the keep halted at the sound.

Rosamund turned as Dagan drew himself to his feet, still partially dazed as he walked to the top of the stairs. He glanced at Champlain, where the knight lay motionless on the floor behind him, then at de Silva, where he lay at the bottom of the stairs. When Rosamund moved into his embrace, he held her close.

Sobbing with joy, Rosamund reveled in the feel of Dagan's mouth on hers. Then she drew back, remaining at his side when he picked up his sword and descended the staircase.

She watched as Dagan looked up at William's knights, who had taken over the kitchen under Martin Venoir's command. It took only a moment for him to assess the situation as Martin saluted him soberly then awaited his orders. Raising his voice so it might be clearly heard, Dagan said, "All those who would stand in William's defense, say aye!"

Ayes echoed loudly, with no man among de Silva's soldiers abstaining, and Dagan nodded. Speaking for the first time to Martin, he ordered, "Take the baron's body away. Have him prepared for a soldier's burial—for whatever he eventually became, he was once one of William's finest."

Turning his back as the men moved to his command, Dagan drew Rosamund into the hallway. Unseen, he held her close against him as he looked down at her and whispered earnestly, "I love you, Rosamund. You are my life, my dreams for the future, my hope. I willingly risk my life for you, and if it takes the rest of that time, I will prove that our futures lie together."

"You have already proven to me what you are, Dagan." Her eyes filled with the love she could no longer deny, Rosamund whispered, "Norman though you are, and Saxon that I will always remain, I can make only one reply . . . that I am yours."

Rosamund closed her eyes when Dagan's lips met hers, and the beauty of their love overwhelmed her. The simple words she had spoken trailed through the back of her mind in solemn litany as Dagan's kiss deepened.

Norman though you are, and Saxon that I will always remain . . . I am yours.

Yea, she was his . . . forever.

Epilogue

I thought you had returned to Normandy. I had not believed I would ever see you again."

Hyacinthe smiled uncertainly at Martin Venoir where he stood opposite her in the castle yard. Weeks had passed since the final clash between Dagan and de Silva when Martin had returned heading a contingent of knights sent directly from William to rescue Dagan. In the time since, Martin had stood steadfastly at Dagan's side while he buried de Silva, emptied the dungeons of prisoners, and saw to it that the construction of the cathedral resumed with proper recompense for all.

Uncertain and unwilling to broach the silence between Martin and herself, Hyacinthe had watched approvingly, yet with a deadening ache inside when she thought of her own, vague future. The wedding between Rosamund and Dagan was only a day away when Martin surprised her by appearing behind her in the yard.

Her heart pounding, Hyacinthe waited for him to speak.

Obviously as uncertain as she, Martin responded cautiously to her greeting. "I want you to know that it was never my intention to abandon my post here and return to Normandy as you assumed, Hyacinthe.

Instead, I felt my only recourse was to go to William as one of his knights and inform him of Dagan's imprisonment, as well as of the baron's true activities in this area."

Hyacinthe's eyes filled unexpectedly as she replied, "You and your men arrived in time to help Dagan and aid in the changes here. I thank you for that."

"You do realize that none of it might have been accomplished, if not for you."

"Because of my vengeful acts . . ."

"Was it vengeance, Hyacinthe?" Martin took a step toward her, his brown-eyed gaze intent. "Or was it instead an instinctive sense of decency that welled up inside you once you were no longer beholden to the monster de Silva had become?"

"*Sense of decency* . . . me?" Hyacinthe short laugh was devoid of mirth as she added, "You know what I am. You know how I became that person, and you know what I have done."

"What have you done, Hyacinthe? You have merely followed the man you loved . . . the man you believed de Silva to be . . . the man to whom you wished to dedicate the rest of your life. When you found that he was not worthy of your love, you attempted to gain recompense."

"Yea, I did that in the only way open to me." Silently aware that Martin understood her like no other, Hyacinthe said, "Yet here I am, still a servant in a strange country . . . still uncertain . . . still alone despite the many admirers who have offered to ease my way."

Taking another step, Martin gripped Hyacinthe's arms tightly as he whispered, "You need not be alone.

You need not be uncertain, and you need not remain in a country where you feel an outsider."

Noting that Martin's gaze had dropped briefly to her lips, Hyacinthe swallowed tightly. Her heart began pounding. "I do not feel that Hendsmille is my home, yet I cannot leave here. The truth is that I have no place to go and no one to take me in."

"That is not true," Martin whispered. "I have always seen the good in you, Hyacinthe. I have always known that you were innocent in de Silva's exploitation of you."

"I was not innocent."

"Yea, you were. You believed in him until the end, while I became aware of the duplicity he practiced much earlier."

"Yet you stayed with him." Hyacinthe shook her head. "Why?"

Martin replied, "Do you truly not know that I stayed because of you . . . because you turned to me when in doubt, because you depended on me to be there and felt the loss when I was not, and because I was bound by my feelings for you?"

"You have always been a beloved friend."

Martin's dark brows knitted at her statement. He replied, "I went to William when I knew I could no longer be of use to you here. I returned with his men, ready to fight de Silva to the death if necessary, but found only a lost shire where chaos had been settled by fate when de Silva tumbled down the stairs and broke his neck. I knew you would be affected by his death, no matter his attitude toward you before he died. For that reason, I forced myself to allow you time to grieve, but I need to speak to you now because it is time for me to leave."

"Leave!"

Her spirits plummeting, Hyacinthe remained silent as Martin continued, "I have already informed Dagan that I intend to go back to Normandy after his wedding to Rosamund, that I have decided it is the best place for me to start my life over, with the past behind me."

Her sense of loss was acute when Hyacinthe asked quietly, "You intend to leave here . . . never to return?"

"Yea, I do. William has already made a place for me there."

Hyacinthe attempted a smile. "I will miss you, Martin."

"That is not my intention." Taking a breath, Martin continued, "It is my heartfelt hope that you will return to Normandy with me."

Stunned, Hyacinthe could not miss Martin's earnest fervor when he rasped, "I have always loved you, Hyacinthe. I can think of no future without you, and no woman I would feel prouder to call my wife."

"Your *wife*?"

"You will learn to love me, Hyacinthe." Martin drew her close against the length of his hard-muscled body and whispered, "I will be good to you. I will make a decent home for you, one like you have never known, and I will love you all my life."

"Martin . . ."

"Do not refuse me, Hyacinthe," Martin said hoarsely, "Do not crush the dream I have cherished longer than you realize."

Tears overflowing her dark eyes, Hyacinthe whispered in return, "I have no desire to crush your dreams as mine were crushed, Martin. Yet I have always considered you a friend. The emotion that I feel for you bears no resemblance to that which I bore for Guilbert, even though I feel more honored by your love than I was ever honored by his, though I feel safer with you than I ever felt with him, and though I feel a sense of peace when I look into your eyes, when his gaze never set me at rest."

"That is something to build on, is it not?"

"I do not know, Martin. Is it?"

"Yea, it is."

Hyacinthe paused at Martin's response. Cupping his cheek with her hand, she replied, "Another truth I did not dare mention is that I have found my life surprisingly empty without you."

Martin asked with hope bright in his eyes, "So you are saying . . ."

"I am saying that I do not deserve you, Martin; but, in truth, I cannot see a future for me without you as a part of it."

"Which means . . ."

"Which means I find that I have no choice in what I must do, since I cannot bear to be separated from you. Yea, whether worthy or not, I will be your wife if you would have me, Martin. And I will be honored and thankful—"

Martin cut short Hyacinthe's reply with his kiss. She felt his love, and her heart swelled. It was a love that she had not expected. It was a love that she did not feel she truly deserved. Yet more important to her than the heartfelt words Martin had spoken was the simple moment when he drew back from his kiss and raised her hand reverently to his lips before clasping it tight in a gesture more binding than a vow.

Her throat thick with unshed tears, Hyacinthe knew that together, Martin and she would share a future filled with love, and that through him, hers would be the future of which she had always dreamed.

The day was brilliantly lit with sunshine. A fresh cover of green blanketed the ground as Dagan and Rosamund stood in the newly constructed altar of the cathedral being built in Hendsmille. Her eyes glowed pure silver with joy, and her delicate features were flushed with emotion as she clutched Dagan's hand tightly. Radiant in the same sumptuous gown that had once brought her to tears, she looked lovingly at Dagan. She saw only him, her bridegroom, resplendent in a luxurious garment of pale gray fitted expertly to his massive proportions. His piercing amber gaze raked over her hungrily, and his raven-black hair was swept back from strong features still bearing the marks of battle in her defense. She swallowed at the realization that the words they would soon speak would bind this handsome man to her for the rest of their lives—lives filled with truth and honor . . . and with love.

So enraptured was Rosamund that she was as unconscious of William's presence in the gallery as she was of the assembly of Saxons who had come to witness the ceremony that would bind them forever to William as their sire. She was grateful that peace had come to the shire with William's decision to award to Dagan all of de Silva's holdings as a wedding present, thereby blending the old with the new, and she was happy, knowing that the children she would bear Dagan would be the first in a long line that would eventually bring an end to the harsh feelings stirred by William's invasion.

Most of all, Rosamund was happy because she loved Dagan. She loved him for his strength, for his honesty, and for the inborn decency that made her certain that in marrying him, she had truly fulfilled her reason for being.

Dagan looked down at Rosamund as she repeated her vows. He saw the beautiful woman she had become and was filled with wonder. He felt her happiness and sensed tentative acceptance and approval from her people . . . from men and women who would soon become *their* people.

Taking her hand as the friar pronounced them man and wife, Dagan took Rosamund into his arms, knowing that fate had somehow destined her for him. He kissed her deeply and cherished the moment, aware that in the blending of their hearts and bodies, there would be peace in Hendsmille at last.

Bonnie Vanak

"...[writes] thrilling adventures, clever plots and unforgettable characters!"   —*Romantic Times BOOKreviews*

The Lady & the Libertine

Read ahead for a sneak peak.

Chapter One

Khamsin camp, Eastern desert of Egypt, 1908

He would not be the virile groom tenderly deflowering her on their wedding night. Her virgin breasts, hidden beneath the white *kuftan*, he would never caress, causing a sigh of passion to wring from her slender throat. The sparkling ruby dangling between them stood out like a blood droplet against a snowy bank. His hands, accustomed to stroking the skin of whores, were not worthy of touching her.

They were, however, quite capable of stealing the ruby, as they had swiped other priceless Egyptian antiquities.

Crouched beneath the shade of a cigar-shaped ben-tree, Nigel Wallenford, rightful earl of Claradon, studied his prey as he clutched an oily rifle in his sweating palms. The silent woman picked up scattered seeds on the ground. Karida was her name. She guarded the ruby he needed to complete the key and locate the treasure of the sleeping golden mummies. All week, during his visit here on the pretext of buying Arabian mares, he'd heard her relatives praise her virtue and honor as if she were not a living, breathing woman but a limestone statue. Nigel wouldn't have cared if she was as corrupt as he; he cared only about the ruby.

Ben-trees, acacia trees, and yellow-green plants peppered the water source near the Khamsin camp. The burning yellow sun played off jagged mountain peaks and peach-colored hills of sandstone. A cooling breeze chased away the sultry afternoon heat shimmering off the tawny sands. Black mountains and endless desert ringed this part of Egypt's eastern desert.

Jabari bin Tarik Hassid, the Khamsin sheikh, thought Nigel was currently at the water source to kill desert hares, but he had chosen the spot to pursue Karida. Each afternoon since his arrival, she came here to gather seeds. Like a good hunter, he'd learned her habits, knew her movements. Like a hare struck down by a bullet, Karida would never know what hit her. The ruby would soon be his.

Karida kept stealing glances at him. Her face, hidden by a half-veil out of courtesy to the visiting al Assayra tribesmen, was expressionless.

A good hunter knew how to disarm his prey, make them feel false security. Nigel set down the rifle and offered his most charming smile. He gestured to the bullet-hard seeds she dropped into her goatskin bag but kept his gaze centered on the ruby. His fingers itched to swipe the stone. Soon. "Are those for eating?"

Karida blinked, as if startled to hear a human voice. "Samna. Cooking oil." Like her Uncle Ramses and the rest of her family, she spoke perfect English. Yet her accent was odd, as if she'd lived somewhere other than here in Egypt. "I'm marrying tonight. This will be my last time gathering the seeds." She gave a little sigh, as if pondering her fate.

"Do you love him?' Nigel blurted, then could have kicked himself. A rude question. But he was a foreigner; maybe she'd forgive him.

"I do not know him." Karida gave a little laugh, as sweet and musical as the jingling of gold bracelets. "I was informed

I was chosen as a bride, but I don't know who has chosen me. All the al Assayra warriors are honorable and noble, however, and so my husband will be." Her large, golden-brown eyes, so exotic and mysterious, seemed to pierce him. "He will never lie to me or steal, and he will be admirable all his days."

Nigel stared at Karida in sudden bleakness, feeling the shadows of old ghosts smother him. She was so damn perfect, an angel compared to the demon lurking inside him. His gaze dropped to his hands, and he rubbed them violently against his khaki trousers, knowing he wasn't fit to touch her.

You would never marry me. I can't father your children. My own sire lied about my birthright because I was sterile, and though I was older, I could not give him an heir like my twin brother. I wouldn't give you my heart, but I could steal away yours.

Or worse. I could kill you.

Screams echoed down a rocky mountainside in Nigel's mind, then silence. Nigel tensed against the memory, guilt swallowing his soul until nothing remained but an inky darkness. He could just shoot Karida, take the damn stone, and leave her corpse here, festering in the blistering heat. One more crime to add to his list.

She glided over to a small brown rock to pluck out the few seeds scattered there. Each movement held an inborn grace. As sinuous as a serpent, so lovely. Unlike Nigel, Karida was not scarred from painful surgeries to fix an arm that would never work quite right. Her skin was flawless, her body smooth and unmarked.

Her exotic gaze centered on him as she straightened. "You won't see many hares at this time. It's too hot. Like the scorpions and the vipers, they like to hide."

"Like Englishmen should," he joked. "Ground's hot

enough to poach an egg."

His gaze dropped to her feet, and he wondered if her toes and ankles were as perfect as the rest of her. Fabric billowed in a sudden gust of wind as the gods answered his prayers, revealing a flash of shapely ankles and well-shaped feet in silver sandals. Nigel licked his lips, imagining his fingers stroking her delicate skin and tickling her toes.

As she moved toward the tree, his eyes caught a sudden movement in the rocky sand. "Christ, watch out!" he yelled.

He raced forward, hooked an arm about her waist, swept her off her feet, and waltzed her away as if they were dancing in a ballroom. The goatskin bag tumbled from her fingers and fell to the ground with a smack just as the viper's head emerged from its sandy nest. Fangs struck the bag instead of her ankle.

Trembling, she remained in his embrace. Nigel became aware of those soft breasts pressed against his chest, the rapid pounding of her heart. A fragrance of orange blossoms and almonds filled his nostrils. For a wild moment, he wanted to rest his cheek against the top of the scarf covering her head and stay there, holding her in his arms.

Reluctantly he set her down and turned, watching the snake disturbed from its afternoon nap. He hunted for a rock to kill it.

"Use this."

Karida handed Nigel a nearby stick he'd seen the Khamsin use for shaking acacia leaves loose to feed their camels and sheep. He grasped it, and his fingers tentatively brushed hers. Nigel trembled violently at the sizzling contact.

Drawing in a sharp breath, he curtly told her to stand back. He lifted the sturdy pole to strike the viper. It lifted its head and, for a moment, its cold, beady gaze seemed to reflect the blackness inside him. Then Nigel struck. Again and again he beat the snake, even after it lay motionless on the ground. Blow after blow, the misery and self-loathing inside him exploded like gunpowder.

A gentle hand tugging on his jacket sleeve caused him to stop. "That's enough, Thomas. I think it's past dead."

Her gentle, teasing tone caught him off guard, almost as much as her use of his false name. Nigel tossed away the stick and turned to stare at her. Dryness filled his mouth.

Bloody hell, she was beautiful. Pure as polished ivory. Radiant as the sun. His gaze dropped to his hands. Hands that killed more than just snakes. Nigel scrubbed them against his trousers.

"Are you all right?" he asked hoarsely.

Karida gave a little nod. She stared back with frank interest. Rapt, he leaned forward. Was it his imagination, a trick of fading sunlight, or did her eyes widen as if she liked what she saw and wanted him as well?

His pulse quickened. Nigel wished he could see more of her face. Was her mouth thin and flat? Did she have a wart on her nose? The flimsy veil was a fabric barrier between his curiosity and answers. *Take it off*, he silently ordered. He began chanting in his mind: *Take it off*.

Karida unhooked the veil and let the fabric flutter down. Breath hitched in Nigel's throat.

Good God. No warts. Nothing but honey-toned smooth skin, a face sculpted by the Egyptian goddess Isis herself. A pert nose, full lips in a cupid's bow, elegant cheekbones, and the most startling caramel eyes he'd ever seen. As her long fingers smoothed over her cheek and she tilted her head, he watched with rapt fascination. Such grace. Her every movement was elegant as a winged ibis taking flight.

His gaze fell to her rounded chin that nonetheless hinted of stubborn pride. The contrast between her graceful femininity and the arrogance of that little chin stirred his blood.

She looked like a fighter. He wondered if she would prove such in bed, wrapping her limbs about his hips as he drove into her, nails raking down his back as she hissed and bit in a fury of desperate need. Blood surged hotly through his veins as he indulged this wild imagining. She was his bride and, on their wedding night, she shyly removed her robes to bare her lovely body for his pleasure.

Nigel's lids lowered, and he daydreamed about cupping her breasts with absolute reverence, their heaviness resting in his palms as he gently kneaded, showering her with tender, adoring kisses. Making love to her through the night, he coaxed shrill cries of pleasure from those rose-red lips, waking up to her in the morning and knowing she was exclusively his, that he'd forever marked her with his passion and she'd never forget him…even though he was a lying dog and she was a beautiful princess.

He shook free of the daydream as she reattached her veil. He turned away, knowing she was a woman of honor bound to marry a man of honor. A sweet innocent like Karida would never lower herself to be with him. The women in his bed were always whores, or liars just like him. His gaze dropped to his thieving fingers. It was time to do what he must. He was in desperate need of money.

In a desert cave was locked a map leading to stolen treasure as vast as King Solomon's. Nigel had the scorpion charm and needed only the ruby, the missing stone atop the stinger, to acquire the map. He soon would return to England, find proof he was the true heir, and drop this absurd masquerade as his twin; the title would be his, the earldom of Claradon, and afterward he'd seek the treasure and become wealthier than the pharaohs.

Tension knotted his stomach as he remembered a hopeful, gaunt face waiting for him in England. Little hands, calloused and scarred by hard labor, eyes far too sad. Damn it all, he was a sinner, not a saint, but he'd get that gold and for once in his miserable life do something right.

Karida had turned to retrieve her dropped goatskin bag. Nigel fished in his pocket for the fake necklace that would replace the treasure around her slender neck. He swallowed hard, but his hand shook violently as he reached out to her.

Silently, he cursed. *Just do it, damn it.*

He had taken but a step forward when he heard a distant thunder. Again, Nigel silently cursed. Too late.

Karida whirled, pivoting like a ballet dancer he'd once seen on stage. Her gaze went strangely flat as a small cluster of Khamsin warriors rode up. Clouds of dust swirled around their horses' hooves. A proud, regal-looking man clad in the indigo *binish* and loose trousers of a Khamsin warrior dismounted with grace. It was Nuri, Karida's father. He gave Nigel a friendly nod.

"Karida, it is time to prepare for the marriage capture."

"Yes, Father." She gestured to Nigel. "Thomas abandoned his watch for the desert hare and caught a viper instead. He saved me."

Gratitude and praises were showered on him, making Nigel's stomach churn with disgust. He accepted their thanks but ruminated in dark amusement that he should learn from the viper's fate. Get too close to Karida, and he, too, would lose everything.

He went to collect his rifle and the goatskin of water he'd brought, turning both physically and mentally away from Karida. Money was all that mattered. Women did not. Especially a woman he could never have, with a full, sensual mouth made for kisses and startlingly clear eyes as exotic as the pyramids. He had one last chance: tonight when she was wed. After that, she would depart with her husband and forever escape the grasp of his dirty hands.

By tonight he'd have the ruby in his possession, and by tomorrow he'd have forgotten her name. So he fervently hoped.

Today was her wedding day, and they were staring at her again.

Back straight as the palm tree shading her, Karida bint Ali Sharif kept her gaze focused upon nothing. Better to pretend aloofness among the other brides awaiting the marriage capture, especially when she was the object of their gossip.

Hot color flushed her cheeks. Whispers rang like shouts in her ears as the women waited for the men to arrive:

"How can any warrior want her? They say she is incapable of bearing children."

"Scarred, and she can't conceive. My mother says she does not bleed each month!"

"Poor Karida. This is the only way she can find a husband. Such a burden to her parents. I wonder if they regret her coming from England and becoming part of their family."

The whispers she could endure. Gossip was hurtful, but she'd endured far worse. Hunger. Beatings. Cold, stark prison walls. Her heart squeezed nonetheless. She was approaching twenty-three, and no Khamsin warrior wanted to marry her. They regarded her as an oddity: the foreigner brought from England by their sheikh's bodyguard, Ramses, who told them she was related to the earl of Smithfield, his wife's father. Even after Ramses's brother Nuri took her into his family, the others treated her differently. Prospective grooms rejected her after hearing the whisper that she was incapable of bearing children. This marriage capture, arranged by the Khamsin sheikh, was indeed her only chance.

Never mind the stares. They always stared at her. For the

first year at the Khamsin camp, Karida had gotten even by stealing from the tribe, resorting back to the ways of the English workhouse where she had lived. She had lied and stolen until the day she'd swiped a pretty ruby necklace from her Uncle Ramses. Expecting a beating like she'd gotten in the workhouse, she'd cringed when Nuri discovered her crime. Instead he had taken her to Ramses, who gave her the ruby and charged her with the important task of guarding both it and the treasure map it was said to unlock. He challenged her to change and become a person of honor, because he trusted and believed in her. That was ten years ago. She now stood to marry a man of honor. No one else would do.

Vibrant energy thrummed through the camp's more than one thousand tribal members. Women fetching water in goatskin bags or making cheese from goat's milk were laughing and talking more than usual. The delicate aroma of jasmine scented the air around the brides.

Men from the al Assayra tribe would soon "raid" the Khamsin maidens. That Bedouin tribe, which lived near the western oasis of Bahariya, had sent warriors here to select eligible women. The Khamsin allowed this marriage capture in order to honor the al Assayra's tradition, but each previously selected maiden would give her silent consent by offering her hand when a warrior approached. Afterward the men would carry off their "captured" women. The warriors would pay their would-be brides' fathers the *kalim*, the bride price. Then the wedding feast would commence, and then the warriors would take their wives to their tents and consummate the marriages.

Karida's heart raced with hope. One man among the al Assayra had requested her hand. She dared to hope it was Kareem, the younger brother of the sheikh. Karida had met him when she and her uncle visited Bahariya and she'd seen the very tomb whose treasure she protected. Kareem's arresting features and piercing brown eyes had sparked a fire in her like a match set to kindling.

Kareem had been impressed by her knowledge in the art of Bedouin jewelry-making, and he had charmed her with his courtly manners and winsome smile. He was only nineteen, home on leave from Oxford. Gossips said he was kind and noble, a fierce warrior in battle, and eager to acquire a bride. He'd seemed to divide his attentions between Karida and another girl, but Layla tended to talk too much. His personal and loyal servant, Saud, had secretly told Karida that Kareem definitely approved of her. Saud's dark eyes danced with mirth as he told her this, and Layla was not now among the waiting brides.

Giggles filled the air. The gaggle of women lounged beneath the cluster of date palms, their hands adorned with intricate patterns of henna. Kohl and other cosmetics were applied to their faces, making their eyes appear huge and mysterious. This was a corral of potential brides, waiting for capture.

To Karida's relief, the conversation switched to the upcoming nuptials and the consummations to follow.

"What do you think it's like? Will I know what to do?" one bride-to-be asked.

Farrah, a girl about two years younger than Karida, tossed her head. "My sister told me everything. It's like a horse mating. The man's stalk becomes stiff, like a camel crop, and he mounts you as you open your legs. He pushes his stalk inside you. It hurts the first time, and you bleed, but then it gets better and you eventually like it."

"How much does it hurt?" another anxious bride asked.

"It depends upon how large the stalk is," Farrah replied. "I hear the more power a man has, the larger the stalk."

"Kareem's stalk must be very large," whispered a third

girl, and the others giggled.

"He is a sheikh's son. Of course he is powerful," said another. She nodded toward a man standing beneath a nearby date palm. "Are the English powerful, as well?"

Karida's heart skipped a beat as she recognized Thomas, the English visitor who had saved her from the viper. He was alone, studying nothing, and yet she sensed he was studying everything. Even her.

"He is very handsome," ventured Farrah. "And virile. I saw him ride out earlier with our sheikh. He sits very well on a horse."

"How large do you think his stalk is?" asked one bride.

Their gazes whipped over to the Englishman. Karida's heart gave a violent thump as Thomas glanced at her, smiled, and then looked away.

Remembering how she had briefly unveiled before him, she flushed. Her breathing grew uneven as she remembered how she had felt in his arms when he'd whisked her away from danger, her soft body pressed against his hard one. Yet his eyes, green as Nile river grass, had shown flashes of a haunting loneliness that echoed her own.

She had never met such an intriguing man. His khaki suit, starched white shirt, brown tie, and shoes dusty from sand made him look like any ordinary Englishman. He had sharp, chiseled features. Sunlight picked out auburn flecks in his thick brown hair. Broad shoulders hinted at arrogance born of breeding. His full mouth, square chin, and dark brows showed a man capable of holding his own among her tribe's fierce warriors.

When their gazes had collided at the spring, she'd read the naughty dare in his eyes. With brazen recklessness, she had answered the demand. It had been worth it to see his eyes widen with bold interest. For a wild moment, she wished he were the one she would marry and give her body to.

Foolish! Would he would want her if he saw her naked?

"I wonder if he would care," she murmured.

The other women glanced at her. "What?" Farrah demanded.

"Nothing," Karida replied. "Just thinking aloud."

A thunder of horses' hooves pounded the pebbled sand. Karida rose to her feet and shaded her eyes. Dust clouds in the distance darkened the air as the sound increased. She joined the other giggling girls who had also stood. Her heart thudded as a group of twenty men on beautiful Arabians rode through the camp center, their robes of deep purple and white flowing behind them. Ululating yells split the air. Women threw their hands up and screamed as the horsemen galloped closer. A phalanx of Khamsin warriors on either side waved scimitars and shouted along.

Anticipation shone in the brides' eyes. Delighted shouts and squeals of laughter erupted in a storm of sound as the men on their fine horses circled. Frantic hope beat inside Karida. This was it; she was about to become a captured bride. True, she was scarred and could not have children, but she still had value and much to offer.

The forgotten dream surfaced once more. A handsome, strong warrior on his white horse swept her away to his bridal tent. He would be noble and honorable, never lie, cheat, or steal. He would defend and protect her, fall upon his sword if she bade it, and make love to her beneath the moon and the stars as the silks in his enormous tent billowed in the breeze. For once, she would have someone who loved her for who she was, not caring about the ugly scars marring her beauty, not pitying her for being a bastard hidden away in the desert like a shameful secret.

Karida's pulse quickened as the riders guided their mounts closer, each cantering over to a giggling girl who offered her hand. Each man lifted his willing captive into his saddle, swinging her before him and galloping away. The stuff of romantic dreams happened here before her wondering eyes. She, too, wanted desperately to be one of the chosen few.

Finally, nearly all the men had ridden off. The Khamsin gathered around, cheering and yelling. The last al Assayra warrior on his mount seemed of prodigious height and carried himself with grace and pride. He unfastened the veil covering the lower half of his face, and Karida's heart raced. Kareem.

He had striking features, high cheekbones, a full mouth, and an arrogant but charismatic air. Seeing Karida standing alone, he guided his mount toward her. The breath caught in her throat. Karida willed her trembling limbs to relax as her heart raced with eager anticipation. Her mind chanted words of hope. *Oh, please, pick me. Yes, pick me. Here I am...*

His dark eyes blazing, Kareem approached on his white steed. A joyous tinkling sound came from the little silver bells adorning the colorful purple and gold tassels on his horse's harness. Kareem gave her a reassuring smile, murmured a greeting, and reached down for her hand. Her fingers trembled as they brushed against his tan skin, so close, just within touch. Her new life, her new hope; someone truly wanted her...

Outraged cries filled the air. Kareem pulled back, confusion furrowing his brow. He stared at a woman pushing through the crowd, determination in each of her pounding steps.

Karida's heart sank. *Oh God, not Rayya.* Layla's mother. *Please, no...*

"As is my right in these matters, I lodge a formal protest. Karida is flawed," the woman called. She pushed her daughter toward the prince. "Take Layla instead."

Kareem's features hardened into a threatening scowl. "Go,

and leave me to my bride and stop your talk."

"Sire, Karida is *najes*. Unclean. She will never bear children."

Karida's heart pounded wildly as Kareem's frown turned into a pensive look. Rayya persisted.

"A future sheikh needs sons. Layla will give you fine sons. She promises to be like myself, strong and fertile. Karida cannot bear children. I have proof she is not fertile," the woman insisted.

Behind her, Nuri struggled in the secure grip of Uncle Ramses. He rained a string of violent curses on Rayya's head.

Regret darkened Kareem's face. He looked torn. Karida knew whatever he did, he must choose and choose now or the contract would not be binding. The prince clucked to his horse, turning the Arabian away. He took the hand of the eager Layla, who laughed as he pulled her up onto the mount. The white Arabian snorted as Kareem settled his bride into the saddle, and loud ululating yells ripped through the air as he galloped away.

Shame brought a blush to Karida's cheeks. Her hand, still outstretched, quivered like silken tent drapes in a hard desert breeze. She let it drop and pretended not to care.

A thousand stares increased the heat in her flaming cheeks. She wanted to shrink back beneath the towering palm and bury herself deep in the sand. Pride forced her to lift her head high instead. She would never let anyone see how deeply she hurt.

The shouts died away, and people gradually drifted off. Karida returned to her carpet beneath the cool palm tree and concentrated on staring straight ahead. She'd pretend as if it never happened. As if nothing mattered. Her chest felt hollow with grief and regret.

When all fell silent around her, she finally dared look.

Eyes that refused to shed a tear regarded the sweep of sand and trees. No one was there…except Thomas, the Englishman, still leaning against the nearby date palm. Hands in his pockets, he regarded her with quiet intensity.

Fresh humiliation poured through her. She lifted her chin, daring him to say something equally cruel as the murmurs and whispers. He merely regarded her with a sad smile, as if he understood. Then he made the most astonishing gesture, one recalled from her distant past in England. The Englishman touched his forelock in grave salute of respect. As if she were an equal, as if she were a woman worthy of respect. Flustered, she looked down at her feet.

When she looked back up, he was gone. A desert wind had swept him silently away.

Chapter Two

Laughter spilled through the camp. Lamb stew with rice and tomatoes was consumed as the wedding feast, and musicians played a wild polyrhythmic beat on their instruments. Crackling flames from several campfires leapt into the air, sparks dancing on the night wind. As the only English visitor, Nigel sat in the honored circle of men that included the sheikh of the Khamsin tribe and Sheikh Zahib of the al Assayra tribe, Kareem's eldest brother.

A short distance away, Karida sat with her family. Her face remained veiled, her carriage stiff. Nigel knew what it was like to be rejected and shunned. He also knew the necessity of pretending to the world it mattered not one whit.

He pushed aside his feelings. They were dangerous. Just as dangerous as the man slithering toward him, eyes dark, flat, and cold, wind billowing the dresslike *thobe* at his ankles. The man was posing as his servant, but Malik Wardi was his partner for this heist.

While exploring for treasure in the Eastern Desert, Nigel found a cave with an ankh and a jackal carved on a rock wall. Malik, whom he'd hired as a digger, confessed in a moment of drunken camaraderie that the symbols marked a secret room hiding a treasure map. For generations, apparently, Malik's family robbed tombs and hid their stolen finds in another. This last sacred tomb was "filled with golden mummies." Malik's ancestor had cleverly placed traps in the tomb to thwart grave robbers like himself, drawn a map to detail the easiest way to find it, and sealed the map inside a secret room inside the cave. From father to son, all the secrets of the tomb's treasure were passed down for use at a later date—passed down until Ali, Malik's father, had altered tradition. Ali refused to tell Malik of the tomb's location or its secrets. Instead, he'd begged protection from the Khamsin when he was threatened by other robbers who desired the treasure, begged protection and claimed to realize that what his family had done was sacrilegious. Ali had given the Khamsin a ruby, the missing half of a key to open the map room. All Nigel needed was that ruby to complete the scorpion amulet key. Then he could recover the treasure map and find the tomb. Karida guarded it.

Nigel trusted Malik as much as he'd trusted the viper he'd killed earlier that day, but he also knew how to keep the man tethered. He'd said if he caught Malik taking the ruby, he'd chop off all his fingers one by one.

Malik asked in English, "Sir, I have seen to your horse for the night, as you asked. Is there anything else you require?"

"Yes, return to my tent and fold my laundry. Immediately," Nigel instructed.

Cold anger entered the man's eyes, but it was matched

by the steel in Nigel's own. Malik finally bowed and left, fingering the curved knife at his side.

"Malik?" Nigel called out.

The man turned.

"If you fail to keep to your word to keep everything clean, you know what your punishment shall be." Nigel held up his hand and waggled his fingers.

Malik swallowed hard, bowed, and scurried off.

On his right, Ramses bin Asad Sharif, the sheikh's bodyguard and Karida's uncle, shot Nigel a questioning glance. "More sweet tea?" The warrior held up a clay pitcher and gestured toward an empty, handleless cup. He regarded Nigel with frank interest.

Nigel nodded.

"That little mare you rode and are considering for purchase is very sturdy. Is everything meeting your expectations with her?" Ramses poured the tea and then replaced the pitcher on a low, round copper table in the middle of their circle.

Nigel nodded.

"You are a man of few words these days, Thomas. On your last visit with Jasmine, you were very talkative." Speculation bloomed in Ramses's amber-colored eyes.

Nigel shrugged.

Ramses studied him and put a hand to the hilt of the long sword always at his side. "How is Jasmine, our beloved Badra's daughter? Have you married yet?"

Bloody hell. Ramses asked the question in Arabic. The Khamsin warrior's gaze was sharp and assessing.

Nigel spoke flawlessly in the same language, lying. "We will marry soon, but first I must return to London to settle old business." In truth, he did have old business to settle— finding proof that his brother's title was legitimately his. The plan was with the consent of his twin. Hell, it had been Thomas's idea. Thomas, who was now living in Cairo with Jasmine, his bride. Thomas, who had locked all the estate funds into a trust that could only be used for repairing the country home and tenant cottages their father had neglected, maintenance of the London townhouse, and as a small allowance for their mother. Nigel would be just as broke as before.

"Congratulations." Ramses's broad shoulders relaxed, and his hand left his sword hilt.

Overhearing the remark, the other men in the circle turned to Nigel. He answered their questions easily, asking polite questions about their families in return. The talk shifted to children.

Ululating yells broke out to the accompaniment of wild drumbeats from the musicians playing near their small circle. A laughing dark-haired girl no older than fourteen ran toward them, threw back her head, and yelled. Then she dashed up to the circle and squatted by Ramses's side. The warrior's fierce expression softened. He chucked her beneath the chin.

Nigel's heart twisted unexpectedly at the clear affection between father and daughter. He thought of the sad, hopeful face that awaited him in England.

"Fatima, why aren't you with your mother and the women?" Ramses asked.

The girl's lovely face creased in a pout. "I could care less about weddings and fuss," she declared in English. "I want to go with Tarik and Asad to see to the al Assayra's horses. Please, Father, *must* I stay with the women?"

"Yes," he told her, giving her a gentle push. "Time enough later for horses. Try to be a lady for once. Your mother would be pleased with your company."

Fatima rolled her eyes. "Yes, Father." She pushed to her feet and bolted away, dust eddies kicked up beneath her racing feet.

"Children." Ramses sighed, but there was pride and warmth in his voice. He glanced at Nigel. "You will soon know how trying they can be."

"Yes, I look forward to finding out," Nigel responded.

His gaze flicked to Karida. "Your niece possesses an admirable dignity. She will make some worthy man a very good wife—a man who understands her inherent value. What will happen to her now? Will she remain here?"

A guarded look covered Ramses's face. His eyes became chips of flint. "You are asking many questions, Thomas."

Nigel thought quickly and offered his most charming smile, one that had softened the steeliest curmudgeons. "Forgive my curiosity. I can't help but think of my beloved Jasmine and the snubs she suffered in England. I wish the best for Karida, and I hope the future holds only joy as it has for my bride-to-be."

Ramses's gaze was steady. "You gave up a great deal in England to live here with Jasmine: the money you made for your English estate, the lifestyle of being an English earl…"

"Giving up those things is easy when the return on my investment is far greater," Nigel replied.

A reluctant smile touched the Khamsin warrior's mouth. It vanished when he glanced at his niece.

Sheikh Zahib leaned forward, following his gaze. "Fear not, Ramses. I am certain a good man will be found. One worthy of your brother's daughter."

Ramses's bearded face became a grimace. "Only the finest would do. Karida is an exceptional woman, pure and moral. A lie never passes her lips, and she sets an example for all Khamsin women."

Again, their praise made her sound more like a statue carved from limestone than a woman, cold but pure. Nigel glanced at the silent Karida. Interest flared. He would wager much that a living heart beat beneath all that honor.

"You chose well in giving her the ruby to guard the map," Sheikh Zahib said gravely. "The treasure of the sleeping golden mummies must never be disturbed. My brother, Kareem, has sworn an oath to guard the tomb with his life, Ramses, as your niece guards the tomb's map. Their marriage would have been a perfect bonding of our two peoples, but my brother is stubborn and guards his own heart as zealously as anything."

Ramses stiffened, as if the sheikh's talk of the treasure bothered him. He glanced at Nigel.

Nigel pretended absorption in his tea but said, "Hearts are far more dangerous than lost tombs. And hide many more secrets."

Zahib gave a deep, rich laugh. "Wise words from the honored guest. But this tomb has extremely dangerous secrets. Traps for the unwary, whose dangers are known only to Kareem, Ramses, and Nuri's daughter. Ali, the tomb robber who stored the treasure there, reputedly took knowledge of the secret traps to his grave and did not pass it on to his sons."

"I have heard of such traps." Nigel gave a casual shrug. "Ancient Egyptian tales to scare off explorers. Tales of traps and curses? Rubbish. Nothing more."

Silence descended like a dark cloud. Nigel glanced up to see the flames flicker eerily over Sheikh Zahib's face. "Do not discard the warnings so lightly, my English friend. Traps and curses carry more power than you can imagine. And the tomb of the sleeping golden mummies has them all."

Malik didn't warn me about that. Cold sweat broke out on Nigel's forehead, and he gave a respectful nod. He was tempted to believe. Bloody hell, how would he maneuver past all that and grab the treasure?

I'll find a way.

"Sheikh Zahib, with all respect," Ramses murmured, "it is not good to speak of that which should lie undisturbed beneath the sands. Many lives have been lost for that treasure."

Zahib dusted off his hands and stood. He began a long speech in Arabic about the joy of the occasion and then gave a blessing for all the new brides and bridegrooms. As the speech ended, a loud ululating yell split the air. The crowds cheered. Startled, Nigel cheered as well. About time. The sheikh was a windbag.

He glanced once more at Karida, his mind working rapidly. Tonight, whatever it took, he would have that ruby in hand. Even if she was a rejected bride surely mourning beneath her facade of celebration.

"Wickedly witty writing and wonderfully entertaining characters are the key ingredients in Bryan's sinfully sexy historical romance."
—*Booklist*

Emily Bryan

Vexing the Viscount

As children they'd sparred with play swords. She'd scarred his chin, and he broke her heart. Now, more than a decade later, the true battle was only beginning…

Daisy Drake needed Lucian Beaumont, Viscount Rutland. Tired of being labeled "on the shelf," she craved adventure. And Lucian held all the clues to a long-buried Roman treasure. Surely her desire to join his search had nothing to do with his dark curls and seductive Italian accent. Too bad Lucian wanted no help from her—until she donned the disguise of an infamous French courtesan and promised to teach him all she knew about the pleasures of the bedchamber. Of course, she only knew what had been written in naughty books. But Daisy had always been a quick learner. And night by naked night, they'd discover treasure neither expected to find.

ISBN 13: 978-0-8439-6134-8

USA Today Bestselling Author
RITA Award Winner

JENNIFER ASHLEY

"Readers who relish deliciously tortured heroes and spirited heroines who can give as good as they get will find much to savor…from the consistently satisfying Ashley."
—John Charles, *Booklist*

It was whispered all through London Society that he was a murderer, that he'd spent his youth in an asylum and was not to be trusted—especially with a lady. Any woman caught in his presence was immediately ruined. Yet Beth found herself inexorably drawn to the Scottish lord whose hint of a brogue wrapped around her like silk and whose touch could draw her into a world of ecstasy. Despite his decadence and intimidating intelligence, she could see he needed help. Her help. Because suddenly the only thing that made sense to her was…

The Madness of Lord Ian Mackenzie

"Jennifer Ashley fills the pages with sensuality."
—Romance Junkies

ISBN 13: 978-0-8439-6043-3

Discover Great Native American Romance

If you crave the turbulent clash of cultures and the heat of forbidden love, don't miss these exciting Native American Romances:

Chosen Woman by Shirl Henke
Coming July 2009

When Fawn meets rough-and-tumble Jack Dillon, she is both infuriated by his cocky self-confidence and irresistibly drawn to his charismatic charm. He is the wolf totem of her dreams and holds the key to unlocking her visionary powers. Together they can save her people, if only he chooses to love her.

Comanche Moon Rising by Constance O'Banyon
Coming August 2009

Struggling to make a new life for herself and her young brother on a rugged ranch in Texas, Shiloh finds an unlikely protector in the chief of a nearby band of Comanches. But when he kidnaps them, she is torn between outrage and the powerful attraction she feels for the virile warrior.

More Great Native American Romance!

Chase the Lightning by Madeline Baker
Chase the Wind by Cindy Holby
Shadow Walker by Connie Mason
Half-Breed's Lady by Bobbi Smith

✂

☐ **YES!**

Sign me up for the Historical Romance Book Club and send my FREE BOOKS! If I choose to stay in the club, I will pay only $8.50* each month, a savings of $6.48!

NAME: _____

ADDRESS: _____

TELEPHONE: _____

EMAIL: _____

☐ I want to pay by credit card.

☐ **VISA**   ☐ **MasterCard**   ☐ **DISCOVER**

ACCOUNT #: _____

EXPIRATION DATE: _____

SIGNATURE: _____

Mail this page along with $2.00 shipping and handling to:
Historical Romance Book Club
PO Box 6640
Wayne, PA 19087
Or fax (must include credit card information) to:
610-995-9274
You can also sign up online at **www.dorchesterpub.com**.
*Plus $2.00 for shipping. Offer open to residents of the U.S. and Canada only.
Canadian residents please call 1-800-481-9191 for pricing information.
If under 18, a parent or guardian must sign. Terms, prices and conditions subject to change. Subscription subject to acceptance. Dorchester Publishing reserves the right to reject any order or cancel any subscription.